A SHIELD OF PARIS

A Shield of Paris

stories by
LARRY SMITH

Adelaide Books
New York / Lisbon
2019

A SHIELD OF PARIS

stories

by Larry Smith

Published by Adelaide Books, New York / Lisbon
adelaidebooks.org

Editor-in-Chief
Stevan V. Nikolic

For any information, please address Adelaide Books
at info@adelaidebooks.org

or write to:

Adelaide Books
244 Fifth Ave. Suite D27
New York, NY, 10001

ISBN-10: 1-949180-95-6
ISBN-13: 978-1-949180-95-4

Printed in the United States of America

Contents

Kid's Friend

William Burroughs and I understood each other perfectly. Never actually friends, we shared a kinship based on class, although the tacit bond crossed significant genealogical barriers. My paternal blood extended farther back than his, to the China Trade, and my mother's stock was older yet, gentry from turn-of-the-eighteenth century Albany and environs. Yet if Burroughs was a parvenu by comparison, he comported himself as quite the genuine number if only by way of (in his case) that horror of pedigree which may often define bona fide pedigree. I think men like Burroughs, more I daresay than someone like myself, I've always been much less uncomfortable with the accidents of lineage, ever prefer some collective historical immolation to the embarrassments of overt distinction. Their lives host a resolute and perennial potlatch finalizing them as in fact the aristocrats they can't help but be.

Only with the caliente reputation that followed on *Naked Lunch* did Burroughs seem at all less distracted by his own birthright, yet the clench-jaw cadences persisted, of course, throughout the many incongruous phases and incarnations of his life and career – he sounded more like one of us than any one of us I have ever known – and it seemed to be a burden he just could not unload. Sometimes when we spoke, even after his famous book was published, he'd still practically twitch at the sound of his own voice. It wasn't, as I say, a discomfort with which I empathized much, having really always seen the superficial trappings of privilege as a rather bland fact of life or, to the extent I could count some picturesque wastrels among my near kin, even a tangible literary asset. But Burroughs raged equally against the Midwestern elite and the debasements of commercial democracy that certain members of that elite, having banked the wealth democracy allowed them to amass, affect to despise. Imagine his dismay at first reading *On the Road*, since all his discomfort must have been sorely tweaked by Kerouac's flippant depiction of the mighty trusts and estates ostensibly in store for the character in the book based on Burroughs (especially since the real Burroughs was at that point for all intents and purposes disinherited), although that relationship, not so much between the two men themselves as between two visions, Burroughs' and Kerouac's, and how two such different ways of reading (and writing) experience could possibly coexist in the same subculture, demand a very long and labyrinthine story indeed.

In any event, since all that kind of socio-cultural abnegation, in Burroughs or in others I've known like him, I find just tiresome, the bond between us was different and deeper than anything simply attitudinal. More to the point, we understood each other at an extraordinarily physical level, a very basic shared experience of physicality itself which people who have, say, merely made love to each other (which he and I never dreamed of doing) don't come close to knowing. Maybe you have to be a Hapsburg with sliver lips and unimaginable capillary disorders contemplating another like-afflicted Hapsburg to begin to understand what I'm talking about. What Burroughs and I shared was scarifying and personal. It begins, fatefully, with a peculiar fastidiousness. Then—and here the bond proves in equal measure irremediable and unutterable—to disencumber ourselves of that fastidiousness amid such fecal regalia as only those for whom the world and the human bodies in it are, finally, impossible contradictions can appreciate, was an equally definitive organic characteristic Burroughs and I had in common.

But nor is it as simple as some purge-and-binge routine when, say, one's retentive little auntie starts to shit her pants all night. The great spiritual quest, and I do sometimes suspect that no one is as equipped to take this journey as those of us who, like Burroughs and myself, were born to nether worlds of such privilege that, Lord knows, someday we may actually be able to hire people to do our shitting for us, the quest, I say, is to maintain the balance; if not resolve the contradictions, at least hold them in exquisite tense abeyance. The love that pitches its whatever in the palace of excrement likewise elegizes New England Indian summers, for sure the happiest times of my life because they were so damn clean, even the mud got caught up in sun showers that scoured the earth we walked on. Lord, I so deeply need to unearth the crap from a young man's gut yet clothe us both in the white roses that feed on and grow from the reeking dump.

Not that a single redemptive stem ever sprouted from the raw carbolic residue the Mexicans or the Arabs or whoever the hell it was left caked like acid soap flakes up Johnny's ass. Yet if our brief but telling conversations, or the rather uncomfortable nods of mutual understanding Burroughs and I exchanged at various times in our lives, did hint at kindred vision of sorts, the green coital putrescence and rotted cytoplasmic matter found throughout *Naked Lunch* and *The Soft Machine* evoked a supporting and, I'd boast, a rather sagacious response on my part, especially since I knew the author and the people he was born to so well. Whatever extraneous critical exegeses these passages may merit as commentaries on the lives of drug users or metaphors of whole social infrastructures framed around meta-addictions of the mind and body or medieval rites that seek palaces of the spirit via journeys straight into and then past the unspeakable buboes sublunary flesh is heir to, it was also because these expressions of the physical were, finally, summative expressions par excellence of the real nature of the social class into which he and I were both born, and against which everything he and I have written must be measured, that, I believe, I understood him so well. These deep dirty things are defining inherited expressions no less than Veblenian predation or whatever other tribal atavisms the various great chronicles trot out. Burroughs had to respect me, if distastefully, because I was one of the few people who understood that his writing, at least as much as my own, is signatory of the upper class situation as it maintains its place in 20th century America.

So that's what I'm talking about. We were two guys from rich families who were hep to each other's scene, you dig? We were mutually aware and wary. Sententious nods re shit on the dick. Johnny's rancid liver tissue dripping off Ahmad's lip. Dull thrill of carbolic. Dicks greased for the kill. Know what I mean? Secret love stuff of Sudbury, Massachusetts wrapped tight under three-piece suits. You should see the way I clean a toilet after I use it. Robert Bennett Forbes one sec, that's me, then his beatnik alter ego shitass secret sharer the next, that's me too. Just like Proust. And Henry James, the way he's so damn fastidious limning every exquisite little fart of a nuance about Maggie Verver this and Isabel Archer that, withholding so much even in the outpouring of verbiage, yet what an outpouring, what expulsions, endless paragraphs – Edmund Wilson even called it Jamesian gas—-passing out the portal of literature like somebody's gotten into somebody else's shithole and out it all comes, two trillion words about what Maggie may or may not think about her father. Refined textual buggery, lessons from the masters, one expostulation in *The Golden Bowl* is the well-honed climax of the class vision, a spectacle of Johnny ripped gutwise and creamed on with blue viscous poison cum juice in *Naked Lunch* or *The Soft Machine*, I can never remember which text is which, is the denouement. Giving everything and holding it all back, and all at the same time, that's us.

I don't know if Burroughs knew tenderness, though I guess maybe he did those later years in Kansas when he lived close by the nuclear test sites with the preppy looking guy, what's his name. I myself have puzzled over tenderness, never quite knowing when or with whom it might be appropriate, as if the great tension which is the real moral imperative of our lives, that Augustan reserve hiding back buckets of shit, and the primal urge to gut-fuck creation itself until it positively drips, have at last precluded what might be called "focused emotional expression." If I am a tender man, and I think I am, it has been all inchoate longing lo these many years, undifferentiated yearning and yearning to express what I yearn to differentiate. Ah me! I have loved, mainly men, and there was depth of feeling, passionate appreciation, all that stuff, yet I have dreamt in vain of the frail little connections, glances just as knowing as the ones Burroughs and I might have exchanged, but not this time darksome predilections of scatology in eschatology historically bequeathed; quite to the contrary, similar-looking nods of acknowledgement to memorialize something fundamentally different, more human no doubt, or at least more merciful, the brief but heartfelt moments of personal concern between two human beings, affections subtle enough that at one and the same time they're imperiled and imperishable. However handsomely I've treated some lovers, and I've treated some very handsomely, such moments, moments I know to naturally occur between the most unlikely boorish or sullen folk, I, I freely admit, I have never known. Nor, though, have I ever expected pity because of that deprivation or myself dwelt on it piteously, yet it's probably a piteous fact in any event, and people if they knew me would probably feel pity for me right now even as I may refuse to feel pity for myself, the whole wretched specter of an aging fag writer, who knows, I might be that and nothing else, all the more piteous-seeming as he begins to recall an incident that's persistently haunted him in recent years involving a kid named Michael Langstrum and Michael's friend Joel Ragula which, and this may be the most piteous thing of all to reflect on, brought him, this old fruit, closer to a feeling of involvement with tenderness, the real McCoy, the actual marvelous incarnation of it, and I don't mean its classic poses, the Pieta or some other archetypal rendition, but rather such tenderness in utterly transient messages between two beings spoken or unspoken and never more than caught on the fly yet betokening the fabulous concern that one of God's children may have for another. I think the chapter in my trilogy where Felix and Betsey are together in Florida approximates what I'm talking about, the half-sentences that pass between them, the pain and fear each feels mainly because the other one suffers pain and is afraid. I wrote that at least ten years before I met Michael and Joel and it does seem to me, in light both of my own best writing, as well as the memorial persistence of these boys, Michael's soothing words to

Joel, Joel's eyes softer on account of the powerful comfort he knew he could count on from his friend, that the actual living of a tender life is, at least from a moral standpoint, no more to be admired (it is certainly more to be envied but, from a moral standpoint, not I think more to be admired) than such reveries as I have been inspired to in subsequent decades. Quite to the contrary, perhaps. Some men are blessedly born to tender delight, some aren't, but abstracting it, essentializing it, and who else but Plato should us butt-fuckers take cues from, salvages it from the rack of time, and salvages them, the kid himself and his friend, from the ravages, not just of age and separation, but of what time may have done to blunt their fine and lovely edges. So here I be, brooding as may be said dove-like o'er the vast proverbial abyss, and what I can still see way down there are the two beautiful young men loving each other beautifully. "Brooding" indeed, for I don't preen myself or dote on the delicious remembered flesh, delicious as it may have been, but instead the memory of Michael and Joel causes me such unending ache I hesitate to revive it as memory much less write about it. Maybe that's why, again if only from a moral standpoint, the abstraction I make cannot be gainsaid simply because the maker himself has never known quite that kind of love in life and might refuse it were it offered. Twenty years are gone by and I'm still aching, and I absolutely do not want to find out what's become of them, dissipated cynics by now, maybe, even overweight Lord knows. But what seems most to the point, if on a scale of values you want to weigh their actual tenderness against my memory of it twenty years after the fact, is that, having almost undone me with a display of the sweetest affection you can imagine between two young boys, which is precisely what they displayed on the day I was with them, having thus made it inevitable that at least on certain subsequent nights I would castigate myself to the core of my harrowed being for never having felt or expressed what these two boys were able to feel and express, I'd still like to point out that, for all we know, at this very moment, *they don't even remember each other*. Excuse my getting emphatic. But I'm here still and I'll bet all that's left of what once they were is me right now. Maybe I don't know how to love, but without me there isn't any.

I met the kid Langstrum in Cleveland when I was guest lecturing at Case Western Reserve University. The main train depot in the center of the city, a tower that still dominates the cityscape, was a pickup scene in those years and I'm still amused it's called the Terminal Tower, death and phallus and ye old terminus too, the city's butthole where mostly decently dressed middle-aged men cruised the boys. I followed Michael out, I recall it was late afternoon, and I found him going to the Publix Book Mart, a very decent store in those days. I can't say I'm ever delighted when a cute kid turns out to be a poetaster, except insofar as it makes it easier for a famous writer to get into his pants. But too often all that literary stuff just obtrudes. I don't disdain meat with a mind, but if I'm getting hot over somebody's rumphole, I hardly care to stop and chat about Faulkner or, God forbid, they'll bring up Vonnegut or, these days, McIlhenny or McInerny, whatever it is.

"I can't believe you're in Cleveland," he said when I introduced myself in the fiction section.

"It's been in the papers," I said. "There was an item in the *Plain Dealer*."

"I missed it," he said, and seemed confused that I'd know the name of the Cleveland newspaper, much less read it.

"Why don't we take a little walk," I said. "It's a lovely, lovely day."

Michael was a slim-waist kid with perfect Mediterranean, more Italian than Greek, features, the Anglo surname aside, and a bushy head of hair in multifarious but not girlish curls. I wanted him right away, the same way I always wanted the kids I'd get. The ones I used to long for, but realize I'd never have, those were vaguer less overtly sexual longings because I kept them vaguer, knowing this hunk was out of my league or that stud too straight even for a blow job. But Michael I wanted with the kind of desire I always felt for the boys I knew I'd crush. I could already just about hear him grunt as we navigated the innocuous moments of the getting-to-know-you crap.

"I can't believe I just met you like this. I always thought I'd maybe meet writers and stuff when I got to New York, but I never thought I'd meet somebody who I read and think about just by going out one day. . ."

". . .To cruise the Terminal Tower," I finished for him, and he stammered a little with a quick smile and fell silent. I could see tight brown nipples inside a brown smart shirt. It was July or August, and none of the kids were wearing undershirts. "I saw you there, and then I saw you walking to the bookstore."

So he was twice disarmed. First, because I knew he liked men. But, knowing that, I also knew he wasn't a street kid, he was denied that protective psychic comfort because I saw that he was educated, pawing away at Faulkner and Kenneth Patchen and even George Mandel. Good old George, *The Breakwater* was in print then. Now there was a man who couldn't stand the sight of me! But I liked *him*. And *The Breakwater* is the best turgid book I've ever read.

Michael said something about not yet quite finishing my whole trilogy, but that the parts of it he read were great poetry. So I told him about a kid I knew who saw Auden walking on

8ᵗʰ Street in New York. "The kid goes up to the old boy and he says, 'Excuse me, Mr. Auden, but I just love your poetry.' So Auden says, 'Well, Sonny, why don't you come up to my apartment and I'll show you some real poetry!'"

Michael laughed, though I don't think he could quite appreciate the rather harsh spirit my anecdote was born of, that manly cynicism all writers share once they grow a little hair on their chest but that, like Auden, they won't let mitigate their commitment or their faith or whatever it is they think they're supposed to have in order to be great writers. My tone softened a little because I liked Michael. "I should stay in Cleveland," I said. "Now that that ninny d. a. levy's killed himself, I could be the poet laureate of the city. Would you be impressed?"

We finished the nine blocks back to the Terminal Tower and watched a portly old well-dressed gent bargaining with a couple of blond kids, prototypical gentile get of the Midwest even if Cleveland wasn't quite the Midwest. "Do you like watching the action?" I asked.

"Oh yeah. I like watching life."

"Not everyone would say this is 'life.'"

"They don't understand."

I took him home and got his clothes off right away. I rubbed his body with the flats of both hands, squeezing the tight tawny ass and then curling my fingertips against his pubic clump and cute little balls. I liked his flesh a lot, and I was delighted at the thought I'd really get to dirty him up. What a thrill it must have been for him being with me, all so unexpected on a summer day in his own dreary home town with a famous writer. Unless, of course, he didn't really like the trilogy, and was just being polite about the poetry crap.

But he was staring hard at my cock, and as I saw him seeing it, I figured he was fascinated because it was mine, after all, and not just because I've got such a big one, but because I was famous, maybe even immortal, like Herman Melville, and here he was playing with my hard dick and he had to know in a thousand years youngsters like himself could be reading the trilogy even if he himself didn't particularly like it.

Then the time came to fuck. It may be that at least in those years I couldn't quite take seriously someone I'd screw, not even if I took pleasure in his company, as I did in Michael's, for he was a very nice young man indeed. But at some level I take all these kids very seriously, for their gasps and grunts aren't simply involuntary tributes I wring from their gullets, but little openings as well into their very beings and, since it is their very beings I want, I do savor the fact that, when I spear them in their shit, the noises they make are theirs and theirs alone. That's a kind of love. Like what I was saying before about the abstraction of tenderness being worth more, at least from a moral standpoint, than the tenderness itself which may be soon forgotten as the abstraction endures. Here, by extension, the need to make them squawk like seals was a kind of objectification which I know is not, in the current social climate, a popular thing to fasten on, but I do maintain, if only from a moral standpoint, that an understanding of people for the objects they also are, in addition to whatever particular and personal individualistic human qualities etc. etc. they may presume to, allows more about them as social and political and moral creatures than what most of the lyrical languages of affection can hope to uncover. For here, the lover truly gets at the essence of someone, the object that the beloved is, no matter how much he might not want to be that object, but the lover knows it's really him, and lusts for it, and wants to get at it with his cock, right up there, right up the beloved's ass. It's like blacks, when you objectify them as niggers, at least in bed, of course they're human and for all I know they could be corporate presidents or goddamn brain surgeons, for Christ's sakes, but they're also niggers, and that's beautiful, it's beautiful to be a piece of meat that everybody in the whole goddamn world has fucked at one time or another, and if you truly love a black person, that's part of what you love about him. Real love seeks the real person, but real persons like French food get cooked in awfully dirty pots, and real persons are never things the persons themselves are usually ever comfortable being. Michael whatever his name was could be dead by now, but the squirming smile on his face, the ecstasy he felt even though he was embarrassed because he farted when I fucked him, that lives on forever.

His body was slightly brown like a fine moist wood in a green forest, and he smelled like talc, natural talc in his blood, not a powder he put on; I felt like I could absorb this splendid fresh flesh right into mine and indeed I did just crawl right up his little fuckhole until I felt it give.

"You're just right," I told him.

"Thank you," he murmured with the big tool in his ass. Hairless body; the kid was so sweet, he managed to smile as I probed him.

"Not too big, not too tight, you're just right," I said.

"Thank you," he said again even as I got him to suddenly grunt a startled effeminate grunt jabbing and groping his shit.

"You're just like the three bears. You're not too this, you're not too that. Oooh, baby, you're just right!"

"I'll always remember you said that," he said almost laughing. I could imagine him writing it down for his memoirs, a tale of me like some silly intimate story of Hemingway or Fitzgerald. A moment later, though, I'd fall in love with the look on his face as I got ready to cum. It was a gracious, encouraging look, he even raised up his ass a little so I could penetrate deeper, and his eyes were urging me, and there was a strange mature respect in his gaze at me the man fucking him that I don't recall I'd seen before in such a young one.

He must have had the presence of mind to take my number off the little plastic strip on the telephone because being famous I have an unlisted number, and I don't generally give it out, not even to sweet kids like Michael. But he kept trying to ring me, as he later confirmed when we finally did meet again. (I often don't pick up the phone when I'm at home either.) One day he left a note on my door urging me to call him because he had something to talk about that he thought I'd find "very appealing." Soon another note appeared, and I had to acknowledge I was a bit intrigued, and I didn't want to hurt his feelings anyway – we should treat people a little better than might sometimes be our wont, since we're not just famous but as famous poets we affect people deeply, so treating them like garbage isn't quite fair—-so after about a week I did call him.

"Hey, I been trying to reach you," he said with no resentment or sense I had tried to avoid him.

"And now you have," I answered, good-naturedly.

"I wanted to talk to you about my friend, Joel. Joel Ragula. He's the closest friend I have, and he thought it was absolutely incredible when I told him about you. He wants to meet you."

Idiot me! Another Johnny waiting, soft drapery around his neck, needs it strung tighter, wants a big gallows cum with a dick up his ass – and there I was wasting time not returning phone calls! Maw for more. Renewable stench of love. Gimme. "Just friends?" I asked, still amiable.

"What do you?. . .Oh, you mean him and me? Kind of. We sort of play with each other, but we never. . .like what you and me did. Joel's actually kind of a virgin. Say, meet me at The Blue Beak and we'll talk more."

Michael ordered a Dubonnet cocktail – a strange drink, I noted, for a young kid, more like something old ladies order when they want to get secretly a little pissed—-and I was aroused again by the sight of the boy looking so fresh, 'kind of a virgin' himself even though I and who knows who else had gotten well up the ass he sat on making it fart like the absurd love meat it is.

"So this Joel, he's never had real sex?"

"Yeah, he has, with me, and with our friend Brook, but, you know, the sex wasn't like what you and I did."

It was intriguing, the way Michael was boldly offering up his friend's body yet tried to be respectful doing so, scrupulous even, he wasn't going to talk too blatantly about a friend, it was another human being after all, and he didn't know how much he had a right to say, but the way he talked, the way he hesitated to say too much, also convinced me the kid's friend could really be an honest-to-goodness cherry ripe for the picking even if it did still sound all too good and I wasn't going to let myself get excited yet.

"And I am to do the honors?" I asked.

"If you'd like that. He'd like that."

"Is Joel easy on the eyes?"

"What do you mean?"

I love boys. One minute they're so sophisticated, the next minute they don't even know a common figure of speech. One minute they're intelligently explicating *One Hundred Years of Solitude*, the next minute you find out the name Wallace Stevens means nothing to them.

"I mean, is he good looking?"

"Oh, he's real pretty. He's got bushy blond hair, there's a little red in it, and he's got the face of an angel. Sometimes just when I look at him, it'll change my whole mood for the better."

"Why is he still a virgin?"

"It's not the kind of thing he's seriously thought he could do, you know what I mean. Until recently."

"Then what caused the sea change in your young friend with respect to being butt fucked?"

"I guess he's just gotten around to wanting to try it."

"And I am to be the recipient of young Joel's newfound craving because I happen to be a well-known writer?"

"Yes, he likes your work, and because I did tell him a few secrets about your dick and stuff."

"Ah, my dick and stuff!"

"And also, this seems strange, but he needs me to see it happen."

"Well, dear, you're welcome to participate as well as observe."

"As a writer, I think this will interest you. It's something Joel and I used to talk about a long time before you and I met, and he came up with the thought that, if I were to see him get fucked for the first time, it would be a way for him to really tell me how much he loves me."

"The two of you are sweet. You're sweethearts."

"I feel like I've known him all my life."

"Why don't you fuck him?"

"I don't do that. But we tell each other everything. You'll love him too."

Joel met us the next day for lunch at Emilio's which I picked because I was hot for the idea of a virgin kid stuffing himself with spaghetti and having a gut full of meatballs before getting fucked up the ass. Food and shit go together, I love my boys to eat a heavy meal before I have them. Michael's friend was everything Michael said and more. The face was better than angelic; it was ruddy and therefore cherubic. And he arrived in a svelte tan leather jacket, the sleek suggestive kink a nimble counterpoint to the ostensible innocence I was primed for. I could tell too, by his wide blue eyes, and the way he smiled, and the staccato talk, that he was geared for it, a life-altering experience as well as pent-up physical release.

As we sat, Joel for whatever reason was comfortable talking about his family. A few minutes into what I soon realized could be a veritable peroration on the subject of the old folks back home (Scranton), I sensed that his talking about them was a mental preparation of sorts for the imminent maiden voyage, an invocation to the elders, as it were, though Mr. and Mrs. Ragula were probably no older than forty-five. Joel was an only child, and they missed him terribly since he had gone off to Cleveland to, well, I don't actually remember why it was he went off to Cleveland or how he and Michael had first met, though one of them did mention it. They had always given him the space he required as a human being, in fact, they knew better than other parents, especially most other parents in a claustrophobic place like Scranton, that that kind of space was something all human beings have a right to. Joel's tone was affecting; he did love them, it was sweet that he did, and there was a natural honesty in how he talked about his mother and father at this important moment of his life an hour or so before I'd be running a poleax up his rear, which, even though I couldn't see it now because he was sitting on it, I knew was a tight what these days they like to call real bubblebutt. Meantime, Michael said nothing about his own parents, which, if I were the sort to psychologize, would have struck me as significant.

Next subject, finally, was another famous writer Joel had met while visiting an uncle or something in Boston. By now, we were warmed up, getting familiar and talking freely. "I thought I'd go all the way with him but I backed off at the last moment, and he just used his mouth on me," Joel recalled.

Joel, with an instinct you often find in boys but it comes as a pleasant surprise anyway, must have seen in some quick shadow fretting my expression that I was concerned he might back off from me as well. "But if Michael's there, it's all definitely cool," Joel reassured. I didn't feel quite the lust I had for Michael the first time, but there was a joy I took in Joel's presence, almost a kind of joviality, that I hadn't felt in Michael's, and it got me hot to fuck him just as hard.

When they were both sitting on my bed, the way they stared at each other, you'd have thought they were going to embrace at once and couple quite grandly as if no one else were there. What a lovely tableaux defined the moment: Joel's eyes sparkling blue, Michael's soft and dark. Joel's cock was a skinny pretty piece the head of it like a tiny white bonnet new babies wear when the weather's nice but just a little chilly. Michael's loomed out of his half-open trousers. The kid was definitely hung, I'd say eight or nine as the crow flies.

But there was a fourth entity in the room: that powerful lyrical longing itself between the two boys which had seized my imagination, which was like to taunt me, and it was that thing, that great ineffable, that I wanted to somehow fuck the bejeesus out of. It was an altogether other-worldly spirit I sensed had bewitched Michael and Joel and held them in its thrall so that they could never or would never fuck each other, but a somber sharing of such a moment as this consecrate their love instead, and maybe for them it was a searing thrill more binding than the warm liquid thrilling feel of their two bodies conjoined.

It was a form of love I'd certainly never seen before. "He's ready for you," said Michael as I stripped. "Oh sweet baby, you're going to get it. You're going to get fucked. He's going to fill up your ass." It was a rare poetry Michael was about to achieve: the physical love he could not express he'd empower in another. Cyrano the proto-poet! "His dick is bursting for you. It's bursting to know you. It's bursting to be inside. He wants to be you. He wants to have all of you, to love you up into little pieces and swallow you and then sleep at last like he was dead."

I was delighted. He hadn't memorized this heated language from the books he read, I was sure of that, nor did I figure it pretentious stuff he might have cooked up by himself or together with Joel in a garret in town holding each other's cocks and poking away at a typewriter. This was the genuine number, love's language yanked right out of him by the gods themselves. I know I sound ridiculous right now, I know what an embarrassing canting old queen I must sound like saying all this, but think about the stuff you can yank out of boys even as you shoot your own knowledge right up into them. If I'm hyperventilating, so did the Greeks in their great glory. Plato proscribed poetry, but it wasn't philosophy he ultimately tore out of his boys or filled them full of. Out instead dripped the very subversive stuff Plato hated, dactylic hexameter ouch! after dactylic hexameter ouch!

Joel was on all fours. When I spread his cheeks and could see his little butthole, I wasn't yet utterly given over with greed for it that I couldn't at that moment also imagine how that pink naked thing would look to Michael as he came around to my side of the bed to see what his own cock wasn't going to fuck but what his heart of hearts yearned for. Then the two boys just broke my heart. As I felt the fuckslot give way and pressed in to mess him up, they *held hands*. Pardon my being emphatic again, but I'm telling you they held hands and were in love.

"Beautiful ass," I said, wishing I could say more.

"Darling Joel," said Michael as I thrust in.

"I can't believe it's happening," said Joel. His back muscles like a young deer's flesh only much paler quivered as I tupped him.

"Love me, love me," said Joel.

"I do," said Michael as I screwed, trying to make it hurt because at that moment I'd have felt safer had he been torn away from his true love and bound to my authority instead. But "I love you," he breathed, only "I love you" to Michael.

"Darling, you're fucked," said Michael, his tone startling and almost eerie because it was a supportive, kindly sound, though full too of recognition, an almost wise paternal acceptance that this person he loved was someone who had to get fucked and, now, finally was getting fucked. The voice was so damn human.

"Eeeeeeh" was the sound of the sound Joel let go as I opened him way up, the very way I like to make a boy my bitch, but then I heard Michael say, "Oh my darling, you have the look of love at last." And he actually started singing the popular song. . .*I can hardly wait to hold you, Feel my arms around you, How long I have waited, Waited just to love you. . .*It seems so ludicrous now, so damn laughable. At the time it was extraordinary, heart-rending. That music. . .*Now that I have found you, Don't ever go. . .*

Like an ethereal music that some bad music seems at certain potent moments to be. But the kids still didn't touch more than by just the smallest intimate clasp of their hands binding them in that same superlative fraternity of theirs. "Back away," I very nearly hissed at Michael, and I don't know if he then let go of Joel's hand, but I do remember covering Joel's whole back and feeling the rosy butt cheeks against me as I creamed inside him at last. I remember the spurt was a warm hot shot almost like I was pissing. And then I felt the anger, which I hid, I hid it completely, saying, "Good kid, good kids both of you, good sweet kids." The anger persisted but it was mixed with fear, and a sense of myself about to die, and wild love and longing passed through me too, longing for the other-worldly creature the boys had created between them with their love, and I was still way down deep inside the one boy the other boy loved like Mary loved Jesus, and I was shocked actually shocked that someone so loved like he was could have so much cock and cum inside him although isn't that what love is when someone truly loves you?

It was while I was still inside him that the persuasive thought I touched on before came to me, that the kingdom of heaven was theirs right now but these kids might not only forget all this ever happened as they got older and paunchy, but maybe even now they couldn't compass the full significance of their own love, and maybe they never would, or, if they did, the knowledge would pass. It was I, I! who would remember the depth of it and preserve it and sanctify it, for I wasn't just a guy in love with a piece of meat, I was the one who'd mount the deer head and memorialize their lovely loving enactment for as I long as I lived, or longer yet if I could get it down on paper so future generations would know all about true love, and it didn't really matter who felt the love versus who pre-served it so long as it was preserved.

A few minutes after I pulled out, they broke my heart again. I awoke after a thirty-second nap – one of those brief little relaxations of the self that produce the most jolting little dreams, and how I wish I can remember what it was at that point of all points in time I dreamed—and sensed the presence of both boys in the bathroom. When I ambled over there, in a scene no painter I can think of can do, Michael was cleaning his friend. His hand was on his shoulder and Joel rested his head on the nape of Michael's neck. They moved in silence as Michael, tissue in hand, worked the violated crack. Thank God I saw them or the scene would have been lost forever.

They persisted in silence for five minutes or more. Joel finally said, "I didn't expect it to hurt so much or that it would be so messy."

"You were beautiful," Michael reassured.

"Thank you," Joel said, and Michael finishing up patted his balls. I backed off toward the bedroom, fixing again in my mind's eye the earlier moment when I fucked him. I saw Joel squat, I heard more now, I heard whimpers I hadn't heard while I was in him. Yet it still seemed a thousand years away, a legend of life already.

We slept through the night and when I awoke the next day, I didn't touch Joel who was lying beside me on his stomach. For the first time, I noticed the freckles on his back, faint irregular designs. I didn't think to touch him. Instead, I got up and cooked breakfast, eggs and bacon. Michael, sleeping on the couch, walked into the kitchen bleary-eyed, cute, as if he were the one who had worked hardest of all the night before.

They were talking about an English professor they knew who taught at Cleveland State named Leon Bieber. They admired him greatly, and were a little intimidated by him. He was a no-nonsense sort, didn't coddle anything that smacked of being sophomoric; his main love was Melville, and he taught Whitman only begrudgingly, despising, he could barely conceal it, all that open-souled stuff for its apparent formal laxity and, worse, absence of ambiguity. That kind of poetry was suspiciously easy to write, he warned, and he made fun of how

Whitman favorably reviewed his own *Leaves of Grass* under a pseudonym.

"Poetry that's life-affirming and that really loves life doesn't do a thing for him," explained Joel, critically but not without respect.

"He's one of a professional multitude," I said, "and I've known them all. If they can't abide Whitman, who's been sanctified by time and collective opinion, what chance does a contemporary Whitman like Kerouac have in academe!"

They huddled over the eggs, impressed by my comment. I continued. "Now, you talk to us, to me or to Clellon Holmes or even Bill Burroughs, who's never written a joyous word in his life, and we'll tell you how great Jack Kerouac really is, greater in some ways than Whitman. But it will be another hundred years before guys like Bieber deign to see it."

"You think Burroughs is a great writer? asked Joel.

"Sure, but sometimes I say, so what? So the whole world's on junk. So the Pope's a fucking junkie. So what! I tell you boys, the world is just dying for all the rhapsodies it can get. There can't be too many. One Whitman is better than none but two or three in the same generation would be glorious. Now finish your food, boys, time's a wastin'."

Punch Line

This is the story of a very great miracle that happened one evening during the first half of the century before the last. The weather that night was horrible. There was a torrential blast, full of lightning and thunder, which was extraordinarily un-usual for this neighborhood that's actually famous for tran-quility. Great and tormented souls have come from this land, but, if they were tormented, it wasn't because their bodies were buffeted by climatic adversity. I've seen knolls of grass here that looked posed and frozen in the sunlight. Such is the usual weather, that only the light dances. Each blade of grass is, as it were, statuesque. The clouds that do roll by are soon brushed away by the sirocco.

Yet unremitting rain was already pounding against Dr. Mathez' cottage at a severe angle, so that the heavy tape his wife had used to seal the sills admitted thin continuous streams. Towels lay on the floor to absorb the moisture. Mathez smiled and nodded as if to say, "there's nothing more you can do." She settled into his arms for their nightly silence, which was better than sexual love had ever been.

Their three children had gone out into the world decades ago. Two were living in the town, one a merchant and the other a merchant's wife. No one understood it, but the third was a seared sort of fellow, painfully shy and hard pressed to make his way. Fortunately, the local clergy were glad to help. They made a place in the church for the young man and, a few years ago, sent him off to a foreign place.

"Do you hear something?" he asked. "Something not thunder?"

A bolt of lightning flashed, forming, it seemed, a whole circle streaking around the house, and the thunder that ensued was so loud his wife didn't even try to make herself heard in reply. When the noise subsided, she nestled against his chest and corralled and caressed each of his fingers, one by one, as had been her pleasant habit for over forty years.

Another sound, though, was certainly not thunder. It was a rhythmic thud repeated half a dozen times. "My word, a knock? Now?" she asked. His body tensed and she undid the embrace. The old man left the room and went into the small passage that led to their front room. She waited, bemused. Returning, his footsteps were just audible, like a rustle of silk under the din from outside.

"I'm needed," he said, gray-faced. His white beard, cropped around the jowls, varied somewhat his sallow complexion. He'd had a bout with hepatitis some years earlier; it took all the color out of his face. At that moment he seemed grayer yet, a little afraid of the weather outside and not at all confident about the chore ahead. His wife scurried to an antechamber and brought his bag: powders, the forceps, a knife, other instruments. She opened it quickly to check that his mask was also inside.

Their eyes met a bit fearfully as he took the bag. "She began six hours ago," he said. "I hope to be back in another six or seven."

He made his way to the carriage waiting outside. The reek of horseflesh was like fresh dung and merged sharply with the smell of the grass, which was likewise stunning and sharp in the wet air. It was unpleasant; Mathez, not expecting the stench, could have fainted. Just the thirty yards from his door to the road was enough to drench him to the bone. The umbrella, which was torn anyway, would not have been of much use against the rain that was blowing at angles of almost 45 degrees.

Horribly, there was no roof on the carriage. It was completely exposed. "What is this!" he shouted at the stable hand who had come to fetch him.

"Their other wagon broke an axle," said the boy. "Just this morning. I couldn't fix it."

Mathez shivered as he accepted a thick cloth hood from the boy. He tried not to anticipate the trip ahead–it was many kilometers from his cottage to the town–and focused instead on the horse, whom he knew: a dark-skinned jumper often shown off around the town by his owner. This beast, although a local entertainer for some time now, neither sought nor got much affection. He often seemed ornery for no reason and Mathez was sure he'd be hard to handle in the storm.

The stable hand was a thin bright-looking kid from a well-liked family in the town. He was known to be an adept rider, no doubt why he'd been asked to fetch the doctor in this dangerous weather. With a sharp lash of the crop he struck at the horse's butt and then repeated the stroke when the horse tried to pull back as if to rear away from the storm. They worked up a canter, but, as the ground heading toward the copse sloped downward (an easy enough curve in normal weather), the horse picked up speed, too much speed, skidding his hooves against the slick stones on the narrow road. The kid pulled back, too late, though, to slow the pace. The horse panicked and leapt, lifting the wagon almost a foot off the ground.

The wheels landed without damage. Mathez was helping. He grabbed on to part of the rein and pulled with all his strength. It seemed a great long time but then the pace slackened. You could hear a thousand sharp raindrops bounce off the animal's head almost like hailstones.

Once past the copse he'd be more than halfway to the town. The trees at their tops looked glued together in the air. Often at night you could make out their shapes in the moonlight. The copse was actually a favorite haunt of his. Sometimes, if a mild breeze worked up, the high branches would sway as if in a slow waltz. But now they all hung together like a herd guarding some secret in their midst.

In the further distance, other trees were alone, bending and shaking to the storm. It was a land of pines and cypresses. There were grapes and almonds and olives growing there too. Further off still rose the great mountain, and some smaller ones as well, with seedlings visible even in this terrible night. Many, though, would not survive the sidewise deluge.

The water soaked through his underwear and Mathez was freezing. Worse, the underside of the cloth supposed to protect his head was also drenched, and the rain invaded every angle. When all was said and done, he grimly realized, he'd probably come down with fever. He was both flattered and resentful. Flattered because, although there were good doctors in the town, and no end of good midwives who'd arrive faster (not to mention more safely), he'd attended this family since their arrival in the province and they wanted no one else. But resentful, because their trust was exhausting and could even kill him.

Up ahead was the town. Tonight he could barely see the stone houses, their soft rock wrung up from the ancient quarry nearby, yet the sound of hooves against cobblestone was clear even in the storm. One of the town's many fountains cast a vague shadow to his right where the church on the other side of the square was also visible. Ahead was their squat, two-story home. Like many of its neighbors close by, its shutters were newly painted, and the facade included a single caryatid abutting elaborate but not ostentatious ironwork. The top floor had been in disrepair for the last few months, though the roof was also freshly painted, a somber green.

The boy tried to shield him from the rain as they raced up the garden path. Mathez smiled appreciatively and patted his shoulder as the gray door opened. "I'll need a large dry towel at once," he said to the maid as she admitted the two men. "And some privacy. Take my bag to the lady's bedroom. And have her pass as much water as she can."

He was escorted to a small closet-like space off the kitchen and handed a dry cloth about six feet long, of very thick rough cotton. First he dried his feet. There probably wasn't enough time to strip and dry off completely, so he removed his waistcoat and hoisted up his shirt to wipe his chest and back. Like rope burns, the towel chafed his skin, which had gotten very soft in the last ten years. He winced. He didn't bother with his pants, although he could still feel the rainwater soaking through.

The master of the house was standing in the middle of the kitchen as Mathez walked out of the closet space. They nodded at each other. "She's in pain," said the man. "But I think there's still time. The stove is hot," he added, pointing toward the other side of the room where a short hallway was lined with cabinets, a small stove and sink. "Five minutes in front of it should help you."

Mathez nodded again. The fire warmed his hands and feet but he couldn't escape the cold wet against his loins and belly. "Take me to her," he said to the maid after only a moment or two by the stove. She walked him through the corridor, past a small rustic sitting room, and into the woman's bedroom. Though he had been in the room on a number of prior occasions, this time it seemed smaller than before; the squall outside was shrinking the whole house.

The woman was a mass of sweat lying on the four-poster bed, a small presence on a mattress that could apparently sleep three. She was panting at regular intervals, and around seven inches dilated. Her eyes blinked open and shut, and she almost smiled, comforted by Mathez' familiar, reassuring presence. Not a very big belly, considering such discomfort. As he caressed her brow and smiled, soothing her, he noted in his peripheral vision that her husband was standing just outside the door: stiff, motionless, not perceptibly very anxious but tense and dutiful. A light in the corner of the sitting room cast the man's shadow across the floor at the entrance to the bedroom. Mathez thought "husband," although he knew they hadn't yet married. Presumably, he would acknowledge and care for the child; otherwise, Mathez thought, he'd take it upon himself to consult the church for help.

So far, all was well. Mathez felt her back in order to be sure that the baby wasn't sitting on the spine. Then, his ear to her belly, he listened to the healthy thump and nodded with a slight smile. The woman saw the smile, as he meant her to; she let out a happy grunt between the agonized yelps. Reaching out for the powders, he called for the maid to bring water. He mixed the sedative in a glass and his patient drank it down. He caressed her again, giving the potion a chance to take effect.

Outside the storm rose higher and stronger. Sometimes miracles happen on the clearest nights of the year so that the stars can guide the visiting kings. But not this miracle, even though it was to be no less a miracle of the light than the birth of Jesus.

The husband stepped into the room. For an odd second, he and Mathez faced each other as if in confrontation. There certainly was something angry in the man's round face; the cheekbones were folded in sharply toward the nose, and thick eyebrows lowered over his features. Neither man blinked. He glared at Mathez as if not trusting him with the responsibility–even though Mathez was the one he chose–before returning to the entrance and waiting there, almost sullenly.

Turning back to the woman, Mathez guessed suddenly what the man's problem may have been. Her nightgown was hiked up to her waist and her legs were spread. The full pubic beard and swollen lips were a sight this husband wanted to claim as a sole prerogative. In an ideal world, all doctors are blind and nothing ever intrudes on the conjugal stake. Maybe, thought Mathez, he had been brought here because a younger doctor could not be tolerated.

Her braids hung in tatters down her cheek. Mathez saw the hips already spreading. She'd be a fat old woman. Maybe fat before then. Her cries now echoed around the room. An expensive gilt crucifix hung on the wall. Its Christ's eyes were shut. No blood on the walnut skin. She reached down to her hip; the bone was bearing the brunt of the pain. Maybe it was the rain outside and some intimacy engendered by it, but Mathez himself began to sweat in sympathy. Maybe the fever he'd been expecting was already coming on; as he began to massage the woman's abdomen, his own hips felt swollen and a leaden weight hung between his legs.

She heaved terribly. An hour passed. Her cries were short yet sharp and came every five seconds until they were like a continuous exhalation. He felt older, and weak under the burden of her pain. Nothing was coming yet. In fact, the dilations had stopped altogether. He became worried. He thought about the knife but it had been years since he had cut, and he didn't want to do it now. Eventually, though, he'd have to do something. Another hour passed.

In all the years, only a half dozen children had died in his hands. Yet the key to his legend was, not a single woman had ever died. When the first one does, he thought, will that be the end? If this one dies, do I die? His nose and chest were congested; he saw, with each gasp of the patient, a specter of his own death. Finally, stronger contractions, and, then rather quickly, full dilation. No fetus in sight, however; he nodded to the maid, who presented him the forceps. He'd pull something out or faint from the chill and his own mucous. Faint, God forbid, and she'd die, and he'd die.

The head rested in the tongs. Mathez now saw a peak of bare cranial flesh between her legs. The maid fetched a small table from the sitting room and spread out the warm linen, then set down the knife he'd use to cut the cord. "Push," said Mathez. The maid, with remarkable aplomb, went behind the bed and reached out to hold high the woman's legs.

But the mother started babbling. "Dozens of them," she kept saying. "Dozens of them."

"Easy, my dear," said Mathez.

"All on the road. Dozens everywhere. Don't stop them, let them wash through, let 'em flow. Tumble each on each."

"Easy, dearest," he said again, worrying again for her life. Then he remembered what he'd done with the Palissy woman a decade ago. He leaned over as if to whisper in her ear, but instead began himself to breathe with full, heavy and regular breaths. He furrowed all his concentration in his own breath; he covered the woman with those breaths. Even in her delirium, he'd get her to echo them and, with such breaths, she'd regain control of the moment, and ride over the unbearable pain and the unbearable incoherent visions.

Legs way up. The head was out, and Mathez let the forceps fall from his hand. Just outside, the husband's shadow loomed large and crossed a foot or two into the bedroom. Mathez watched the top shoulder approach birth: an extrusion as slow as geology. Again, he worried: Had there been enough oxygen?

"It's a boy," he said, finally.

"A boy! A boy!" said the mother.

The husband stepped closer to the bed. "Is he whole?"

"He's whole, so far."

"End it soon," he said, sounding more put upon than weary. "Finish soon, can you?"

As if to oblige, the child's feet sidled out of the mother's womb. The woman's thighs were glistening with sweat, and she was almost blinded by the water dripping from her scraggly braids. But the ordeal wasn't over. There was no sound, not even a splutter of air, after the first slap. Mathez landed another, harder. The moisture on his brow turned cold and he felt it cling to his skin; he felt it chill and clammy inside his head. A third slap, and he heard what sounded like a faint cough, although it didn't seem to come from the baby. It sounded distant, like something lost out there in the storm. Mathez dared not look at either parent. He blasted, at last, the newborn back with the side of his fist, and a rasp of a cough broke loose.

The infant began to cry but it was a cry Mathez in all these years had never heard before. Not a shrill cry, nor rising ululation, it was a low moaning call that harmonized oddly with the sounds of the rain beating against the windows. Only gradually did it begin to rise, until becoming at last the healthy sound of real life.

Mathez himself could barely see through his own sweat as he counted the toes. "Completely whole," he said, and let the baby rest against his mother's belly instead of lying him down on the linen. Mathez cut the cord. The maid hurried over with towels to collect the afterbirth and sop up the blood. As she leaned over, Mathez came close to her fleshy face and smiled. "You're a fine woman," he said, loud enough for her employer to hear. "This has been a very hard one. Thank you."

"Thank you," she said with a self-effacing smile, still holding the cloth full of afterbirth.

"You can get rid of that now," Mathez advised her.

He checked the mother. No fever, no sign of infection. But her mouth was ajar, and she seemed insensate. "I was expecting it to be difficult," he said. "Bear the pain. It will pass."

The maid came up with the swaddling cloth, and Mathez, stepping back, felt faint again, this time with exhaustion. He was too old for this, too old for such struggle. The father, impassive but no longer quite so stiff, approached him with the coins. "As in the past, we thank you for your considerable efforts," he said.

"Send a message tomorrow with the stable boy," he told the man, "even if it's only to say she's resting peacefully." And to the maid he said, "Check her for any excessive redness in the morning. If she's too warm, tell the master. Any discomfort she mentions, have me informed."

Mathez walked to the threshold and looked back at the woman. At last she was smiling, happily, as the baby rested on her breast. Outside, the vast pouring rain. As he surveyed the sky, he opened his mouth almost in awe, like he was about to call out to the world. He might have, had he had something to say to the rain. The boy brought the carriage over and Mathez hopped on, using another thick cloth over his head for whatever protection it would provide.

The moon jumped out of the clouds in a sudden blur of bright white and illuminated the whole landscape ahead of him. Everything shone in unprecedented clarity. Never had he seen forms at midnight so well defined. Pieces of bark on the trees hung over each other in a sharply outlined quilt work. The world never looked like this. The distant hills ambled in the moonlight like clay gargantuas about to reshape themselves. Nature was playing with itself, and he felt like an intruder–as if he had caught the world unawares and was about to see its secrets.

He glanced at the stable hand manning the reins. The boy seemed to be seeing something too, but both were quiet.

Actually, the young man was in some pain. The rain was whipping his cheeks and neck, and he was wincing at every turn. The horse barreling resolutely over the land was behaving as if he were angry. Mathez imagined the horse's eyes: red and glaring, mad at the world for heaving up a child on a night like this. Or perhaps the apparent mystery in the air was unsettling the beast, who was bolting now and almost skidding down the road. But Mathez was less anxious than before, or perhaps he was just resigned to fate.

On the other hand, he wanted to see his wife again. Again, he reached over to help the boy rein in the wild steed. Suddenly they veered over the rim of a ditch, and Mathez heard a perilous sound of horse hooves scratching. He glanced downward as they passed and saw the mud flooded like a deep bog, crisscrossed on the surface by fallen branches. The whole carriage tilted as if to crash, and the two riders braced themselves for the worst. But two of the wheels hewed to fairly solid ground, and the trip continued.

"I guess I don't want to die yet," he muttered to the boy, who didn't respond. Mathez thought of the man who was the child's father without quite resenting him, even though he lacked the common decency to offer a bed for the night or shelter until the storm subsided. Mathez would have accepted such an offer, of course, and perhaps should even have solicited so basic a consideration. Yet there was about this travail, this deluge of nonpareil clarity, something of a force of inevitability for him.

"And I want to see my wife again," he added. This time the boy nodded in reply, almost sympathetically.

Harder and harder they pulled on the reins as their steed charged on. Mathez' arm was throbbing and there was a slight gaseous pain in his chest. A heart attack wouldn't surprise. He knew his body was being racked. He knew such vessels as his own weren't fit for this.

The mud saved them. The whole backside of the horse was lurching forward with great resoluteness but the momentum slowed as the wet mud rose ever higher along the road. Soon the beast was a veritable contortionist picking its way forward with exaggerated movements and grinding to less than a trot as his dark legs dug into the quag.

The deceleration made for another problem, however: lightning. Streaks of it were everywhere; the air itself was a lodestone. The young driver was apparently troubled as well. Where just a moment ago he'd been straining to rein in the animal, now he was whipping it almost furiously. One bolt flashed just above their heads, in an instant illuminating countless raindrops for miles in the distance. Not only his own death, Mathez regarded the poor boy beside him who'd never had a chance to live.

"I give up," he whispered aloud to himself. "I'm as good as dead."

Yet as if nature were contriving to be merciful, the mud before them hardened and their pace picked up. Mathez glanced at the driver, who also looked relieved. They'd apparently gotten past a small network of streams that had swollen and badly swamped the road. Of course, the lightning could still kill them, or the horse once again accelerate dangerously, but at least now they didn't feel as if they were just sitting still, waiting for their luck to run out and a thunderbolt hit.

Mathez breathed even deeper when he realized that the copse was well behind them, so their destination could not be too far ahead. "You sleep in the kitchen tonight," he said to the driver, who nodded back with an appreciative smile. "You can put your horse in my neighbor's barn."

"I hope my mother doesn't worry too much," said the boy. "I think we'll be all right as long as no tree falls down on us."

That was actually a serious consideration. A few older trees hovering over the road were creaking in the wind and rain. But finally Mathez spotted it: the limey green-white facade of his cottage, no more than five hundred yards away. The other-worldly clarity that so affected him at the outset of the return trip had faded – although, as they neared the house, and the garden by the front door, Mathez did see the bent heads of the white and red roses in their beds also hung in sharp, eerie outline. The gaslight inside fanned out through the front room. One hundred yards away now, he thought he could make out his wife busying herself about the room.

She embraced her husband as the boy ran off to lodge the horse. Now the cold really afflicted him. Trembling, he peeled off his shirt and pants as his wife brought hot compresses. "I'll make more for the boy when he comes in," she said.

He wrapped himself in a long white sheet and hunched up by the fireplace. He lost consciousness before the fumes, which had overpowered him but loosened the oppressive congestion in his head. He opened his eyes to find his wife standing beside him, and he rose to accept her sympathetic caress. Some time had passed, apparently. The stable hand was already settled inside with a mug of tea.

"Tell me you'll be all right," she said as she poured him a cup.

"I will," he said. The back of his head was heavy with indescribable exhaustion but his throat was just a little sore.

Finally, they lay down together. "I've never seen you look so tired before," she said.

"I've never felt so tired before."

"It must have been a hard trip."

"It was," he answered. "The delivery was hard too. It was all very hard."

"Why?" she asked.

"Because it was Cezanne. Tonight, I delivered Paul Cezanne."

Stone in the Bone

They said Mary Modesto was pregnant sometime in 1955, I
think it was sometime around June, they being Dr. Heath and
the nurse and an obstetrician who stops by from Glens Falls
on a regular basis. Mary did not have a husband but we didn't
hold that against her, we being me and most of the people in
town that I know. Unlike what a lot of people say, people in
towns like ours can be pretty fair-minded, and we hold our
judgment and we who are not without sin do not throw first
stones, especially when we like you, and everybody likes Mary
or at least there's no reason not to. She's regular people, she
treats those around her pretty good for the most part, and she
doesn't put on airs or act in strange or defiant ways because
her parents came from someplace else, not New York City in
her case but some place like that where the people who come
over from the old country are all looking to start up their lives
fresh in order for their children to find a better life in America.
When Mary said she didn't know who the father was, we just
kind of glanced at each other but we held our peace. We tried
not to pass judgment. Somebody, I recall it might have been
Toby McFalls, said it was likely Gil Berry, who was always, even
when he was thirteen and fourteen, kind of a tomcat. Then,
when we heard that Mary told her best friend Amy Kuhn that

she was still a virgin, we still didn't say much. But you could tell people might now be thinking there was something odd about Mary. But like I say, even then we didn't say much.

All kinds of people have passed through our town over the years. There's good hunting here, deer and pheasants, and good fishing too in the many streams that float along just outside the town limits. But just as much as that, we're on a pretty direct line with Cornell University to the west and Skidmore east and a little more north. Also, people come over from High Falls and Woodstock, just poking around for the most part but sometimes they'll stay a few weeks, they rent rooms in the old dormitory from the McPhersons, and they stay awhile often for the relaxation you can get here and the peacefulness and the opportunity to do their work, art work and photography and poetry too, without their ever being disturbed in the nice bright warm sunshine. Some of them are odd sorts, I must say. The oddest one I ever met was a painter who lived in Albany because his wife had a job there with the government, and they had a child, poor fellow, who was handicapped with autism. For safety's sake he wore a helmet to protect his head, and his father used to smear paint on the helmet so that when the boy banged his head it would leave interesting patterns on the wall, which his dad would copy out blotch by blotch on the canvas that painters like him use.

But getting back to Mary Modesto, 1956 came along and soon it was the summer of that year, a cool pleasant summer as I recall, and then the winds picked up and by and by the snow fell and it was Christmas, which comes but once a year but it does come every year for sure. It was very confusing for all of us, for Mary's friends and well-wishers and even for some of the visitors who learned about it by chatting with Chet over at the hotel or with the McPhersons at the dormitory. Mary Modesto was still pregnant, isn't that odd? Mary looked around six months pregnant, but nothing was moving, her belly was the same size as it had been over the summer of 1956 and back in late 1955, and meanwhile nobody was getting born. I assume she hadn't had her monthly since 1955, but that was no business of mine and I'm not the kind of guy to ask.

So we started wondering if Dr. Heath and the nurse and the obstetrician from Glens Falls who visits us regular were necessarily correct in their diagnosis. I'm not sure "diagnosis" is the right word when it comes to pregnancy, but you get my point.

Anyway, Dr. Heath was having lunch at the hotel, and Chet tells me he went over to him and said, "May not be my business, Doc, but this thing with Mary Modesto has got us all wondering."

"Got me wondering too," said Dr. Heath.

"What about that fellah from Glens Falls?" asked Chet.

"Oh yeah, him too. He's wondering a bunch."

"Well, so what can it mean?"

"Don't actually know at this point," said Dr. Heath.

"Gee, when are you going to know?" asked Chet.

"Can't really say. All we can do is run more tests."

Mary, for her part, was walking around in sort of a daze and you could tell it was hard for her to answer the questions that some people were starting to ask, though they were as polite as they could be in asking them. Amy, as I said, was her best friend, but all Amy could say was "I don't know. Nobody knows." Dr. Heath and the obstetrician from Glens Falls tested and retested. Nothing had changed, they said. She was pregnant and there were the sounds of life inside of her. They took x-rays and they said they saw it. More months went by and Mary Modesto could be seen walking through the streets, into stores like the hardware store she went into one day because she said she needed a hammer and screwdriver to fix things. We worried she was going to do something rash and violent to end the ordeal but Amy said no, she really did need a hammer and screwdriver to fix things,

As 1957 went on and nothing changed, people started thinking of reasons for it. Some called it a medical mystery. Others had a kind of theory that Mary could trace her roots back to dark places in the old country, and that, you never know, there was a spell on her and hers. I thought that was pretty ignorant talk but I didn't have anything better to offer by way of explanation. Meantime word spread around and curiosity seekers arrived from as far off as New York City, Montreal, as far west as from Pittsburgh. Newspapermen came from local papers in Troy and from all the way in Boston and were asking people questions. Dr. Heath made himself scarce and so did the obstetrician from Glens Falls. A team of specialists from the state university was summoned, I guess by Dr. Heath, and their examination confirmed that she was six months pregnant and that there was certainly a living thing inside of her. 1957 wore on, and most of the newspapers lost interest, understandably. How many times can you tell the world that a baby has not been born?

I saw Mary on the street, I think it was around September of 1957, and she said, "I'm so tired of being poked at."

Meantime, things in the world didn't stop happening. In fact, big things were happening, and not such good things, like when the Russians sent up their Sputnik. That scared people. It sure scared me. What if they could shoot at us from outer space and we couldn't do diddly in response? And I sure didn't know the Russians were that smart in the first place. Now I knew. So we all walked over to the meadow out by Rocky Ryan Park, which is so pretty in the fall of the year, even as late as October, and we looked for Sputnik in the sky and nobody could see it. Except Mary Modesto came by, and she said, "I think I saw it."

"Maybe she's in with the Russians," Gabe Lessing said on the sly.

"Go fiddle your fanny," I heard sweet old Dorothy Young answer him. Good for Dorothy. Dorothy is the sweetest soul, always has been. She knows it's not Mary's fault if she's just six months pregnant after getting pregnant two years earlier. And overall it was so nice to see Dorothy Young then, it was such a sweet comfort to see her face which was so sweet even though the Russians just mounted space.

By late 1958, Dr. Heath and the obstetrician from Glens Falls were reckoning that Mary might be seven months pregnant, but they didn't seem so sure even of that. Sometimes you could see Mary sitting over by Toby McFalls', or sometimes on the bench in front of the hardware store, just hanging down her head and seeming to mutter who knows what. A funny thing also happened in late 1958 at Tuff's Diner when Gil Berry was eating there, and Gil just stood up and proclaimed, "I got nothing to do with it! I got nothing to do with it!" There were a bunch of people at the diner at the time but, honestly, nobody really cared at this point who the father was, seeing as how they were a lot more concerned with what the father, whoever he was, was the father of.

That's about the time when I saw Brad Jaeger at the Easy Time Lounge, and he said to me, "You know what I think?"

"What? You talking about poor Mary?"

"Yeah, I don't think it's a baby at all."

"What do you think it is?" I asked him.

"I think it's a stone in the bone."

Sounded plausible, I guess, and word spread. Now you know, a thought like that can get to be general consensus, and general consensus is just about impossible to hide from anyone and, in this case, everyone included Mary Modesto. From what I could learn, that consensus just broke poor Mary's heart once she heard of it and thought about what it meant if it were true. I have it from Amy Kuhn, God bless her, Amy who to this day is such a loyal friend of Mary's. Mary confides in her and tells Amy her deepest most painful secrets. Amy doesn't betray those confidences but sometimes just out of concern for Mary and because her own heart is breaking she just has to say something. Amy's father was like that too, he was always telling you something about somebody because it was deeply troubling him. So Amy told me this.

Amy told me that Mary has been loving her baby so much since 1955. She caresses her belly. She talks to the baby. She tells the baby how much she will care for and cuddle with and kiss and tickle and tease. She tells the baby his name will be Shane if you are a boy or Leigh Ann if you are a girl. She tells the baby how happy life will be in the town but that you can still have wonderful adventures all over the world and then come back home to be loved again and hugged again, always and forever and always.

So you can imagine how awful Mary Modesto must feel to think that the baby inside her isn't really a baby at all, but just a big old stone in her bone.

"How do you get a stone in your bone?" Amy asked me one day when I saw her coming out of Mary's little house that she shared with old lady Davis and a handyman named Weil who also rented rooms from the Fry family that owned the property. We were strolling down Walnut Lane together.

"I guess something just starts to calcify," I said. "I don't actually know the details."

"So maybe she really is a virgin?" asked Amy.

"I sure don't know," I said.

"But this has never happened to anybody before, don't you think?"

"I never heard of it before, but I guess I don't know," I said.

"Gosh," she said. "How does it start? Does something get put inside you or is it already there?"

"I wish I could tell you," I said.

I remember when 1960 came and Mary was still six months pregnant, there was a kind of quiet recognition around town that a new decade was dawning and still there was Mary still carrying it around. It was all a fixture by now, for sure. Most of us by now were figuring it was really a stone in the bone. There wasn't actually all that much more to say or talk about. Even people's curiosity about it was less than what it once was, with the passage of time and all. "There's Mary and that stone," people would think to themselves, I guess, and then just go about their business. Me, sometimes I'd think to myself, "Maybe we should give the stone a name." I don't know why I thought that. I don't know why I thought that might have been a kindly thing to do. Probably not such a kindly thing, as I reconsidered. Probably just make Mary Modesto feel like even more of a freak if what she was carrying were to have a name like Joe or Sally.

Time was passing and other things were going on in the world as the years went by. In 1962, there was the Cuban

Missile Crisis, for example. Everybody was afraid they'd die. One evening that time in October when the park and the meadow are still so pretty even this late in the fall, we were all sort of gathered in Rocky Ryan Park, and we were looking for Russian missiles in the sky and nobody said anything except when Mary Modesto got there, she said, "I wish I could see something."

"You're better off not seeing anything," said Brad Jaeger, and Mary stood there and didn't say anything more, she seemed so tired, and Amy Kuhn stood by her side and didn't say anything either. That was a tense time. We finally started walking away, it must have been close to midnight, and Amy whispered to me, "Can I talk to you a little bit tomorrow?"

"Poor Mary," she said the next day as I gave her a cup of coffee. "There's something she don't tell anybody but me, but I hope I can get some advice from you anyway."

"I won't tell anyone."

"Mary is a good-looking woman," said Amy. "Even now that she's older, she's good-looking. Maybe better looking. Except for her stomach, she has a good body too. But damn, she gets lonely. She wants a man. She wants to know what it's like."

"That's only natural," I said and looked away, I guess I looked away in case Amy was hinting something to me seeing as how I'd been alone for the past couple of years.

"I feel so bad for her," said Amy.

"You know what scares me?" I said. "It's bad enough that Mary can't get what's natural for her to want. But what scares me is that some guy might want her just because she has a stone in her bone. You know, like it would be a novelty experience. That would be worse for her than being all alone and pining away."

"I was thinking the same thing," said Amy. She got up and said goodbye and no more was said about it.

By 1969, Dr. Heath was passed away and so was the nurse and the obstetrician from Glens Falls retired. That was the year man first walked on the moon. Instead of heading out to Rocky Ryan Park, we gathered around our televisions, at home and at the Easy Time Lounge and we heard the astronaut say it was one small step for a man but a giant leap for mankind. They brought rocks back from the moon and it got you to wondering what was next. I would often look up and say to myself, "A human being has walked on that moon, actually walked on it, and only once in all of history and it was during my lifetime!" Even so, the moon still seems to be as cold and mysterious and silent as it always was to me before.

I didn't see Mary Modesto for weeks afterward, I guess it was just happenstance that I didn't see her, but one day I did see her waiting for her order on the take-out line at Tuff's Diner. I guess there's not much more to tell, at least not as yet. I wish I could tell you more right now about how things are working out, but I can't. You know what they always say: The more things change, the more they stay the same.

The Queen of Astoria

The Prounis family had the time of its life. Maybe a lot of the other people, even well-meaning friends, were looking down on them with disapproval. The Asimakopoulos', for example, all thought the Prounis' were getting too carried away, that the new ways which weren't their ways had gone to their heads.

Not that the Asimakopoulos' weren't real Americans like everyone else; the wonderful John Asimakopoulos had died at Bataan, for heaven's sake! But dying for your country didn't mean forgetting what's important to your own people, or behaving like giddy teenage children. John Asimakopoulos' descendants would always gladly break bread with the Prounis', but sometimes they seemed to need a warning.

Others could think no wrong of Nick Prounis, his wife Eleni, their sons John and George, the lovely daughter Joyce, and Nick's brother Ari, who you'd think lived more at Nick's house on 34th off 31st Avenue than at his own place closer to Steinway St. The enthusiasms of such people as the Prounis', so figured the Panagiotopoulos', the Kapochunas', even the Papadopoulos', who were in some ways as old-fashioned as the Asimakopoulos', couldn't be so very bad after all. Who were they hurting? It might not be how they themselves would ever feel comfortable living their lives, but what was so indecent?

Nothing at all! The Prounis' were good neighbors, ever since they moved over from Nauplia.

You could say a certain respectful forbearance reigned among their detractors, while the approbation of their supporters was not without a faintly heedful anxiety. A lot of the people figured it was Ari who made the Prounis' a little different. It was interesting that it didn't really matter how long people were over here. The Asimakopoulos' came to the United States a long time ago, since before the 1930s, yet sometimes they still acted like people who pulled water out of a cistern. The Prounis family was here less than twenty years, but they had Ari, and Ari had a real flare for America. Sometimes he was also critical of what he saw, not so much of how Americans behaved as of how people lived here, as when he compared linoleum to tile. "Remember the way our floors used to look, and how they were colorful and looked like a human being had made them, and had real dignity even when they got dirty," he declared once at the diner after a third or fourth whiskey. "They felt so fine and chilly against your bare feet. And they were pretty. The blue tiles on the yellow, and the white ones at the baseboards."

Life here was too much linoleum. The home supply stores on Steinway that vended the endless sheets of the stuff oppressed Ari just to walk past, especially since he knew there wasn't much point trying to use anything better. Unless you were a rich man, the aesthetic struggle was wholly intractable. It was, for example, no use painting the apartments fresh every year, because the dirty light and dust wore down the sheen in just a few months. Meanwhile, the facades built up inexorable accretions of soot, block after samish block. No way to freshen or change them. Once he went to see his friends the Donleavy brothers who lived with their grandfather Al on 30th St. It looked just like his own apartment except smaller. The sight of the place as you walked in was like an unpleasant modern painting, because all there was to see were three rooms that weren't very big, with each of the three bordering floors a different color of light-toned linoleum.

But the way Ari kept telling it to Nick, there was still a great life here waiting to be lived, and it wasn't just the money you could make. It was all the thousands of miles in every direction, with people everywhere and room for more, having adventures and never knowing what the next day would bring. That was why people kept coming here, and why Joyce, who was an angel, was old enough at eighteen to go to the dance after the big dinner. Everyone from the neighborhood, and others they never saw or met before from Long Island City and even Manhattan, would be going, all except the Asimakopoulos', who would let their three daughters only go to the dinner. The Kapochunas' were undecided, and said they'd wait as late as Friday before making up their minds about Antigone.

Eleni Prounis giggled a little when she looked at Ari and Joyce, only pretending she'd be on their side in case Nick had second thoughts about Joyce going to the dance. Beautiful Mama! When Eleni called Ari on the phone, what she had to say filled him with gladness. "I saw a beautiful dress on 31st Ave. It was very elegant and it wasn't too expensive. It's a dress that if Joyce wears it on Saturday everybody will remember."

"That will make old man Asimakopoulos think twice!" exclaimed Ari.

"Like the whole world is going crazy!" laughed Eleni.

"And passing him by!" said Ari.

"I can't wait until you see it," said Eleni. She described it vaguely: a little low cut, just a little, but the white lace at the bosom made her seem an angel. Swirls of braided beige overlay snaked on down to her ankles. "It's a little revealing," admitted Eleni, "but it's decent."

That evening when he visited, Ari shook his head sternly in mock disapproval. He clucked his tongue, and told Joyce her Mama had told him all about the dress for the party, and that he and her father were both outraged. Nick, playing along, affected a sour, tragic face as he put his hand on his brother's shoulder. "After all my hard work," said Papa, "you turn out to be such a bad girl!"

Joyce was that day wearing blue jeans and a sweater, just like all the girls from Astoria and Long Island City who'd already gotten started in the public school when she and Mama and Papa were still in Nauplia. She picked up the cue. She scowled with her hands on her hips. "Shame on you, shame on you both! I'm a good girl!"

"We're sending you back right now," said Ari. "You'll go home and marry a fisherman."

"And your mother, we're sending her back too!" exclaimed Nick.

"So I'll have a nice cruise!" Eleni called out from the kitchen, where she'd gone to see to dinner. "Send me to Thera."

Ari was bursting with joy inside. It could have been the sense alive within him that, in the ten years since he came to New York, this was the very first time he was really embracing the new life and feeling himself a part of the great hurly-burlies. Not that Greece hadn't made him feel alive too, especially around the islands, or when he went as far as Heraklion, where he was friendly with a prostitute who confided her secrets whenever he visited.

He was a small dark man whose rugged lined face was always a little stubbly. It was his wont to jostle things affectionately, like this very way he enjoyed teasing his beloved niece.

Nick often played along, but Nick was a much quieter and less ambitious man, ambitious in the sense of how some men always want to swallow up life. Ari was a conqueror by nature, in the best sense of the word. Ever since he'd landed in the United States, he felt almost a responsibility to gorge on life here too, and to feel it just as keenly as when he used to sail the other side.

Ari's dream was to drive a car clear across to California, but he knew he'd never get away long enough from the liquor warehouse in Maspeth where he worked. That was a shame. He wanted to see the Grand Canyon and the Mississippi River. The squat grime of Queens didn't fit, never could fit, he knew, the bursting emotion that was the rest of the great city, the real city, much less the endless wonderment of the whole big recumbent country itself. It had been awfully frustrating, to be here and yet not quite taste it.

Joyce was a way to taste it, especially since, although he loved adventure, he hated being away from his family. He was pulled in two directions, and his family usually won him over. But Joyce was both adventure and love, the deep tie to the family that grew even deeper after she was born, a joy in the heart when she was a child, always happy and tugging at you, she was, at your face and nose and shirt collar. Now that she was a lady, it was as if the family had accomplished a great thing, because something had flowered here which, even in Greece, might have gotten lost in ancient linen and perpetual custom and the smell of new paint on old clapboard. That this lovely thing was Nick's, was his brother's own, made their bond yet stronger, and caused him too to love his brother's wife as if she were his own sister. It was such a joy to be so close to a beautiful woman like Eleni, so physically close, without lust intruding or being allowed to intrude. What an achievement

for a man, to feel that way so close beside a beautiful woman–
and, as she got older and her figure grew wonderfully full,
Joyce too. The smell of her was also intensely like a woman's.

Let's have a party before the party," Ari said. "A family
party, to celebrate your beautiful new dress. Just us and your
brothers and maybe the Panagiotopoulos'. Invite them for
Thursday. A preview!"

"I'll be embarrassed," said Joyce.

"It's a rehearsal," said Uncle Ari. "There has to be a rehearsal. One step at a time. Soon you'll be a star, the first girl
since Maria Callas to marry a billionaire. You'll marry Onassis!"

"He's dead, and when he was alive he was fat," pouted
Joyce. "I want to marry Mel Gibson."

The Panagiotopoulos' came, toting the Croat who'd married Melina Panagiotopoulos' sister, and who drank too much.
He did so again tonight, leering at Joyce even before she put
on the dress. No one cared much. There was gaiety in the air,
and the Croat was a pathetic soul. The usual thing was to feel
sorry for his wife.

"Last year the dinner was fine but the party later got too
wild, I think," said Melina, referring a little suggestively to the
upcoming event, but not, really, with all that much concern
or censure in her tone.

"What, 'wild'?" argued Ari.

"Some of the Irish kids were fighting outside in the parking
lot," laughed Eleni. "They had bloody noses, but now they're
friends again."

"I know their family," intoned the Croat. "The Riordan
family. Good people."

Ari rested his eyes on the icons in high relief on the part
of the kitchen door jutting into the living room. In the other
corner of the kitchen, John and George were watching an old

Perry Mason rerun on the small TV by the window. A buzzer sounded for Eleni to take the food out of the oven. Joyce helped with the plates. The saffron-smelling seasoning she given the big casserole of orzo and lamb seemed a little foreign to the house, as if from another part of the world.

"Things like that fight," warned Nick, "give Asimako-poulos something to worry about."

"So let them look down their noses," said Ari.

"Asimakopoulos is a good man," said Melinda.

"I didn't say he wasn't," answered Ari.

"Maybe Greeks stick together too much," commented Nick, without bitterness.

After dinner, they called for the dress. Joyce hurried off, a little embarrassed but savoring the attention. It was a chance to conspire with her beloved uncle against the whole world. The Panagiotopoulos' sat back to wait. "Put them all to shame," Ari called out toward the bedroom where Joyce was changing.

"We don't need you, you bum, to tell us what a beautiful girl this is," said the old grandmother, Helen Panagiotopoulos, who lived in New Jersey but, for some reason, came and stayed for month-long visits every spring. It was one of those strange family habits that no one ever quite understands or asks about, but it made Ari squirm a little, like it was something odd, both old-fashioned and oddly compulsive, that was too often accepted without question. Maybe Greeks do stick together too much, thought Ari, even more than the Italians.

Joyce was lovely! As the beige braid work followed her long legs to the floor, the elegance of the thing seemed to work on her own mind, and on her whole notion of herself. She even arched her back in a grander manner than the family was used to. The beginnings of her breasts were visible but not lurid, more like how statuary shows anatomy if stone could be made warm and slightly dark to the senses. Her black eyes glimmered, proudly, and a little mischievously.

What excitement there was in the neighborhood the night of the dinner that the masons had been sponsoring every year for the past six years, along with the special gala party for the younger kids which the local Astoria order threw separately at the party hall on 27th St. Even strangers on the street seemed to sense an effervescence that carried over from school into the diners, and to the cafes where a younger alien but friendly bunch of young people who worked in Manhattan lately gathered, mainly on the weekends. To Joyce, at least, its life abounding was ubiquitous.

That very night, though, Joyce would frighten herself a little, because she couldn't stop looking at herself naked before she put her dress on. Such an intimate moment with herself she'd only have once in awhile on certain nights just before going to sleep or right after taking a warm bath. A few hairs dangled around her nipples, and she reached for a scissors to snip them. But then she blanched. Why should she be doing this now? It shouldn't make any difference whether there were hairs there or not. She was a good girl, and she blushed naked for a second or two as she dashed the guilty thoughts out of her mind.

She put the dress on and felt it cling to her undergarments. The bravado she'd shown for Uncle Ari and the Panagiotopoulos' at the party before the party was gone. She was excited, but a little bewildered. She heard Mama open the apartment door for Ari. Her thoughts went there with them, relieved, feeling alive because the beloved and incredible uncle was with her now and she wouldn't need to be worried or ashamed about anything.

Uncle had come to wish her a good time. "It's like you're brand new!" he exclaimed, his eyes jubilating up and down the dress, like to feast on the silken fibers. "You won't be a wall flower tonight. That would be wrong."

Beautiful Mama was right behind him. Her head was lowered a little, and she was smiling a warm little smile that, at one moment, suggested a joyful giggle inside her also, coyly, trying to hide. "Ari," she said to her brother-in-law, "it's not girls' fault when no one wants to dance with them. Some just aren't so attractive."

"It is their fault when they don't want to be a success," said Ari. "Or when they dress so old-fashioned, nobody wants to dance with them."

By the same token, it wasn't as if people were looking down their noses at the half-dozen or so girls who did come to the dinner that night dressed conservatively in stitched wool sweaters, colorful but wholly covering the contours of their bodies. Such girls were inevitable parts of the scenery in this Greek neighborhood and were, for that matter, a welcome sight to some of the men who figured they'd ultimately be safer falling in love and marrying them than more modern types like Joyce.

Who would fall in love with Joyce? He'd be a teacher, maybe, someone who taught engineering in Athens, and was waiting for a job in the United States or was going for an advanced degree. He'd be very modern in his attitudes. Maybe he'd be a businessman, working for an American company rather than one of those slightly shady Greek entrepreneurs you'd see sometimes around the neighborhood visiting their parents. Joyce's husband would expect her to think in a forward-looking manner. With such prospects before her, even the small and private moments of life ahead might be wonderful in a way many of her friends could never understand. Life would be exciting all the time. Sometimes, when she was alone, and was in the right mood, and wasn't embarrassed to think about such things, Joyce thought about kissing and hugging, and what it would mean in terms of love-making to marry a forward-thinking man, and how modernity might improve on Old World models.

It was a consanguinity too close, perhaps, for Uncle Ari to approve of, but the Croatians, the ones living by the church on 33rd right off 31st avenue (not the crowd of the Panagiotopoulos' Croat, who was from Jackson Heights), were all seated together at the dinner. Papa probably wouldn't approve either. "It's our fault too," she once heard him say, after a local confirmation party where some friends of the Papadopoulos' had politely invited some Irish families, but who then huddled together in a corner by themselves throughout. "We share our food and our drink, but we don't really give of ourselves," he said.

The dinner was lovely. Mr. Papadopoulos kept nodding at her and smiling throughout, as if he were happy to be with her even though she was dressed—as he had begrudgingly complimented her upon their being seated—"oh like a real society lady!" It must be admitted, Joyce was a little disappointed that the only people her own age at the table were Helen Papadopoulos, a numbingly silent 16-year old, and George Parisis, a neighbor of the Kapochunas', a sweet boy but a little immature, who kept staring at her dress, particularly when she bent slightly to drink her egg soup. He always made very crude jokes. There was the one famous time he nearly got expelled from school because of a remark. They were reading *The Greek Way* by Edith Hamilton in history class. Mr. Parker asked a broad and challenging question: "Sum up for me, what is the Greek way?" George bellowed out something in reply about people's rear ends. Not only was it gross, Joyce couldn't imagine such things. No one she ever met would do that. Why did they say these things about the Greeks? Why did the Greeks say such things about themselves?

They had their choice of chicken or fish in big helpings with nice tomato sauces, although Joyce never expected cooking at restaurants or public gatherings to be as sumptuous as what people served in their own homes, including her own. She worried sometimes, if she married someone who was forward-looking, and they moved to Manhattan, or to another city, maybe a foreign city, would they only eat delicious food when they came home for a visit to Astoria? On the other hand, she herself could always cook the good stews and broil fish like she was used to. But then she worried if a forward-looking man, even a Greek from a Greek family, would appreciate her kind of food.

She was able to circulate after eating and go chat with the Malanos twins at another table. Theo Kampani was there too, one of the more personable boys who'd already gotten early acceptance to go to Stanford University. She wished her family knew his better. Once she even planned to mention them to Uncle Ari in hopes he'd make an effort to cultivate their friendship. Not that the Kampanis stood out particularly in the neighborhood – Theo was the first Kampani to go to a great school like Stanford – but something about their company was invigorating and it was a treat to see the family at neighborhood gatherings. It was even in the way they smiled. Admittedly, Joyce felt, by way of contrast, a certain contempt for the Papadopoulos' sitting through the dinner hardly speaking, or feeling much of an obligation to do so. Their attentions were focused entirely on the food, and the extent to which the meal enhanced the aggregate quality of their lives or failed to do so. That was a cautionary lesson, perhaps: maybe she herself shouldn't be worrying so much about food when she pondered the future and envisioned the forward-looking man she'd someday marry.

The party on 27th Street was loud and warm and full of young people jumping and gyrating on the dance floor. The hall was decorated with big signs welcoming different youth groups: Welcome, 34th St. Wildcats. Welcome, Achilles Warriors. Welcome, Fighting 43rd. There were trophies everywhere and bright paper decorations fluttering, and helium balloons hovering. She'd felt a little overdressed at the dinner, as if the splendid dress Mama and she picked out and tried on and paid (Joyce guessed) $200 or more for, had finally been only for the dubious benefit of the Papadopoulos clan. But here it was different. Here dark young eyes lit up at the sight of her. At first she was a little nervous being so prominent, but many of the boys were friends of hers, while other boys she'd just chatted with on occasion in school or around the neighborhood gathered around her for conversation. Other young men she'd never met kept staring. What fancy fine pedigrees and great adventurous biographies they must be imagining in their heads to explain someone as elegant as herself! But it wasn't her fault if they were misled. She wasn't lying or misrepresenting herself. She was simply dressing well, and if people she didn't know thought she was some kind of a queen because of it, well, she had no control over what they thought.

It was additionally thrilling because there were young people here from throughout the area, a variety the Astoria masons had arranged on purpose. They wanted their children mixing with other people's children so everything wouldn't always just be Greek, with a few Croats tossed in from time to time. You could tell most of the couples in the middle of the dance floor were Italians. That was sometimes a disadvantage in mixing, that some groups can't help but start to take over. Joyce didn't mind too much, though, especially when she recognized Tony and Joe Vecchio, whose father, the older man who owned the newsstand on Steinway, was always so nice. Tony and Joe were sort of naughty guys, but they were always sweet, never obnoxious like George Parisis, and they meant no harm.

What if she didn't marry a Greek? What would happen then? Uncle Ari might be happy, and she guessed Mama and Daddy would be too. But then what if there were some kind of trouble? What if they suffered marital discord? It would be like confirming what everyone predicted and would have warned her against had they felt at liberty to do so. The thought of her tail stuck between her legs because she'd married an Italian or an Irishman who turned out to not be worthy of her was just too awful. It would be like everything she had tried to be, everything she believed in, would be disproved to people who were too smug and small to ever believe in living differently from the way they were.

Tony and Joe made a big deal of her dress by starting in to tease her. "Hey, fox, you wanna move closer to Steinway?" called Tony. "Look who'd you'd be right next door to."

"No kidding, Joyce, we wouldn't let you go walking by yourself," said Joe, "especially not wearin' that thing. Whoa!"

Two others she'd never seen before were standing just behind Tony and Joe and smiling broadly. They seemed very nice. One appeared to be Irish or just plain American. The other had an Italian complexion, but she couldn't quite tell. And then a third figure appeared, hard to see behind those two. "I'm surprised we've never met you before," said the young half-hidden man. "We're in this neighborhood a lot."

"Yeah, I'm here a lot too," said the Italian-looking one, his voice, unexpectedly, a most displeasing nasal twang. "I was in Greece once," he continued. "Ever hear of Epidaurus?" The twang vibrated with a sudden pride in its ability to say the name of that distant and ancient place. "They got a big theater there where all the old-time people went to see plays. You go all the way to the back of the theater and they drop coins on the stage, which you can hear perfect from the all the way in the back. That's how good the acoustics were even though it was in ancient times. You can sit there and even hear dimes."

"Sure," said Joyce. "My family is from Nauplia, which isn't really too far from there."

"Oh I was there too," said the twangy guy. "They got real fresh fish there. I love real fresh fish," he said as his companions smiled broadly and even a little strangely.

She started dancing with George Trypanis from school. George's mother was once very close to Eleni before something happened, a mysterious and very personal dispute that Mama never talked about and no one asked about. Then Tony Vecchio cut in. As the music got faster, the American-looking guy she'd never seen before cut in and, as he gyrated, loomed real close toward Joyce. The tempo redoubled and Joyce flushed from the motion, then blushed at the sudden intensity with which she and the others were moving. She backed off.

"Sorry," said the young man, nodding deferentially toward Tony as well. "I certainly didn't mean to be forward."

"You know them?" asked Jay Trypanis, George's brother. She shook her head. "No one else here does either."

The American-type returned to Joyce's side and asked, respectfully, almost too respectfully, to dance with her again. Joyce was interested in being fair, as well in being open-minded, and she thought he was an interesting-looking sort, with a face kind of craggy beyond his years. He had on a string tie no one else in the neighborhood ever wore. As he led, wonderfully, Joyce caught sight of a coterie of Greek girls, each of whom she knew by name but never really conversed with, huddled together, whispering among themselves but mainly saying nothing. It was so strange to Joyce, as her partner whirled her to the music of the band and the appreciative scrutiny of the band members who were all crimson shirts and darkish ties and soft, almost effeminate faces with pronounced mustaches. So strange: these girls, one of whom she too might easily be but for circumstance, easily draped like one of them in a black dress, a pubescent widow. It was a staring dark conspiratorial circle but for the occasional girlish giggle.

The dance ended and Joyce accompanied her partner as he rejoined his friends. "How you getting home?" asked the Italian-looking boy with the twang.

"My father and uncle are picking me up at 12:30," she answered matter-of-factly, pleasantly.

"And here I was, figuring to get a hot kiss goodnight," said the twang, laughing as he said it and blushing a mite to boot. Joyce smelled beer on his breath.

Joyce moved away, put off and scared a little but excited at the same time. She sat, just far enough from George Parisis so they wouldn't have to talk, on a small sofa by the wall where she could snatch a moment of her own to reflect and wonder if this was finally it: that she was a young woman now, that she'd entered a forbidden realm of talk and knowledge and unspoken messages that yet wasn't so forbidden people like Mama and Daddy hadn't themselves been here and known the feelings and cherished the memories. Repellent things, like the beer smell, were part of it too, something adults realized had to be accepted as part of life. George Parisis was different: her disgust with him was the disgust of an adult for a child. Maybe that's why she'd chosen to sit down not far from him after the more intimidating presence of the Italian with the twang. George was only harmlessly ridiculous.

As she sat coldly ignoring George so as not to let his ridiculous presence obtrude on her burgeoning mood, she felt the dress slink up a little over her ankles. End now, she thought to herself. Everything, the evening and the dance and life maybe even, end now while it's all so perfect. End like this in one big bubble right here and now.

By midnight, she and the other girls from the school were out in the parking lot waiting for rides home. Others there, mainly a few young men who lived close enough to walk home, were dawdling and hoping to flirt. The young man in the string tie came up behind Joyce. "Can I see you again?" he asked, stepping so close she was taken aback. "I'll show you around. I'll show you Brooklyn Heights and parts of Manhattan you've never been to."

Joyce was silent as he continued. "I'll show you nightclubs in Brighton Beach where no one else goes to eat and dance except Russian gangsters. I'll take you to live shows in Greenwich Village and Soho in New York where they do things too weird to do on Broadway." Then he said his name, Robert Adams.

Next day, the Prounis' were nonplussed when she told them about this invitation. These were adventures no one in the family had had, not even Uncle Ari, but they weren't necessarily disapproving. Mama and Papa were even a little excited for her. It was five years since Eleni spent a whole evening in Manhattan. All she said was, "you've got to be careful in New York."

"You used to go to Athens all by yourself," Joyce reminded her. "Remember you told me about how a handsome French foreigner tried to talk to you at the cafe on Lykabettos!"

Mama blushed. "Oh, all he asked was what he should see in the city, and how to best get there."

"What if Robert calls?" asked Joyce in a lowered tone, intent on getting a definite answer.

"You can go," said Nick. His smile of gentle approbation!

The call came two days later. "I thought we could take in an early show at Radio City on Wednesday and then have dinner. Ever been to Rock Center?" He said 'Rock Center' in the blithe way a real Manhattanite would say it.

Excited, she phoned Uncle Ari, and he was excited with her. She put the dress on that very afternoon, not that she was necessarily planning to wear it on Wednesday, but it had such a feel to it, the way the white cotton clung, and the top of her breasts peeked out, and the braided thread migrated so pronouncedly to her ankles, that it made the excitement of life itself echo in the apartment. Only her generation among the clans had ever had such opportunities.

Mama called upstairs to say she was leaving for Steinway to shop. Minutes later, Joyce felt it jubilate and bolt inside her, an impulse to show off again. She'd walk the opposite direction from Steinway, so Mama wouldn't see her, traipse the repetitive side streets and drink up the quizzical, the few disapproving but mainly admiring glances from the workers on the street and the old ladies in their lawn chairs.

Outside, it was a cool spring day, and the breeze pressed with the cotton against her thighs. She was so conscious of her thighs...28th St. 29th, 30th, then an alley she had never seen before. The rutted asphalt wedged between two liquor stores. Beyond the stores, there was nothing, more asphalt and an empty lot full of weeds. Being alone in her dress was a pleasure all to itself as she strode majestically down the homely road, almost as if she were in a dream.

But she wasn't alone. There were footsteps behind here, and she didn't feel at all comfortable about turning around to see whose they were, not so much because she was afraid as from some sense that it would be improper to do so. Meanwhile, there was no one and nothing in front of her, and the brief alleyways on her left and right were likewise empty. Then she heard it, a kind of hollowness, an eerie empty clomp in the footfalls behind her. She felt a sudden terror, yet couldn't bring herself to quicken her pace. Her legs were like ice. And she felt a kind of indecency, a terror at herself for having capriciously and without reason worn the dress. It covered her up, she wasn't being a bad girl, yet inexplicably she felt like a helpless and audacious intruder in her own neighborhood.

She knew the alley would let out at last on a busy street. Yet it was as if space itself was weirdly funneled; she couldn't see the point, only a few hundred yards away, where the lonely byway ended. She'd keep walking, arrive at last at some street or, who knows, some bridge or tunnel – but then where would she be? Someplace else, someplace strange when she craved the listless comfort of her own neighborhood. She was lost.

Joyce now resolved to turn around and walk back to where she'd started, but the hollow ringing footsteps were louder and more insistent now. There was no going back, so she forced herself to run and, when she did, her worst fears were confirmed. The footsteps were running after her, faster now, until they were upon her. Then the dress was in tatters and the stuff that was softer than cotton and the cool inner cloth were rent and, before she felt hands upon her or a hot male's rancid breath, she mainly heard the hissing sound of fabric being ripped. Then a sharp cut, a warm release—she couldn't tell from what part of her body—and all was dark.

Nick Prounis faced away from the window, unblinking, at the edge of the wall framing the sill, away too from the murmuring people inside. Aristotle Prounis gazed full-faced out the window toward one of the dull trees squatting at the curb, planted some long-gone time ago in the history of the great city. Each sob audible behind him lay heavily on his mind. Virgins are so fine and clean, and Joyce was the sweetest and sunniest one of all. The defiled body lay a few feet away, posed in a white gown the funeral home had provided, very much the flower which lives only a few days before the first chill descends. If he tried hard enough, he could quicken his sense of smell to pick up something too faint for the others, but which he knew to be – but couldn't bear to think of – as – decomposition. It was, at the very least, the end of his own hopes.

The Asimakopoulos' filed in, dutifully somber, yet theirs were faces subtly self-justifying, as if, a wiser and more prudent crew, death and despair couldn't touch them. Not just Ari, but Eleni too in her silent grief took note of it. A simpler person, perhaps, than her brother-in-law, it thus hurt her more, this invidiousness in such old friends. Who'd have expected her to have to bear another hurt on top of the indescribable hurt?

"She only wanted to live a little," said John Prounis. Joyce's brother sounded angry, although whether he too had perceived the tacit censure of the Asimakopoulos', or whether it was the unspeakable fact of what had happened to his sister that enraged him, Eleni couldn't tell. She wanted to comfort him. There was a hush, as if people were indeed waiting for a comment from someone, a suggestion the blame did lay with Joyce and her family. Blessedly, none came.

"Saints don't suffer like this," said Eleni aloud, although her voice was surprisingly steady. Perhaps it was a little defiance that made her stalwart. Part of her was poised to defend the dead daughter who'd walked alone on the streets with cool cotton clinging to her brownish body.

Ari's senses quickened. He rose toward his brother but Nick was buried in his trance, closing his eyes and hunching his shoulders closer to the wall as Ari approached. There was a violence inside Ari as he loomed above his beloved brother; he could only retreat back to his chair where he turned his attention, or, rather, hurled it, back out the window, toward the ungainly trees in their dry clumps of soil.

"She's with God now," added Timos Panagiotopoulos. Ari, his vision darkening beyond endurance, heard in that good man's tone the slight lilt of someone glad it wasn't his daughter butchered like an animal. The Kapochunas' filed in late, with Antigone bewildered in her dark eyes. Her mother loosed a few platitudes. They had finally allowed Antigone to go to the dance after the party, but Ari assumed many years would now go by before that leash was ever loosened again. They had—what was the expression?—dodged a bullet, and were thanking heaven they'd been taught a lesson they'd never dare forget.

That morning, Ari had felt fear for himself, a cold sweat at the thought his own good name was to be besmirched behind his back, or, worse yet, his very presence spurned by openly hostile neighbors laying all the blame on him for the new, foolish ideas that had brought his brother's family to this horrible ruin. Then grief for Joyce supplanted his fears, and, for all he cared, the world could drop its ax and eradicate him utterly—Ari swore he'd never dishonor Joyce again with anxieties about so paltry a thing as his own good name in a world of such mean-spirited peasants—yet how he couldn't stop hating everything they stood for. Worse, if his dream still lived, there was no one to live it. His nephews John and George were fine men but too simple to dare it, especially since it seemed their charge now to mainly attend the devastated parents. Their lives were set.

And Nick? Ari couldn't bear to let his imagination roam that future, so he squelched the clammy fear his brother would blame him too, though say nothing in the unbroken silence that would stretch on for decades ahead. And Eleni, whom he loved? Eleni, so little resentful by nature, could yet grow bitter with the years until time itself pushes her to find and flay some convenient, close-by paschal lamb. He stopped thinking about it all. There wasn't the time now for these grieving premonitions of further loss. He'd bear them later, and bury now instead the young queen in her virgin white.

It was when the Trypanis' arrived, and the long-estranged Olympia Trypanis embraced her, that Eleni finally let go her nonpareil keening. The depth of it was greater, it seemed to Ari, for whatever old wounds had once separated the two women. Nick Prounis emerged from his trance long enough to glance in their direction; Ari, seeing him, thought to make another effort to approach. But it was no good. He was afraid, at least for now, to test his brother's love, though his own was desperate. Again, he bent back toward the window and took up surveillance of the trees outside.

Melina Panagiotopoulos stood at the table and poured whiskey for her husband. "These days, it could have been anyone who did it," she commented tersely.

"They'll never catch him," said her husband. Melina glared at him for the thoughtless remark, even though his point was already implicit in what she herself had just said. Ari saw his nephews tense up; their faces were like granite. Now, suddenly, he was hearing another awful unspoken supposition in the room: "What if a nigger did it! What if a nigger had her before her killed her?" In a minute, not just rape and death, but a likelihood of primal defilement hung over the scene.

"Could have been anyone," repeated Melina. "Even someone who saw her at the dance."

"We'll never know," her husband said, still being thoughtless.

Nick Prounis, with such ineffable drama because he'd been so still and silent so long, spoke at last. "I hope it was a stranger," he said. "Better that than one of us."

Ari glanced passionately at his brother, who had stunned the room with this unexpected oracular pronouncement. His beloved Nick! Nick still understood how beautiful Joyce was, and how what Joyce wanted to become was always neither more nor less than another metamorphosis of beauty. Thank God, thank God for Nick! But the room was full of angry incomprehension. One of us? One of us? What does he mean?

Their silence was deep as death. Nick and Ari could see with the same eyes this population of pitiless creatures, their neighbors. Maybe, like himself, Nick could envision too that whole other new world stretched before him, its flickering bulbs in a million ranch homes in the dark nights of Kansas and Arizona, or track-house facades of suburban Virginia and Ohio just as dull but cleaner and bigger than Astoria, and full of untold condescending strangers crying crocodile tears for the sad family that tried but could not fit in. From Old World and New, the cry We Told You So rang down on the dead girl like a thunderbolt, as all that yet could be, the dazzling light, must now await some new Greek queen in clinging windblown cotton white.

Hecuba to Him

He fell sick very soon after he got to his father's house on the island. It was a debilitating torpor. There was no specific pain except a dull ache everywhere. His father was crestfallen, and had the bed in the master bedroom made up for him. He lay there for days in the gentle light. His father's wife knocked a few times a day and graciously asked after him. Her smile was all affection. Her eyes were warm and guileless. She was in her early forties, more than ten years younger than his father.

They had first met shortly before she married his father. He had only been back to the island once after the wedding for a short visit. He was healthy that time. And he was usually healthy whenever he was not on the island. But this time on the island he broke down and was sick.

She asked if he wanted any music. He said yes, softly. The music was soft too, when she provided it. Her arms were prematurely wrinkled. Her skin was pallid. But she was a healthy woman. She moved about self-confidently. But it was never strident self-confidence.

The doctor came and prescribed something. It didn't help. On another island, far away, he recalled a woman in love with her husband's son. She accused him of raping her. Her husband saw to his own son's death. The woman killed herself and so did her maid who had tried to do her best but made matters worse. He dozed recalling the story. Words merged as he dozed, nearly feverish. A different eye land. Another I land.

When he awoke, his father was standing there. He was a stately tall man. He'd worn a beard for some years but it was shaved now. His face was craggy. His eyes were as kindly as his wife's. "You'll get better soon," he said solicitously. "And when you do, we'll go out and have a fine time."

"I want that," he answered. He did, because he always enjoyed being on the island the half-dozen or so times he was.

"There are some good shows off-Broadway," his father said. "And you haven't seen MOMA since it was redesigned."

"I'd like to, very much," he said.

In his preface to *Phedre*, Racine says that, while in Euripides and Seneca Hippolytus is accused of having raped his mother-in-law, in his version he is accused of no more than wanting to. Racine wished to avoid making Theseus less agreeable to the audience by such imputations. But Hughes translates Theseus thus:

> After your ravenous lust
> Has sated itself in your father's bed
> You dare to confront him?

And thus:

> You assumed that Phedre, for shame,
> Would hide her defilement…

Either Racine or Hughes has lost the text. I hope Racine lest Hughes' monumental work be at all fundamentally obviated.

He had brought a beautiful woman as his guest to their wedding. It was seven years ago. His father and his bride were proud of how beautiful the young woman was. The bride too was beautiful, in demure blue. The look in her face was encouraging. They danced. She smelled the same way now as she did then. It was a fresh scent. The scent went with her bright generous eyes. The scent was all the more appealing as, by contrast, her skin was now wrinkled and pallid.

Who seems most queenly is the queen. He always worried that he did not amuse her. But she was always warm to him. He liked it that she liked literature, Homer and Shakespeare. That she read Homer for pleasure. She had traveled a lot too. So had he. They talked about Turkey and the Homeric ruins there. But he didn't see much of her after the wedding. "Your mother was very beautiful," she said to him once.

"She was," he said, and smiled sheepishly. She smiled too.

His brother was landlocked in the Midwest, a businessman. He and his father had a respectful but not particularly warm relationship. Another brother was alcoholic. He'd been wounded since childhood by what neither he nor his father could articulate in the few melancholy chats they'd had about it over the years. "I can't remember doing anything wrong," his father sadly said. "I can't remember your mother doing anything wrong."

"These things don't necessarily happen because someone's done something wrong," he said.

"I know that," his father sighed.

Closer to him than either of his brothers had been a friend who pined away and died from no discernible medical cause. But he knew and could see what figured to be the source if not the direct cause. So could his father. A dark look on his father's face one day bespoke his understanding. "An unfortunate situation," his father described it.

His father and his wife lived a gracious life. Their affluence enabled sufficient leisure after years of dedicated labor. Both had worked and succeeded. His father had come to see him on a number of occasions, alone. Only once was he accompanied by his wife. "You should come with him more often," he ventured.

"Thank you," she said. She planned to the next time but her brother died suddenly in Mexico.

He could barely turn over in bed. He felt like crying but had not the energy even for that. He was his father's favorite, which was a badly kept secret. His father returned to the room. He hovered again, concerned. His wife accompanied him the next time after that. "Won't you eat something?" she asked.

"I'll try," he said.

He knew so little of her life before she married his father. His father's life also seemed distant to him, at least those years of it spent to build his empire. There were sketchy tales of adversaries overcome, of old strife on the island, which in those years he'd visit every day, and from which he emerged victorious over other men equally determined to claim a fiefdom. His mother played an active part in that saga and moved with him here to the island, to this very bedroom where now he languished and was too tired to cry remembering his mother. He had never been strong, yet was always his father's favorite. There were unchartered places in his father's heart, he knew that. It held inexplicable passions, wise passions.

"We'll take care of everything," she said. "Won't we?" she addressed her husband.

"Yes," his father answered, hovering now with her over his bed.

"I want to get better," he said. The two of them practically shivered to hear it. They were wise in their generation.

The next morning she knocked and brought him tea. "Lift your head and try to drink it," she said.

"Nice of you," he said. "The maid could have."

"I'm happy to."

"I hope you and my father will go about your business," he said.

"We have no business," she said.

"I hate to be a nuisance."

"We love you," she said.

He drank the tea. "Are you able to eat anything?" she asked.

"Maybe an egg."

"I'll see to it."

"Thank you."

She left and came back. The egg was scrambled and he ate half of it. Then there was a silence and she smiled generously. "No hospital," he said, apropos of nothing.

She only bent her head a little in response. "Say, I've never asked you. Whatever happened to that beautiful young lady you brought to our wedding? Have the two of you kept in touch over the years?"

"She married someone," he said. "They live someplace."

"Aha," she said.

That afternoon he slept and had a vivid dream. His father and his wife were being led away in chains by faceless men in armor. They struggled across a vast white plain. He was behind them and could see a line of pale blue in the distance. It was the sea. He didn't know if that was where they were going. But he was afraid that a great storm would roll in from the sea and over the plain. He was more afraid of that than of the men in armor. Sand started blowing against his father's face and he squinted in sympathy. His wife's body stuck closely to the white cloth she was draped in. He wanted to cry out but couldn't think what he wanted to say were he to do so. He did not wonder why this was happening. It had a sort of inevitability about it. He turned around to look back at a ruined citadel behind them. Then there was some kind of music and, in his subsequent wakeful torpor, that was all he remembered.

The dull ache grew sharper. It became more like a prong than a vise; like something stuck in him was urging itself forward. "Maybe it's a cancer," he thought. "Very like a cancer," but the physician on another visit could see no related symptoms. He heard them converse outside his door. "They want to do tests," his father said, returning.

"No," he said. "Not necessary." His father looked at him thoughtfully and said nothing. He wondered how many unarticulated thoughts he and his father shared, but he was too weary to think too hard about it.

"Shall I turn on some music?" his father asked.

"Yes," he said, and his father left, saying he'd be back shortly.

During the three months his friend had lingered in just such a state, he paid two visits, one to his home and one during the final days in hospital. "There's air but I'm too tired to breathe it," his friend said.

He did not reply. There were many questions he could have asked, many perceptions he could have shared, but he demurred. "I don't want to die," his friend said. Stark moments passed until his friend added, "But I can't live."

"I understand," he said.

His father returned. He stared up at the hovering figure. Neither man blinked much. His father's face in the gathering shadows had a gaunt look he'd never seen before. There was no energy in him with which to silently focus a single thought that his father, by listening with his inner ear, would hear at all. He could only hope that some truth might emanate like an unmistakable vapor from his immobilized flesh. His father bent his head and stared for a brief moment at the floor. Then he lifted it again and fixed his gaze once more on his son.

He saw his father part his lips as if to speak, but he closed them together again. He lifted his hand to his mouth and kept it there, still gazing upon his son in the bed. Then his hand fell slowly away from his mouth and he asked, "What can I give you to make you well?"

"Your wife," he answered.

His father nodded, a kinglier figure with tightly knitted brows and piercing eyes. "I will speak to her," he said, and disappeared beyond the shadows.

Kazantzakis At Home

He was so old that some of the kids said he took the very first shit that ever made the olives grow. Many of the people on the block believed that he was over one-hundred, although he himself wasn't sure. His people may have come from Africa originally, or at least that's what he remembers his grandmother saying, or perhaps it was a dear friend of his grandmother whose family also transported over that said it. Somewhere in his mind he still saw sand so white that, when the sun struck it, the light bounced back up again, like a burning mirror in the thick hot air. But he could recall no strange animals, only the familiar ones of this country. And while he was the darkest person they'd ever seen, he wasn't dark like the jet black people who lived over there.

This land had its own deep white gleam every spring when the people repainted their houses. The heavy lacquer mixed sweetly with the orchids and gave April a gummy distinctive smell. For a long time now he's been sitting on the front stoop watching and not saying too much. He's a tall man, almost bald, with a wispy grayish beard that falls down straight along his cheeks and chin.

Perhaps the family had to fight for its life when they first came to Crete. Their enemies could have been anyone. He let his mind wander back to those days. If he closed his eyes tight enough, could he hear the world as he had heard it from inside his mother's womb: musket sounds, cries in the night, whispers of insurrection? He remembers as much as he can. He figures they all probably landed in Heraklion off some rude skiff, beneficiaries of a week's calm wind on the sea. Maybe the Turks had already subdued the forlorn island, if not the enduring rage of its inhabitants, raped his grandmother as she wandered about, herself darker than the Turks, darting between alcoves in the dusty city. Or, who knows, maybe they chose instead to throw in their lot with the usurpers: themselves grim invaders spying on the townsfolk and peeking out from behind blood-spattered walls when the soldiers cut down the day's conspirators. But no one had condemned him, and of course the people here, who find out everything, never forgive or forget. Someone would have known about grandmother's furtive visits to the police had she been a teller of deadly tales.

It wasn't much of a trek from the city to what would be their home for the next century or so. Due south through the city past the ramparts built by earlier invaders, then past the Turks' new office buildings, to the lamb and fish shops full of life where crones even more ancient than grandmother bargained for the day's catch. Then to the magnificent fountain older than all the crones those crones ever knew. Past old walls and ditches still full of goats grazing on scattered patches of grass. Plenty of space, finally, to build a house or rout a beggar from another house abandoned by some other family in flight, maybe, from the Turks and heading for the sea. Later they built the great wall against the invaders and, when he was already old, he watched them bury the famous writer. How sullen the priests who followed him up, how uncomfortable they seemed carrying this strange dead child of theirs. Surrounded by the winding walls, they laid him on top of the Martinengo Bastion and put many beautiful flowers there.

He had never learned to read, and he spoke very little. Only to his sister would he relate those of the day's events he saw that seemed worth relating. Over the course of his many years he did indeed see a few worth the telling. For example, he'd seen adultery once, which he knew they'd find out about and kill someone for. From the very beginning he watched as John Tzortzis started hating his wife; there was a flicker in Tzortzis' face one day, and for the next ten years the old man saw it harden and become a shadow growing darker and darker. He mentioned what he saw to his sister, who nodded and kept her silence. Tzortzis finally met a young girl living over by the Church of St. Catherine, and they disappeared together. His wife went screeching along the road and through the big ditch, scattering the goats, who raised their own cacophony. Her brother and the young girl's father went out after the elopers and when they brought back the girl some weeks later no one asked where Tzortzis was.

As time went by he saw more and more. Many strangers came, most of them fair-skinned and with pleasant manners. They would hike along the ditch, amused by the goats, and head for the Martinengo Bastion. Often the kids followed them up on bicycles. Sometimes as he lay down on his bed against the wall, he'd hear the footsteps heading in that direction. One night he doubted it was a stranger's walk.

The next day as he sat on the stoop, George, a local policeman, came by to see his niece. George's heavy eyes were unblinking, their lids held back as if propped by little sticks. They spoke awhile, then his niece's husband strolled along. The niece and her husband nodded and shrugged as George spoke. He heard all three of them grunt quietly and cluck their tongues.

George walked past him, moving on toward the city. But before he had gone thirty paces the old man spoke up. "It was a light step I heard last night," he shouted over to the policeman. "A young man's. But his shoes were heavy, and struck up some dust, and echoed in my ear for a count of ten before it settled."

The policeman, taciturn child of a race of perfect detectives, nodded thank you and continued his way.

They saw the old man sitting on the stoop just off the road as they skirted the goats on Evans St. By what Connery could read of the map in the old guidebook, Kazantzakis was buried on a kind of high rampart, or perhaps a natural plateau, which was called the Martinengo Bastion. "Somebody here might have heard of this 'bastion,'" he said to Thalia.

"I'll try that," she said, and approached the old man. He looked up with a blank expression as she spoke to him in Greek. The early sunset was taking the bite out of the day's heat, and there was a slight breeze. Connery had drunk some Domestica but not even half the bottle. If he felt settled inside himself at that moment, satisfied while not quite serene, oblivious at least to the usual torments, it was apparently some natural gladness. It was perhaps these last few pleasant weeks in Greece that had given him surcease.

He'd been told Kazantzakis' grave was worth a look, that it would be especially restful after the torturous intellectual-seeming Knossos. This, unlike most of Greece, was a place where history could be recollected in tranquility. Not that Greece agitated him; quite to the contrary, he had driven around Thessalonica like a native and, in Athens, even enjoyed the sooty outdoor cafes. The other tourists hadn't bothered him. And, when he got off the ferry from Kavalla and saw Thasos' rugged beauty, he decided to stay a week. For a day or two, he enjoyed being alone; then, when he met Thalia Voutas, he was delighted to stay the extra time with her. They continued traveling on together when the week was over.

"Sit with me, of course," she said at the tavern. Although he seldom hungered for women, Connery attracted them easily. His pocked and homely face was a gentle one. He was, in fact, a gentle man, when not too drunk, or set upon by the obscure and at times only half-articulated demands of a parent or cousin or brother. Women like Thalia, also of upper class origins, raised in Paris by her mother and a succession of stepfathers, naturally gravitated his way without much effort.

There was no pretense of love, yet he may never have loved a naked body this much, not just the sculptured breasts and butt which were easy to admire along conventionally aesthetic lines, but also the ungainly dash of moist hair winding around from her crotch to the crack in her ass. Of course he couldn't put his mouth between her legs—he could never do that—but she was kind enough not to ask, which he appreciated.

"You like American men?" he asked her in bed.

"I've only got you to go by," she said, teasing. "It's funny, though. I don't think of you as an American. I think of you as an Irishman."

"And you give allowances to the Irish that you don't to others?

"Yes, very simpatico—but not because of the poets you've made. It's because of the church..."

"That unmade us?" he interrupted with a wink.

"Just so!"

Hers was a sympathy given lightheartedly, without condescension, so he accepted it without shame. Besides which, she seemed to enjoy him so much, even love him a little after a fashion. Next day she put her mouth on him, it happened on the beach, and that he was willing to allow.

Something in all of this he loved. Himself a poet, that evening he wrote

No one ever recovers,
but I will soothe your ancient wound
and lave your sand-encrusted skin,
like death laves its phantoms.

He stopped writing and took a walk over to the little museum, but you couldn't get into it even during the day unless you found the caretaker. So he went back to the inn, and worked by the window as Thalia was falling asleep:

Wait for me,
wail for me,
finish, read me

the monologue
you pass as dream
and, lapped in my ear,

I'll cradle you
like earth's first tulip
bellied with dew,

peeking toward the sun,
proudly, astonishingly black.
Purge the verbs,

fire each new word to world,

thick as night,
echoing like day–

the truth of you
your endless whispered
reverie holds!

My part is old hunger
lined in sawdust,
a rhythm seeking embrace:

O Thasos, Thasos,
yours is the music
all worlds dance to.

The family claims were stupendous. The great-grandfather
came from Ireland, though no one knew for sure which part.
Somewhere he had stolen a horse and sold it for a pot of porridge then sold two portions of porridge which left him enough
to buy more porridge and a few potatoes as well, which, once
sold, was enough to book passage to America. When he landed
in New York, he began the horse and porridge cycle all over
again, except now instead of more porridge he bought a seat
on the New York Stock Exchange and, from there, through
conspicuous international vistas, diamond mines, canals, and
the ear of kings.

His children were feeble. One was kicked off the Exchange, another committed suicide. The grandchildren were
only slightly better. One raised horses and subsidized an-
ti-communist paramilitary groups. His brother, Connery's father, took over one of the world's largest typewriter companies
and within a decade had turned it into one of the smallest.

Sometimes he'd forget his son's first name, which was William. All his affections, such as they were, were tied up in his daughters, while Connery's mother followed her husband about in a haze of gin and bitters.

The family branched. Some of William's cousins went back to Ireland and rested there. Nieces and nephews materialized at parties in New York. During visits to the family estate in Westchester, or throughout long summers at the house in Canada, the eyes of others fastened hard upon him. They were as drunk as he was, as feckless, and, for all their pride in pedigree, just as rootless. But, equating impotence with privilege, they utterly despised Connery, who was too honest not to know himself a sad shambles of a man. And he showed them he knew it, if only in the way he'd avert his eyes or lower his head. Although he really loved only poetry, in the last analysis the redoubtable lineage thrilled him too. Poor Connery, he hated himself for not rising to the fabled family aureole even as he saw through it.

He wrote:

Our child is monster;
he has perfumed the once-strong satraps,
and now Persia is sweet meat
strung for the Northern tribes.

Scenes booze helped erase. The worst, of course, was the boarding school his father had picked out for him. Having gone there himself in the 1930s, he'd remained piously loyal, as well as philanthropic. When the seniors, tacitly approved by the winking priests, buggered the freshmen, Connery shivered to see the callous and disembodied face of the father at each window, peering fiercely. No one came to the rescue. Fear soon obscured those memories; they grew so indistinct, he saw upperclassmen, all smirks and puckered jowls, without really remembering if they were ones who laid him or roughly used his face, or only made him watch as they set upon the weakest of the newer boys. Yet he didn't grow up to hate homosexuality. Just Catholicism.

College, a hotbed of European intellectualism, was a great haven for awhile, and the professors there refugees in their own right. Connery felt the world well lost but for the passion in ideas they'd salvaged from the flames. Even Keats they recast; the clerical hacks who raised him wouldn't recognize their old world now! At home, though, his own unkempt old world awaited, the gothic tableaux unchanged albeit a little worse for alcoholic wear. One day, after visiting with a Jewish friend from school, his mother slurped, "Watch what he wants from you!"

"I don't understand," he said. "We have nothing he could possibly want."

"William!" barked the old man from the other side of the room, rebuking the perceived insolence.

"But we haven't," he said, more confused than defiant.

"If you don't learn what we have to teach you, then—" at once Connery saw his father was drunk and probably didn't know what the conversation was about—"then it's something only long and hard experience will lead to, and a learning experience that you'll have to learn without the help of experience."

Connery mumbled in defense of his friend. "His father just acquired the – Corp."

"But with only the narrowest majority of stockholders approving!" exclaimed mother.

When finally he went out into the world, it was as a clerk in an antiques store. Half the people he waited on also came from great families and the other half were nouveau riche, but, once they found out who he was, everyone sought his acquaintanceship. It was, he wearily realized, the saving grace of his class that, while success, enterprise, all the predatory graces came naturally to some of his own, others like himself were sufficiently picturesque to be exempt from such expectations.

He watched Thalia approach the dark old man as the goats scampered up the side of the ditch. They tore at the small clumps of grass and meandered back down again. He did love her somehow; he did not want to part from her! The waning sun shone through the light green dress against her buttocks. "Martinengo Bastion," he called out to remind her what to ask for. Thalia, her Greek a flat nasal whine, begged the old man's pardon and inquired about the locale. But "Martinengo Bastion" didn't seem to mean much to him, or at least he didn't respond to the name. She started to walk away.

"Kazantzakis!" he called out abruptly. His long spindly arm pointed up toward the road to their right.

They looked out past his grave across the hill. It was an open structure, the wall against the Turks winding down as far as they could see. And it was beautiful, just as Connery was promised. The grave itself was a simple stone sculpture bedecked with a half-dozen bouquets. One shrub with blue flowers seemed to grow out of the grave itself, Kazantzakis' flesh feeding the roots. Not like that other flower, he thought, the single daisy plopped mockingly amid the unspeakable ooze. Little Sheehey, was it? A flower, alone and upright and absurd, which someone stuck in him as he lay there after the seniors finished with him...He drove away the image, as he always had. Not like that, these flowers here for blessed remembrance.

"You know I'm a cold bitch," she whispered to him suddenly, incongruously. "Always been."

"You?" he said. "Never."

"It was my upbringing." She lifted an eyebrow. "Just like you, I was taught to despise everything around me, but we had no illusions about ourselves either. My mother told me that nothing was genuine, everything is for sale. Grace and style and breeding are commodities on a market." She nodded toward the grave. "My mother would say this too is a commodity. A great writer buried in a beautiful spot, that's something the Cretans can sell us, and, even more important, it's something we can sell ourselves. A beautiful experience to sell ourselves, so we'll believe it was, after all, worthwhile to wake up and live through this day. A dreary way of looking at life, no?"

"Was your mother's cynicism as eloquent as yours?"

"Perhaps not," Thalia smiled, "but she made me a democrat in a snide way. We were so full of contempt, it made us respectful. My mother would say, 'Don't look down on the merchants because of their manners or because you despise whatever it is they're selling. The rest of us aren't very different. We're all mercantile under the skin.'"

"Did you always believe her?"

"Once I argued with her when I was very young. It was during my first period and I was very emotional. I was bleeding so heavy, I couldn't believe then that everything wasn't real, so real!" Thalia curled her lips and smiled narrowly. "'You'll get over it,' my mother said, and she wouldn't argue with me. She never argued."

Flowers always made Thalia think of sex. She often imagined orchids between her legs, and when she bent over a bouquet it was her own cunt, or another woman's, she was savoring. Sometimes the sight of a rose reminded her of the first time, and, if she closed her eyes tight enough, she could hear the soft hissing sound of herself being deflowered. Sex at least seemed real, and she had had many lovers. Her intentions were always indisputably heartfelt. The first dinner with Connery at the tavern, for example, her legs were spread under the table. How that thrilled her, his not knowing she had already opened wide. And she liked his poems so much, after she read them she asked him to recite a few.

> O my woman,
> purge the verb to love;
> score from old thunder
>
> the new moon song.
> Sing, I am no wayfarer.
> Sing, I am here to die.

The early evening breeze over Kazantzakis' grave. They'd been holding hands. "At least you're not pitiful," he said to her.

"Oh William," she said, full of compassion. Still arm in arm, they descended the steps on the opposite side of the grave. Walking up toward them was the policeman, George. His jet black eyebrows cast an almost glowering shadow but he smiled at them pleasantly. Thalia said hello and, pausing on a step, he asked her in Greek if they were enjoying their visit.

"It's a beautiful monument the people gave this man," she said. He agreed, commenting that Kazantzakis was a great poet. He started up past them but then stopped short and turned back to speak again. He spoke somberly, his voice lowering to a near whisper as he finished.

When they reached the bottom of the stairs, Connery saw that Thalia's eyes were alive–startled, aroused, yet a little amused as well. "What was that all about?" he asked.

"The policeman said that a few days ago someone smeared shit on Kazantzakis' grave."

"No kidding," said Connery.

"He said they were going to find whoever did it."

"I don't doubt they will," he said.

"And when they find him," said Thalia, her eyes wide and her voice vibrant with the inescapable reality of the matter, "when they find him, he says they'll kill him."

The Testament of Betty Sue Williams

My name is Betty Sue Williams and I am almost certainly the only woman with whom Sirhan Sirhan, the accused assassin of Senator Robert Kennedy, has ever had sexual intercourse. The affair in question transpired in the spring of 1968, a few months before the killing. I want to make the nature of our relationship as clear as possible as quickly as possible. This was no mere dalliance on either his part or mine. Nor was it for me some brief, mindlessly physical fling with a dark stranger. Quite to the contrary, I entertained some thought of marriage and, had Sirhan not been so self-knowingly in thrall to his rarer and most terrible destiny, I'm sure he would have responded in kind. Finally, regardless of whatever sort of bestiality you might associate with the man, let me hasten to assure you that, though there was much hunger in his love, he was never rough or lascivious.

I always knew him to be a gracious, generous lover. If he had his odd moments, both in bed and out, I attribute them to the supreme tensions generated by the arduous path that lay before him. Yes, there were desperate kisses, hot advances, ungodly sounds in the dark of night, but nothing this man did could ever be perverse to *me*. Yet I am no apologist. I understand the enormity of his deed and, being somewhat of a naif when it comes to politics, I really have no idea whether or not his action was justified by any threat Bobby Kennedy posed to the Palestinians. I must say, however, I do know that the hopes and dreams of many good men and women were dashed the day Kennedy fell. Many of these people are old and good friends of mine. It is out of deference to them, therefore, that I have consented to call this entry in my testament "A Great Beast Adores Me."

First a few words about myself. I am tall and thin. My black hair falls in a tangle on my shoulders, which are too bony. My finest feature is my nose, straight and perfectly sculpted against my face, which is a bit long. I have always loved my nose. My original home was Houston, Texas. I moved by myself to California after one of my sisters discovered me in the bedroom with two GIs. It was my first experience. I was naked, the soldiers were in full uniform. It must have been a shattering night for Cathy Mae. They were pulling on the parts of my body as if I was a farm animal. She told my other sisters and, though I don't think anything was ever said to Mom and Dad, a vast silence fell over our home. Glances were averted, sentences were short, polysyllabic constructions were avoided at all costs. We walked through that silence as if it had actual substance, like a gelatin that hung invisibly throughout the house. It was awful. Consciousness began each morning with the drear anticipation of the interminable quiet that lay ahead. No one seemed even tempted to break it. I couldn't stand it anymore. I left.

And yet, looking back now, I realize that I must have been seeking some sort of repetition of this torment, for so many of the hours I spent with Sirhan were likewise endured in nervous silence. So preoccupied was this man with his fantastic ambition that even the days he spent following me—trailing me on the street, in what seems an awesomely distant past before we ever made love—were for him days of distraction. I'd glance backward at him, feigning irritation, and see, of all odd pursuers, the oddest. His head was frequently down, his eyes raised only enough to keep me in his sights. I felt half-cheapened by this apparently desultory sexual attention. It may indeed have been nothing more than outraged vanity which prompted me to finally speak out. "Are you following me?" I asked.

"Oh yes," he said, as if it had taken him a minute to figure out what I was talking about. "I need a woman."

"Go away," I said sharply.

"Please," he said. "I've never been with a woman before and I think I'm going to die soon. I'm so tense. I have so much stored up. You look so kind. Please let me love you."

I found this unbelievable in a way that insulted my intelligence. But I let him buy me coffee, that day and the next day, while on the third day he kissed my cheek. I never brought up the subject of his impending doom, and I was willing to forget that he had ever contrived such a cheaply grandiose come-on. I was getting to like him. There were moments he wanted me so much, yet would insist on total self-control. Even his fists were clenched in sexual restraint. I found it all rather charming, rather exciting. Finally, on the fifth day, he said, "Can I have you? When can I have you?"

"Tonight," I said, smiling warmly. I had never before felt so safe saying yes. I surveyed that small dark body drawn back like a bow. I was aroused.

That evening Sirhan glared at me as I undressed, his eyes full of incipient fervor. It was a controlled frenzy tinged with great sadness. I presented myself to him and he ran his hands

across my body. I like Sirhan's fingers. They're dark, well manicured; they were full of conviction that first time as he gripped
me at the waist and bent me slightly backward. I opened my
legs and gave his hands full play. He rubbed my hole as if he
were affectionately patting a large dog. I've heard men groan
as they fucked, but with Sirhan it was a gut wrenching moan,
a veritable wheeze as he came. He burrowed his lips at my
shoulder and sucked its flesh with immense hunger. I think
this hunger had been his since first he wriggled loose from
his mother's body. I think he would have sucked me there the
same way had he never even dreamed of assassinating Bobby
Kennedy.

He awoke the next morning with a wonderful hard-on.
But he made no move toward me. Instead he lay there on
his side, holding it, just holding it. His eyes were full of fear.
"What, my darling?" I asked. "What is it?"

"I can't tell you. It's too terrible."

"Is something wrong with you?" I asked, vaguely remembering his earlier prediction that he would soon die.

"Not yet."

I lunged forward and stalled above his body. It was an
uncharacteristically aggressive pose for me. Caused by fear, it
frightened him as well, for he let go of his penis and his eyes
widened yet again. The words seemed jolted out of him. "I'm
going to kill someone. Someone great and famous."

"Lyndon Johnson?" I asked.

"No, Bobby Kennedy."

My immediate reaction was relief that Sirhan was not suffering from cancer or schizophrenic hallucinations. And, if I
experienced fear at that moment, it was not fear for Sirhan's
safety, nor agony that, in a few weeks, I would most likely
lose this loveliest of lovers. No, it was instead a terror wholly

appropriate to the immensity of the proposed deed. I felt a distinctive Biblical dread that our great globe would split at our feet, and Sirhan and I and Bob Kennedy, and everyone and everything around us would be hurled to the earth's center, and then out the other end to plummet endlessly through empty space.

I lay back down at his side and in a moment it was over. In a moment there was no terror at all, but simply a sense of some abstract, unnamable force at our backs. All great lovers had their arch-nemeses, like Montagues or Capulets, like death or old age. Ours was this. Terror passed to supreme weariness, and I said only, "Rest beside me, my darling."

Sex on the morning of the last day of Bob Kennedy's life was exceptional, but, again, it wasn't the terror, or despair, or some pornographic blood lust that made it so. It was love. Sirhan and I weren't fools. We knew this would be the last. Imagine a lover withdrawing from your body on the eve of holocaust, imagine what the shaft and tip of his penis must then feel like as they slowly slip out. It was a part of my own body that was slipping out, a gigantic excretion. But I didn't ask him to love me once more; that, I felt, would have been sheer torture. We finished, and then we wept.

As Sirhan set off for the California Primary, I went to church to pray. I found a deserted chapel, a rather desolate nook in a poor Spanish neighborhood. The chapel was sur-mounted by a garishly adorned Virgin; her blue gown was sorely in need of refurbishment. I knelt before this Lady of the Chipping Paint and begged her to either relieve Sirhan of his historic burden or somehow transform Kennedy into whatever Sirhan might want him to be. And I prayed for my own soul too, for love would not permit me to call out a warning to the world that yet another epochal horror lay ahead. Though not myself a Catholic, I felt that here, amid the voluptuous icons and flaking walls, here if anywhere grace might abound for all.

I watched it on TV. The happy throng milled gaily. My heart ached in pity for the violence that would denude their lovely vitality, perhaps forever. Then the Senator emerged. What a delightful-looking gentleman! My eyes followed him; I almost called out to the television, to beware, beware. My heart beat mercilessly. Then the shot, and the shouts, and I glimpsed my beloved, and then it was over.

My subsequent impulse was to disappear, but then I decided to take constructive action. I decided to seek out Ethel Kennedy and to comfort her for her loss. But of that adventure, of how she threw me out of her home, of how I wandered back West and became a kind of goddess—what they call a Spider Woman—for a small band of outcast Navajos, I must tell some other time, in another entry to my testament that will be entitled, "A Broken Heart Abhors Me."

The Desert by the Sea: An Anthology

I.

Betty Sue was as far from where Sirhan killed Kennedy as she could get under the circumstances. The crones in the village she came to mumbled on as she listened about the dark riders who haunt Santa Clara. They may have meant it as a warning. From what she could glean, the riders swoop down from both sides, stiff atop their horses. Even were you able to outrun the fearsome steeds, there'd be nowhere to run to. The undertow at Santa Clara is swift and strong, and it is difficult to swim there. The riders on the shore leave the women they catch naked and alone in the late afternoon just before the sun goes down, on the sand the sun beats down on all morning and afternoon.

She saw the first rider in the west. At first he was a dot, indistinct in the far distance. Then he was fury itself fast approaching. The rider from the east who was behind her she heard first as an ominous distant hum. Then soon a tramping roar beat beneath the sand at her feet as he rode closer. How fast they arrive, how suddenly they scoop them up and strip them bare. They straggle back to the village. They are defined as the ones the riders take. The villagers have seen it before just as their parents saw it before, and their parents' parents. She tried to get out of their way by stepping toward the surf but they circled around her and reversed directions. The one who had been in the east was now in the west, and the one who had been in the west was now in the east.

Since time immemorial the horsemen have swooped down on women walking the shore here alone. Some women are dazed wending their way back naked through the village, barely aware of the dark children following them and staring silently. Some as they walk caress themselves where they were taken. The crones find clothes for them, as they always have. The one from the west corralled her and for a few wild moments her belly hugged the hot horse flanks until he pulled her up. His penis was already unsheathed, and she was fucked quickly with her thighs dangling down against his hips, the trousers belted with hemp. He rode as he fucked driving the horse forward and then as he stopped fucking pulled the horse a herky-jerky full circle until the one riding from the east reached over for her neck and pulled her off his brother's penis and onto his own which was also unsheathed and ready.

So it goes. Very different was this power from Sirhan Sirhan's who in his fucking was small and lithe like a moth. The women smell the horseflesh while they're fucked because the animals are sweating so and, as the riders drive them forward, the sunlight drenches the shore with their heavy sweating flesh. When the rider from the east finishes the woman, he drops her on the sand and gallops away not looking back. The rider from the west continues his way as well. Who knows if and when these two meet again until the next time!

Always, the women are left alone and naked, their clothes lost in the sand or caught by the surf as at last the sun starts going down. The air is thick with the many women who've been taken here. A quiet world thick with the fading sun is heavy with their cries. But they don't actually cry aloud. The sound of their own cries would startle them. The dark riders are so old. They are world weary, cunt weary. They are all the more beautiful because their eyes are like lead. Their big cocks stick up when they ride and, scooping the women, their powerful arms are just like scythes as they come by.

"Please no," she whispered when the rider from the west came upon her. But he held her up above his loins holding the rein with one arm and pulled down her pants and panties with the other even as he kept her fast with the same arm. It must take many minutes to accomplish their undoing, to strip them cloth by cloth, and tear button by button, but they ride so fast it seems a single ferocious uninterrupted moment. Who knows what distances they cover, sand after sand the same hot sun-drenched terrain, as the rider in the west speeds from west to east and back again to join his brother. Who knows how far they go. Time and space are relative.

She tumbled down at last as the rider having her from the east shot his hot jizz in her. Her cunt was wind-burnt. Sirhan's jizz was caked there, one of the immortal accretions. Then she was naked and alone on the shore wandering as they'd all wandered from time immemorial. Students from the university on archaeological digs. Ambassadors' wives. Military wenches. The women Cortez and Pizarro brought and somehow lost in their gold-crazed shuffles. When she came naked to the village, a vague humming noise, like flies, only stronger, stirred the mud huts freshly painted bright turquoise. Like a ritualistic call, the drone was near and far at once, omen that, as the crones said just hours before, another naked woman would stagger the cobbled street as naked women had staggered the cobbled or anciently mud-caked streets when their parents and their parents' parents were still alive to keep this vigil.

They clothed and fed her, also as their parents and parents' parents had done in the olden times that will always seem like these times, the blankest stretch of time, and dune after dune on the shore you can't tell just by looking at if you actually went anywhere on, even though you've gone on forever and ever. Everyone in the village was expressionless, somber attendants on the ancient rite of the fucking of the women who came from far away by the dark and nameless riders who came from no one knows where. The silence on the shore was immense, yet if you go there, you see such great inscrutable corridors. Amid these most immense silences, year after endless year with nothing there to hear, because there is nothing there to hear, even the turf is caught up in the terrific silence, yet you have no choice but to see and to see and to see.

Which is why, I wean, paintings like *Faraway* would be forgotten if they were books and painters like Wyeth would be forgotten (painters like Wyeth; sketch makers are another matter) if they were writers. Painters stand a good chance to parlay momentary celebrity into enduring reputation because you've got no choice but to see such things as and where they're hung. But it's easy for anyone not to read, which thus mandates a mighty willful act if writers are to compel generations to pry open such quaint portraits of consciousness as they'd bequeath. Then too the generations must also be captured there, in the pages. By contrast, a sky can merely be and shorelines just meander.

II.

When it was finally nighttime on the shore, Irena came to crouch on the rocks as she had for many nights past. Often, on those nights, and on the past nights, she heard a faint murmur out by the outlying rocks, which, though not quite fifty yards away, was a jagged path to get to in the shallow water, abrasive even wearing slippers. It was not a stretch she'd traverse however much she might want to explore the dim site in the moonlight the hum seemed to come from. From where she sat, she could listen with curiosity, and she was curious indeed, and rather captivated, by what seemed an altogether different sound from what the waves made, or from what the night birds sang, or from what her own girlish breaths sounded like in the great darkness that was settling on Santa Clara.

Each night the hum grew a little more insistent. Each night she couldn't wait to slip away and listen. It was, she knew, something fabulous. Finally, that night, the wind off the water gathered the sound up as if from out a burial place on the shoals. The imponderable hum became a voice then speaking as it must have for centuries whenever the right wind stirred and lifted it strong enough to be heard over the surf. When she heard it, it delighted her, it was a lovely flat voice, a low voice, but a woman's voice or, if not a woman's voice, a voice that was womanly like an old person's yet also sweet like a lover's.

She sat on the rock listening hard to hear it. "I see you every night," it called at last, a lilting affable voice, not at all jarring even in the stark surf-swept night.

"I come here every night," she giggled. This was a great mystery, for there was a spirit in the rocks and it knew her. She drew up her legs against her chest showing the bottom of her thighs to the sea, innocently, in the same way she might have shown her stuck-out tongue or bare feet or naked armpits with their cute clumps of hair to the little boys in the village who shouted out naughty things at her, but they were just little boys. They loved her like everybody else.

She listened hard but heard nothing more. She kept listening, still heard nothing. "Are you there?" she called out. Her girlish voice was like a little tern's quavering in the air above the waves. The next night she went back to the same spot, all alone as always in the warm night, to tempt back the spirit like a friendly woman's. The moon was blood orange at first and then chalky white as it rose higher, and she waited. If she closed her eyes, maybe she'd hear it.

"You're so beautiful," it finally said. She was thrilled to be adored by a fantastic spirit in the moonlit sea. "I adore dreaming about how you dream."

"You dream about me?" she giggled.

"I dream about you dreaming."

"I don't understand."

"At night when you touch yourself, I see you."

"Oh my Jesus!" she said, shocked by that, and startled further to hear nothing more, for it was so preemptory, to have that said in the night like that, and then, in a second, for nothing more to be said. She opened her eyes. "Are you there?" she called out. "Come back!" But the shore was silent. She was unsettled and for the first time afraid. "My sweet Jesus," she said. She was afraid, yet her secrets were all the sweeter for no longer being quite hers alone. . .

The next night from her perch as the surf pounded the outlying rocks she resolved to walk toward them over the jagged stones so numerous and sharp they could cut right through your slippers. But she stopped midway as the water swirled to her thighs because the sea spray as it creased her pretty black hair blew in her eyes and confused her in the dark. "Are you there?" she called.

"Of course I'm here," it answered.

"Can I see you?" she called.

"I love you," it said, like a mother would.

"You do?" She made her way a further few yards toward the outlying rocks but now, when the tide pounded down in fuller force, on the outlying rocks and on the ones just beyond them, the fierce spray blinded her completely. The undertow shifted beneath and, frightened, she struggled to keep balance. Retreating back toward the shore, she called out again, over her shoulder, "Are you still there?"

She heard a woman's voice call out "Yes" but then fade away as if it were being drowned or was en route back to some vast thing too strange and mysterious to describe and from which it had first come a long time ago. But for all that it was a friend's voice she could still long for. It was someone to hold hands with in the water. They'd touch each other, a little naughty in secret, and share dreams no one else must know. The next night she left her bed and put on a soft orange robe she loved to wear, it was the one she often wore when she dreamed secret dreams, to go there without anybody knowing it, because this spirit, which could have been the Holy Mother, or it could have been a pretty girl just like herself to dream dreams with, could not have drowned the night before, it was immortal, and, since it sees everything, she wasn't going to be ashamed, she would tell it all, for, whatever it was, she was loved despite or even because of everything secret it saw of her when she was alone and full of dreams.

It called her name with a tender longing this night that she hadn't quite heard the other nights.

"I love you too," she cried back to the outlying rocks as the tide ebbed and the moon bore down on the stiller waters.

"You are so beautiful," it said.

"So are you!" she answered.

"You dream of love, but love is not always kind," it said.

"I know," she said. "It doesn't have to be." Her heart was leaping inside her.

"I know your deepest dreams," it said.

"You do?"

"I know everything."

"Can I see you?"

"Sit on the rock tomorrow night, be still tomorrow night and wait. Be as beautiful as you are right now, and wait, say nothing. Tell no one."

"I don't."

The next night there was no moon at all and just a scattering of stars. The sands shone with a gold crystalline light that frightened her a little to gaze on, so luminous they seemed in the pitch-black night. "I'm waiting," she whispered, but only whispered because she remembered the previous night's command to say nothing.

"Close your eyes," she heard the soft mother's voice.

She felt a presence, a stirring in the warm night air. Without being told to, she opened her eyes. A beautiful young man was standing there. He was naked and his penis was erect. She had never seen a man like that before. She was startled. "You tricked me," she said.

His broad smile was luminous and kind. "Yes," he said. He put both hands on his hips.

"You tricked me," she said again. Remembering her dreams, she quivered to know he knew them too. She wondered who he was, and where he came from, and how he could possibly have known her. How had he spied, ridden down on her so? Because he knew, she relinquished all hope of escape. What point was there in trying to escape? She could not escape his knowing. She tasted her fingers each time she touched herself, and he knew it. She crouched to make soft animal sounds when she was all alone, and he knew that too. She could not escape, unless she killed him, or herself.

He came near then and did all she ever dreamed. She closed her eyes, and when she opened them again, not to her surprise, he was gone. Naked at the edge of the surf, there was nowhere for her to go. She had gambled and lost as all children lose when they hear voices in the nighttime. The darkness on the shore was immense. All you saw was the night, and you saw it everywhere.

One understands, as Shaw might have understood, and as I myself said long ago, or will eventually get around to saying, that Verdi's Iago is a lesson in craft for Englishmen and Americans to heed well, guts up, for this Iago has no motive whatsoever, nor needs one, save his Act I Credo juxtaposed baldly to the love duet. He is plain darkness, he believes in darkness, he implements darkness. That said, note Shaw's myopic, "Shakespeare plunged through [the play] so impetuously that he had it finished before he had made up his mind as to the character and motives of a single person in it." Quite to the contrary, the characters, especially Iago, are if anything over-determined. Shaw, being sexless, probably underestimates by half Iago's cuckold frenzy, that Othello and Cassio and half the Mediterranean have humped Emelia. Nor is the racial dread merely our own latter day imputation but a visionary exercise on the part of the author. Centuries before colonialism made it one of life's dispositive facts, how could Shakespeare have known or cared that white men fear black cock? He gleaned it. No words to such effect are found in the play, nor could they be. You cannot hear this darkness. You can only see it.

III.

By next morning Michael couldn't walk anymore, he'd been walking so long, but he couldn't sleep either for the ache in him was like a feral baby bursting to be born. The bonfires behind him on the shore were all gone out and the sun would now be drenching the sands as it had the day before and the day before that. Soon he'd refresh himself in the surf but not go too far out as he'd been warned the undertow here was treacherous. It was just a bit past dawn, yet already the sands were burning his bare feet, and his face and arms were already sticky from the sun shining down in a cloudless sky. He'd been wanting to jump out of his body for a long time.

Maybe it was a mirage, but he thought he saw a crouched form like a bug on the sand further down the shore, who knew how far down. Like a buoy, it anchored his sight as he watched the fixed point grow clearer in the hazy light ahead. As he walked, he saw finally it was human. Then he saw it was two humans, and then that a young man and a young woman were huddled on the sand having slept there perhaps last night and now waking up together.

They sat close to the surf so that when he passed he passed close by. They were naked. When the woman saw him, she lay down on her stomach in order to hide her tits and cunt. But she kept her eyes raised up toward him and smiled coyly holding the man's hand as she lay there. Normally he'd have nodded a brief courtesy and then averted his eyes, but their expressions were bold enough in their way so that he kept a gaze on them and even turned his head back a little so they'd stay in sight as he walked past.

They haunted him as he made his way further down the barren shore. Their flesh on the sand was so ponderous, so real and eerily unreal suspended on the terrain. It didn't seem a place for human beings at all, yet there they were, incongruously human in this empty place. Their smiles, which he continued to conjure up in his mind's eye, increasingly lascivious with each quick memorial flash, tore like zippers into the inhuman white light that hung everywhere as far as you could see. He turned around. They were holding each other again as they had when first he came upon them. But they saw him returning almost at once and when they did, the woman draped herself around the man with her back to the surf, and hid herself that way.

The man smiled. It was a confiding smile that implied complicity. He knew he'd seem ridiculous were he to just walk past them again, as if just wanting another chance to peep on their nudity. He didn't want to seem lecherous. "Lascivious," with its associations with Roman emperors or dissolute artists, implied power. It was willful, active debauchery. But "lecherous" is an old man's nature, impotent and absurd. No, he was too close to impotence to tolerate the thought of himself as "lecherous" or the thought of others thinking him so. Having turned back, he would now have to say something. He'd have to offer something. He'd committed himself.

Not that there was anything in particular he wanted to offer. The feel of strange bodies against his own was a hollow unwanted pleasure as he grew older. Not loving anyone, he had not made love in many years. Yet he must have turned back for a reason, their stark presence on the worldless shore had lured him somehow. They were only a few yards away now and, as he struggled to find and speak the thing to offer, or at least find something not wholly ignoble or absurd to say, he saw himself as altogether small, anonymous, an ancillary part of their lust just as the sand they lay on this day, or the bed they'd tumble in on another, were mere fact patterns.

"I can narrate for you," he said. It surprised him to say it but the sound of it, the intent of it, reverberated the second he said it. In fact, he had stumbled on the very nub of his desire in this matter. He wanted to be a part of their coupling like the foam forking in on them from the sea, but no more than that. He'd narrate, and when he was done, he'd be done.

"Huh?" asked the man. The woman, still holding tight to his chest, turned her head a bit when she heard the strange suggestion.

He felt as naked as they, what with this strange suggestion of his, this oddest of expostulations they might not possibly begin to understand. "Pardon me, I'm not trying to intrude on you," he said, but the man nodded at him almost jovially, in a way that was at least encouraging. "I only mean that you might enjoy having someone describe the two of you together. It could be pleasant."

"You mean while we screw?" asked the man.

"Well..." he started.

"That's wild," said the man, with a sympathetic guffaw.

"That's crazy," said the woman, more suspiciously.

He heard his voice tremble a little for fear he might be making himself ridiculous. He didn't want that at all, he couldn't stand that. "I intend it to be respectful," he said.

"Okay," said the man, chortling again.

"I mean 'respectful' because I'd try to be poetic, and don't you think all poetry is kind of respectful?" he asked. He was losing a sense of place as he stood there. The moment, and its potential, whatever it might be, drove him forward. "I might start by saying something like, 'Her breasts were full and sweet against his chest as they embraced.'" He slipped down to his knees on the sand some discreet yardage away, turning his body a little toward the west so as not to face them quite so directly.

"'Full and sweet,'" quoted the woman, ironically.

"Yeah, 'full and sweet,'" said the man, with a little twinkle.

He continued, "As they kissed, he remembered the other taste of her between her legs, and thrilled at the thought of all their secret kisses." The language was coming on him strangely fast, fast and importunate in the thick morning heat, as if something at last was prying loose. The couple was moved by the language, they liked it a lot. The woman smiled for the first time. "His hand groped for her between her legs," he went on, "and she touched his big balls with the tips of her fingers, exalting at the power concentrate and tight there for her." How he loved this special language! It was the first time he ever shared it with anyone.

Again the woman exclaimed, "This is crazy," but not so sharply this time. "You really going to fuck me in front of this guy?"

He wouldn't let the man answer but took over the voice, the man's very volition, answering, "Kid, I'll topple you for all the world to see." The man laughed once more and murmured delightedly at the rhythm of the apparent game, aping its narrative as he pinned the woman's knees to the sand. Going on, the ache in him found voice, exultant as if this was their first time and the very birth of things vouchsafed him to describe. "She felt the hard head of the cock she adored probe her and she cried out gratefully, in gleeful counterpoint."

Abashed a little, he was, to hear himself well-night pant the words, but the couple, not at all laughing as he might have feared they would, kissed as if in love they fucked. "Only the plashing combs of the incoming surf," he continued, "and nothing else, not the hot timeless sun, nor the vast borderless sands, shared the four-cornered frame of their palpable world. Only the fringes of the surf insinuating themselves against the edges of their flesh returned in soft power reminders of who they were and how they loved. As she felt him probe, words she wanted to utter in raw gratitude came as animal grunts instead. Then it was he knew he had her, really had her, he knew he'd formed her into the pure sweet fuckmeat she was born to be."

"Oh gee!" the woman gasped. "This is crazy," she said once more. But her eyes were narrow and intent, her tone irrevocable and acquiescent. The man in his sudden throes thrust his muscular young butt as if part of the tidal landscape, taking and giving, drawing back and pressing in. The sun kept rising and rising over the bland and endless landscape pouring down its thick, thick heat.

"It was the very man who selfless had sought her through time and tide, he whom her soul loveth was this very man," he intoned. "She felt her soul's surrender as it were pure gladness. The power took her and became her and all she knew was that she was fuckmeat, she had become fuckmeat, that she was made to be fuckmeat, and on the shore where the sun rose ever higher in order to beat down ever hotter, that this hard cock that was..."

He broke off allowing his mind to clear and closed his eyes in the strange and windless, worldless hot place they dwelt in then. When he opened them again, her soles were raised aloft on the windless shore. "The cock immense inside her knocked her up, the hot jizz was turned into a child," he continued, "and each day she was pregnant, she kissed his tool and his big, big balls in tribute because it was that tool and those big, big balls that had done her so." The man was growling now, to hear him, and she was tearful as she grunted, so far so fast had he taken them from the casual adventure they'd consented to, and as he watched the man strain on top of the naked sweating female flesh, he felt his power as he hadn't maybe for years or maybe ever, and he continued, "'I'm fuckmeat for you, fuckmeat!' she called out. "She felt the gun in her cunt like to fire and when it did, she grabbed his neck and held his face to hers, and said, 'Sweetie, sweetie, I love you so!'"

She grabbed him by the neck and held his face to hers, and said, "Sweetie, sweetie, I love you so!" She was meat, by word and deed happily the text he empowered. He fell backward, off his knees and onto the sand, continuing, "She never loved him more than when after such a fucking his cock softened inside her and, no longer the creature who made her fuckmeat, he was the man again she'd sleep with and wake to through the endless cycles of time."

He closed his eyes and lying there heard nothing more of the couple stirring. Time went by as the sun rose higher. The surf distantly humming was monstrously devoid of human voice. There was only his own voice broken out of him again like a long buried ache. "When she came to see him," he said, "she said she could not give herself again. She was so full of rage and sorrow. She needed to pluck beauty, not have it plucked. The small tight cunt between her legs he remembered was the most beautiful thing he ever saw she could not stand plucked or played, not in this world, its maw, the terror, the terror..."

The narrative line he groped for now was so distant it seemed the narrowest ungraspable thread of a fading consciousness. But he groped still. "'I brought a girl to my room,' she told him, 'and I sucked all the sugar from her young crotch, and I turned her over and I spread her cheeks and tasted her there too. The whimpering sounds, such music, you only hear it when you hear it, it fades away, it's evanescent, it's gone. You can't hear anything. I loved her...' She loved her, and she held his hand when she told him, and asked, 'Are you sorry I came to see you and tell you this? Are you sorry you ever knew me?' And he said, 'even I, I you can't stand to have strip you naked, and lavish love on your still small spread, and kiss that cunt of yours as beautiful as anything I ever saw?' And she said..."

The narrative was now garbled. Such a somber tide, the wanting and never getting, the getting and never having, and so forth and so on. He opened his eyes and not to his surprise found he was alone. The couple was just a dot. Away off down the shore they'd gone, steadily westward over the immense tracts of sand. He searched for more ideas and found none. He was bone dry.

Sassanids, etc.

He'd been on his knees all morning the second day when first he saw her. It was the only time in his life he saw truth in a female's face. Others who had served him were always deferential. Others obligingly aped lust. Today it was real, and unbearable. She was the daughter of someone, who was the brother of someone, and distantly related to the king, who in turn was a direct heir of Sapor or possibly Narses. The lineage was not in any event so indistinct that she could not derive a palpably regal satisfaction knowing who and what he was, and how delicious this ungainly subjugation.

They dressed him in plated tin on both sides from thigh to shoulder. Eagles with fierce glares, half like their own and half like the Roman, were thinly embossed on the twin slabs. His bare butt was exposed between. They made him wear ladies' slippers. Whenever he was given occasion to rise or change position, his penis and testicles would partially hang out the flimsy cloth covering that hooked down from the sidings. Rome was a hot shaming memory as he, of all its emperors, was the one to become this literal footstool to the Eastern enemy. His place in history was thus defined. He raged at first but no one cared. The soldiers and the indifferent courtiers and the relatives of the royal administrators let the rage expend itself. These Persian surfaces were impervious, and soon he blew himself out resigned to his fate.

They strung thick silk on his back between the mocking tin plates. Prone, he awaited the king. The king's feet were tiny; his velvet slippers, striped like tiger skin, grazed his neck and chin. A quiet ripple as of contained mirth swept around the palace. And in this fashion they sat out the first day, the king and his retainers savoring the new human tool.

The next day sundry visitors arrived, including the woman with the great and unbearable truth in her face. "He's a most accommodating emperor, this Roman," said the Persian king to the woman as his feet nestled downward.

She said nothing, only nodding. As she nodded, he gazed up from his knees and saw an almond-dark face with fleshy puckered cheeks and paper-thin black lips. Her almond eyes sparkled with dark light. A courtier smiling softly placed his hand on her shoulder as sidling by her side he offered up a flower, a rich lily with a trumpet-like bulb. There were shining trumpets in his mind's eye envisioning the lost imperial past as peering up from his knees he saw the awful unremitting sparkle of the almond-dark stare. She bore down, studying his face. The Sassanid monarch tickled his chin playfully, his big toe teasing the beardless chin, which caused the courtier to snicker and an even deeper dark light in the woman's awful almond eyes to sparkle. "Hail Caesar," said the courtier as the setting sun poured in through the side portals. It poured in from a northwesterly direction, from Armenia where he and his legion had been captured.

As the crowd pushed him toward where the bodies were trussed upside down, he saw furious men, with thin women, and with fat women, with haggard-looking women toting dark boy and girl children, plucking at Mussolini's face like birds who had come to pluck away his eyes. Mussolini's eyeballs were protruding so far out, it was as if many crows had already come and plundered. The men in the crowd formed a semicircle around the woman who hung there beside him. Her dress was torn off and her ankles were tied at the ends of two ropes that forced her legs wide apart. Everybody wanted to see the dead woman's cunt. They wanted to see the cunt that Mussolini loved to fuck. One night ten years earlier when he was twelve years old in Siena he had peeked into his mother's bedroom to see her naked. He had seen her naked before, but this time he peeped with renewed curiosity. It was only after he saw his mother's naked crotch with its modest crotch hair that he dimly comprehended what it was he was peeping in to try to see. He dimly comprehended that it was no longer quite the same hole that he had first crawled out of, because the great man had since then chosen during an official visit, while he strutted self-entitled from room to room in their new model apartment building, to fill it for a few minutes. "Fascist swine," the crowd shouted.

Two hundred years later, the lady's gorgeous face with its tight smile and shining eyes so close to being wicked, to the winking lewdnesses of the Restoration and beyond, still astonished him. It was the woman in the Lawrence portrait at the Metropolitan Museum in New York. He'd made her acting debut in an early performance of *She Stoops to Conquer.* Her skin was so soft. He imagined that her smile in the portrait was the same unbearable smile she'd wear if some military swain were to sidle up and have her from behind. She remembered the unctuous smile on Peter Lawford's face when Kennedy put his hand down her pants. The senator's wife, forced by Caligula, awaits her husband's return and dreads in advance the poor man's battered twitching mouth now his treasure was state property. Faces of women kissed by Rasputin. Ransacked. Essex' joy, when first he knew how Elizabeth tasted between her legs. Elizabeth's wet lips, stunning to his tongue. When Marie Antoinette was beheaded, one boy ran to the basket because he wanted to capture a braid. A soldier chased him away and the head was then taken to a cemetery or else salvaged for a special place in the sacred grove where the priests of the cult of the mysteries of decapitated beauty honor the ungainly remnants. Jayne Mansfield's last lop. Nicole Simpson's.

He eyed Sirhan across the yard. They always guarded him so carefully but that just made him hotter to somehow have him. The little Arab was cute. His rump was tight. Once he masturbated imagining how he'd force a way inside. How he'd make the little fellow grunt. He wanted to proclaim to the world: I fucked Sirhan Sirhan. I creamed in his world-famous Jordanian love bucket.

Too bad we're not back east. Then I'd say: I fucked Sirhan Sirhan in Sing Sing! Ha ha!

"Can't I just make friends with him," he asked Abrisse, the guard.

"No, you sure as hell can't," said Abrisse.

How vast the clothing! What revelations: fold after petticoat fold until at last her blond and manicured pubic strands were bare to see. "Oh!" he exclaimed.

"Well now," she winked, legs spread as if plucked apart. Her thighs creamy white as a child's were bare to see, though her knees were still draped in the pinkish taffeta that bundled on down to her ankles. Her beauty was one lascivious wink. She winked from everywhere. He felt like he was smiling stupidly. "You mustn't keep a lady waiting," she said with a low insinuating grunt.

Elizabeth Farren was her name. She was the daughter of a prominent surgeon and became Countess of Derby when she married the widower Earl in 1797. Lawrence's portrait, the long body bent gracefully, heavily, was shown at the Royal Academy and further popularized through an engraving by Bartolozzi. "This young man begins where I leave off," said Reynolds in praise of Lawrence's portrait.

Many harsh courtiers and soldiers mounted her, and she was the topic of whispered confidences at gala events. "She simply exulted in my balls," joked one lieutenant to his boon companions. Other men were afraid of her, she was wicked in the way she winked. They feared the clipped soft strange accent that had a little Irish in it; they feared its lilted mocking sound were they to fail between her legs. I would particularly like to know if Thomas Jefferson or Benjamin Franklin might have tupped her during official visits to the defeated colonial power.

One wants form to emerge naturally from the lineaments of how we feel. The truest form, in its earliest evolution, must have done just that. One doesn't imagine Homer consciously paralleling the taking of Briseis by Agamemnon to the taking of Helen by Paris, though both were rash love acts that redrew the lines of epochal battlement. Knowing that Agamemnon stood by her bed not daring to suck the tiny berrylike breasts tight against her skin, he sang it, and sang the great consequent fiasco, thousands dead because of it. Knowing that Paris ravened Helen's cunt because it was golden and glistened with regal fluids, and that she had sobbed in her pleasures because nothing on earth or in the heavens could have persuaded her to spare the world this love, he sang it, and sang the great consequent fiasco, thousands dead because of it. But he sang, not thought. Form grew like a stalk from song. Pure song was loosened in the world as the spirit moves like wind in language. There is, to be sure, such a thing to decry as "decadent formalism." But form, as when the story of Agamemnon and Briseis reconfigures the story of Paris and Helen, is an accident that comes of pure spirit, much like creation itself was probably just such an accident. Alas, the Soviet ukase indicted this pure free spirit of form along with self-conscious convolution for the sake of convolution, or stale rigor for the sake of rigor, and, in so doing, nearly made life itself hardly worth the bother.

She crouched on all fours. The lace panties, black and white, were cut slightly in the middle to allow easy access. There was a rose in the lips of her twat. She wore a persistent smile as would please him. She was a gift to him arranged for by his mistress. She was a tribute to him from that lady. Black stockings ran up her thighs and then suddenly stopped.

Her butt was uplifted a little, the suggestion being that he could have her there if he chose to. She had painted her fingernails crimson red. There was harsh black ink accentuating her eyebrows. She'd been assured these would please.

"Happy Christmas, my sweetest best one!" Thus breathed the lady as they entered the chamber together.

He was delighted, was Gustavus Adolphus, unsheathing a fat member. As he waved it about, he laughed, and his mistress laughed too. I'm fairly certain it was Gustavus Adolphus, although it may really have been Maximillian II, in the salad days before he yielded up parts of Hungary to the Turks. Who knows, maybe it was even Francis Duke of Guise, who was assassinated soon after. No matter, they all left a mark thereabouts.

Her Memoir: Part Seven

Now we get to the part of my life that takes place in prison. I get this funny feeling as I start to write that maybe it ought to have been the first part I wrote about or maybe even the only part. There are a lot of reasons why I think that might be. When you're in prison, it's like nothing else has ever happened to you. The past is a dream and the future is a great uncertainty. All the day-to-day experiences you have in prison are so awful and so intense that it seems they're the only experiences you ever actually had. There are the fights where you think somebody's going to die. There's being naked in the shower where everybody sees you and you have to see everybody. There's the moans and groans in the night which make you know that Lord Broomstick's up to her old tricks again.

I guess that's what hell is. It's the feeling that pain is eternal, that it always was and always will be. Not that you don't remember what happened before, and feel sorry that what happened before is what got you here. On the other hand, I have no regrets, no regrets whatsoever.

But there's another reason why maybe prison should have been the first thing or even the only thing I write about. For me, prison is a metaphor. That means, it symbolizes everything that's ever happened to me. It's what my life is all about.

It defines my life. I've always been in prison in one way or another. Even when I was in love, so much in love that I shot someone, that was a kind of prison too.

"Anytime you want me, babe, you got me, " he said to me. I wanted it all the time. So that meant I was his prisoner, and that love itself was a prison.

Sometimes he was my prisoner. "I could get in real trouble because of you," he said to me once.

So why don't you just go away somewhere, I asked him. But he didn't. He kept coming back for more.

I just thought of another reason why being in prison defines my whole life. I became a big celebrity in the regular world and in this world I'm looked upon as an even bigger celebrity, even more so than if I were a Mafia guy or a serial killer. A regular person like me who happened to commit a famous crime isn't someone these other prisoners usually get to see. They all follow me around or whisper behind my back or try to get into my pants knowing that it's an extraordinary thing that they got to be locked up with somebody from a higher rank of society that everybody on the outside is always still talking about.

They all want me, but they don't want me for me. They want me because I'm famous. And I'll confess that something did actually happen. There was one woman who was pretty strong and rubbed up against me in the kitchen when we were both working there. I hated what she did but it was very interesting now that I think about it. Even the atmosphere was interesting. There was all this steam from the vents, and there were big blasts of heat coming out of the ovens, and the only other woman there besides me and Carol was old Carla, an old Puerto Rican lady who was in jail for a long time and was kind of half-witted and didn't know who I was or care about what was going on.

But Carol sure knew who I was. She forced me against the side of one of the ovens that wasn't hot because it wasn't being used and started pulling at my pants. "Get off me, you stupid nigger," I said.

"Don't make me go get a knife," she said.

"I'll get one too," I said, but I was bluffing.

"C'mon, I just want to see what it looks like," she said, and I said, "you seen it in the shower."

"I haven't," she said. "Besides, I want to see it now."

So, to make a long story short, she got my pants down and reached in to my puss with her finger. I was going to hit her or scream, except she fascinated me because she kept repeating my name as she felt around inside me and I realized it wasn't me she wanted or even my body that she wanted. She wanted my name, she wanted to do my name, and I could see her getting very excited as she said it over and over again, as if she were feeling around inside of something more incredibly special than anything she'd ever known before. It was as good for her as if I were a movie star, maybe better. She was so glad to be feeling the puss that made the name famous.

It got around, of course, what happened, so I tried to stay more and more to myself lest everyone want the glory of knowing what I'm like inside and telling everybody they did. But then I saw something that disturbed me even more than if I had been raped, although it was nothing that did me any direct harm. In fact, you'd think it was the kind of thing that would flatter anybody's ego and make her feel like a goddess, but it actually bothered me quite a bit because of what it says about how weird people can be. Even prisoners shouldn't be this weird.

What it was was that a prisoner named Melissa had built a shrine to me in her cell. There were pictures of me from the newspapers, and drawings she had done, and articles all cut up and pasted together in a big collage, like a whole map of me, on the wall. She'd lie on her back and stare, not masturbating or anything, but just contemplating the pictures.

"That girl's got a thing for you," laughed one of the women.

"It's really something, your being here and all," Melissa said to me in a dreamy kind of a way after I called her a crazy bitch. But she never tried to touch me or anything. Melissa was in for shooting somebody too, but it wasn't that she identified with me because we had done similar crimes. As I say, it was just because I was so famous, the most famous person of my kind until the O.J. Simpson murder happened.

They'd be even hotter for my name if they knew some secrets about me that even the newspapers never found out, but that I'll tell you about right now. My parents aren't my real parents, but they got to adopt me because they have the same last name as my real father, who gave me to them to live with partially because of the coincidence of the names, so that I'd be raised with his.

He was a very famous entertainer in his day, who shall remain nameless, but he fell on hard times. He was very handsome and a wonderful singer with a clear deep voice, although not quite a baritone. It was a perfect voice and he had many hit records. But he fell on hard times because he left his wife for a famous movie star, and the public condemned him for that. Then the famous movie star left him for another famous movie star, and the public mocked him for that.

I never really met him and, in recent years, I understand he's been drinking a lot and taking pills. But I have a beautiful letter he wrote me three years ago, which I memorized, and which said:

My fine daughter,

    I hope you are enjoying your life with your fine family. Things are going well for me, and I'll actually be coming east soon to perform at the Harms Theater in New Jersey. Maybe someday we could meet, because I'm sure you're growing up to be a fine young lady and that would make me very proud.
    Your loving father

My mother was someone he met while he was singing at the Westbury Theater in the Round, a woman who came back stage after the show to try to meet Joan Rivers, who was headlining, and had to settle for meeting him instead. It was a one-night stand but my father was really supportive when my mother got pregnant with me and he bought her a little house in Queens. But she had what's called the wanderlust, and she called him when I was a baby and, according to what I was told, she said, "you better do something about this kid because I'm out of here." That's when his agent contacted my adopted parents, and, in truth, the fact that they have the same last name wasn't the only reason they were chosen. My father's agent thought they were also very nice and stable people, and I guess they are. I'm sorry for the pain I've caused them, although I don't regret anything, not a thing. I'm also sorry about the pain I've caused my real father, except he may be too loaded to give a shit. If so, I guess that would be a blessing.

    Oh my papa! Sometimes I think I could follow in his footsteps by becoming an entertainer after I get out of prison. Who wouldn't want to pay to see me, if only because of the novelty? But then that would wear off because I think I have some real talent, and in the fullness of time that's mainly what people pay attention to, like the black chick who was Miss America until she bumped pussies in the magazine but now the only thing people really think about is what a great singer she is.

Did you ever stop and wonder why they made such a fucking big deal about me and the crime I committed? I mean, people get shot all the time, and people get fucked all the time. And people get shot all the time because they're getting fucked or because, like in my case, the shooter's the one getting fucked. So why me? Was it him that got our story on the front page because he's so fascinating and all? I don't think so. Big dumb shits like him are everywhere and so are little cuties like me.

Maybe it's because most of the people who read the *Daily News* and the *New York Post* are a lot like me in terms of family background, and the things we do for a living, which could be either very blue-collar like being a garage mechanic, or very white-collar like being an insurance salesman. Sometimes I talk to insurance salesmen and they don't sound a lot different from guys who load trucks even though they wear different kinds of clothes to work. They've got the same views of things and the same tone in their voice when they express themselves. I remember I was at a bar in Kew Gardens and a guy who was wearing a suit and tie and looked like he was a manager in a bank was talking about capital punishment and he said, "They should just kill those animals and not let a bunch of damn politicians stand in the way." That very same week, I see this construction worker or something like that because he was wearing a hard hat, I see him on the street in Manhattan, and I overhear him say to his friend, "They should kill those animals and not worry about it." I assume he was talking about capital punishment too but even if he wasn't, it must have been a similar subject, and the choice of words and the tone of voice were so similar, I made a mental note of it.

So if you go from bankers to construction workers, and they're all similar enough to people like us to identify with us, and to really pay attention and be fascinated if we shoot somebody, especially when there's sex involved, then you've got an incredible big audience of readers.

That would explain why the newspapers pick one thing and not another, and why something that's not really a big deal gets to be a big deal. In New York City alone, not counting Newark or Poughkeepsie or whatever, do you know all the shit that niggers are getting into, and all the shit that's happening to them? And when you take a whole look at the Tri-State area, holy shit! In just the week or two before I got sent to prison, and was still reading the papers, they found one black baby in a cardboard box on the West Side Highway, they arrested a woman in the Bronx who froze her two-year old in a freezer, a drug dealer was found in little bitty pieces, a family got burned to death in Jersey because the guy thought his woman was doing somebody else, a girl in South Ozone Park was gang raped, a girl in South Jamaica was gang raped, a woman in East New York shot her husband and 10-year old son, and a junkie was found in her apartment still alive but her baby was eaten by a dog because the dumb fucking junkie forgot to feed the goddamn dog. And me? What did I do? I took one shot at one woman, who never even came close to dying but has a slight handicap that will probably go away in time.

I conclude from all of this that the newspapers don't care about niggers or what they do or what happens to them, which is ok as far as I'm concerned, but what hypocrites! They're always preaching about the evils of racism, and supporting the niggers when they give speeches and such. But they know that what actually happens to niggers won't sell any newspapers, so they come after me instead. It's like that Steinberg case they made such a big deal of. I think that guy Steinberg was a piece of shit who deserves to die, but there's a million Steinbergs right now doing their own kids or somebody else's kids, but they single him out because he's white and supposed to be middle-class and professional and all that, and supposed to up-hold middle-class and professional values, and what does he do instead? He goes and does his own adopted fucking daughter, or at least he beats the fucking crap out of her. But is that kid's life worth more than some little nigger's?

And do you know what else Steinberg was? You got it! Steinberg was a Jew and isn't supposed to do such things. I mean, if Jews behave like this, then what hope is there for mankind? Starting to catch on? You know what I am, don't you? You bet I am!

I wouldn't say it's anti-Semitism or anything, especially since most of the newspaper editors are Jews themselves, or else micks that like to hang with Jews. But it's really playing on all kinds of public attitudes about Jews, and not just the thought that Jews are supposed to be more upright than others. I think there's also a sex thing here. Guys love Jewish puss. It's exotic, because it's different, but also because we're supposed to be hungry bitches. So when they see somebody like me, and I have a horny look in my face in the papers or on TV, and they see I've got these slim, pretty, delicate hips, but the guy's probably got a donkey cock between his legs, they read the story in the papers and they say, "whoa, that must have been some kind of fucking!"

I'll tell you a real secret about something that, assuming he still has it, he could make a million dollars or more selling it to Hugh Hefner or one of those people. One day he comes to me and he says, "Babe, I want to take your picture."

"Sure," I said, because I didn't really mind if there was a nudie of me floating around, and in fact it kind of excited me. He'd have even more control of me because he had the picture, but I'd have even more control of him because I could always say he photographed it. So he says we should meet at the regular motel and he named the time.

We meet in the driveway–I took a bus there that day–and as I see him signing in, he's carrying a big leather case in which I know he has the camera, because who checks into a motel room carrying a camera? That would be a little obvious, don't you think? So fine, we're in the room, and I say, "do you want pictures of me doing myself?"

"Later," he says.

"Later? What do you mean later?" I say. "I thought you could do one of me in bra and panties, and a few more of me doing myself in different poses."

"Oh yeah, I'm all for that," he said. "But first there's one I've been dying to take. Stretch out naked."

I took my clothes off and lay down on the bed. He told me to put my hands behind my head, which I did. Then he told me to open my legs just a little, which I did. Then he reaches in for the camera, and he says, "Babe, you're gonna love this."

But I didn't love it. In fact, I thought it was insulting. You know what he did? He reaches into the case and pulls out a brand new white yarmulke. "What the fuck?" I asked.

"I bought it over in Forest Hills," he says, and with that he puts it on my cunt, and takes the photograph.

"This turns you on, you pig?" I ask.

He laughs, and says, "I think it's funny, like you just swallowed up some Jewish guy in your cunt, and all that's left of him is his little beanie cap between your legs."

"Frame it," I said, "and call the picture, 'Man Eater.'"

I hope he does sell it and make a fortune, so he can send his kids to some college where they'll teach them not to be a big dumb guinea like their father. Maybe that's what I'll do after I get out of here. Open up a school for little guineas, like a finishing school, so they can grow up with a little class. Ha ha!

It's odd, though, that when we all became such celebrities, I wasn't particularly surprised. You'd think I would be. People like President Kennedy were raised expecting to be famous in the media every day. But then other times history just seems to swoop down and pick people out. It happens a lot to simple people like Pope John XXIII, and to another great pope hundreds of years ago who was called Pope Celestine V. I'm not a peasant or anything, but I am a simple person, or at least I don't come from a family like the Kennedys, yet I was picked anyway.

History will ask, why did she do it? Right now, until I tell you, no one but me knows why. First, you have to understand what I loved about him from a sexual standpoint. It wasn't just that he had a big dick, but he used it in a bold and powerful way, and I respected how he might knock a girl around without ever hurting her. You could tell he didn't want to hurt anybody. Sometimes I'd slap him when I thought he was being presumptuous in the things he'd do with his dick, but then he'd hold back my arms so I couldn't hit anybody and he'd screw harder and faster like his thing was a pneumatic drill and he was doing a job fixing up 34th St. or something. You have to be a hell of a guy to make a girl feel like she's 34th St. I could never love a guy with a small wiener, yet more and more I was beginning to feel that a big one wasn't enough for me either unless the guy had a genuine sense of his own personal value to go along with it. And, for those of you who do think a big dick is all you need let me tell you, I've heard about real flamers who have big dicks, but they're guys in drag who take it up the butt for joy.

Sometimes I got to imagine what it would be like if I were married and he were doing me like this behind hubby's back. Hubby would be the ultimate schmuck, don't you think? He'd be owned. It's almost like when your wife gets fucked so hard and fine by somebody else, you're getting fucked too. That turned me on, except I wasn't married.

But here's the thing. I loved him so much at times that I wanted to be him. Sometimes I wanted to be him fucking me, but that wore off as a fantasy because, after all, he *was* fucking me. So then maybe I thought I could be him doing him, crazy as that sounds, or turn him into a woman, and make a fool out of his husband, but he doesn't have a husband and it's hard to imagine him having a husband or what kind of guy could ever be his husband. But he does have a wife, if you can see where I'm going. And that idea really worked, it stayed alive inside me, and, as time went on, I started wanting to do his wife real bad, but not as a woman doing another woman, but as a stud doing the spouse of the lover he loves.

Then it got even heavier. The more I thought about it, and the more I dreamed of being him, the more I could really feel what he was feeling and want what he was wanting. So never mind all the hot cheat on your spouse stuff. Love and love alone, love in all its glory, took over. As I remember, the very moment when I was loading that gun, I was thinking about what it must look like when he does his wife or when his wife does him and at that moment I wanted to be him loving up his wife just like a man should.

So I didn't hate the woman. Quite to the contrary, I loved her husband ever so much that I wanted to be him and fuck my wife and really take her over with a big banging she wouldn't ever forget. But if I strapped on a dildo, or even if I could grow my own dick, she would have just told me to go packing, and, besides, I didn't want to play-act like a man. So I took the gun, figuring that would be a satisfying thing to do her with, and of course I wouldn't kill her, I'd only wing her a little, just like Chin Gigante winged Frank Costello in the old days, and in the same part of the body—which just happens to be a part of the body a lot of women use in a very adoring and loving and humble way to give men sexual satisfaction. I loved him so much, I feel like a saint who sacrificed everything for love. I'm not Catholic but isn't that what saints do? Give it up, and all for love?

Anyway, so that's why I shot her. I shot her because I was changed from what I used to be, love had changed me, and shooting her made the change as real as the flesh on my bones and the blood in my veins. I'm no longer the hot little Jew girl who passes out blow jobs around the neighborhood. I'm no longer the bitch who teases dorky guys while she secretly dreams of the stud she's been longing for. I'm no longer the wayward kid who needs a shrink. I'm no longer even the celebrity that pitiful bitches in prison dream about. All I am now is my lover's penis, and that is all I ever want to be.

The Shield of Paris

(Based on the author's "Fields of Force: A Crisscrossing of Real Love and Real War," originally published in *Pre-Hellenic Artifacts and Antiquities*, Universities Collective Press, June 2004)

His name boldly titles the entire masterpiece. But that it was found in old Trikka suggests that it is a work of, not by Paris, and, as the four floral configurations etched into the small gilt inset at the lower right corner are the same Thessalian medical guild emblems that Bertelsman dates to around 1200 BC, the work may well have been commissioned by actual disciples of Asclepius' son Machaon, who'd been wounded by Paris and perished later during a separate encounter. If so, the composition becomes all the more haunting for having been forged apparently in tribute to Paris by artisans with every reason (by our lights) to loathe the mention of his name. Indeed, Machaon had even directly ministered to Menelaus himself. Yet not just a monument, it is a shield to protect – to protect whom? To protect their patron's near-vanquisher? A ravished clan thus sculpts a masterpiece for the safeguarding of its ravisher and with no apparent coercion to do so – and in a war that the ravisher's nation was even destined to lose?

Such attribution as well as the thing itself is sufficient reminder indeed that this prince was War as well as Love as no one else has ever been both, having after all slain Achilles himself and mounted Helen herself. You see the god of war and the goddess of love drawn on opposite corners of the shield, an explicit comment by the artist on Paris' dual preeminence. I wonder why Homer, relating all of Paris' war exploits, never remarks on how nonpareil the triumphs of this prince are in the parallel realms.

The shield amazes, in any event, as does the well-known accident by which Ellis and his students stumbled upon it. Their destination had been Dimini, to join those Adrimi-Sismani excavations that would soon disclose their own treasures. But a wind-fed blaze sweeping through a row of abandoned huts forced the closing of local roads. By next morning, where parts of the earth had been chewed up by fire and hectic brigades, the shield of Paris was extruding from the dirt, seared out onto the surface of the ground within a grove on the northeastern corner of the town. Had Ellis's party not been delayed the previous day, the locals might have mistaken it for an old wall brace of some sort and maybe used it for firewood.

Ellis had the surface scraped and was the first of all of us to marvel at the massive complexity, the weaving in and out of the forms that define this masterpiece. Helen it is likely depicted in the central figure snaking from top to bottom and back again, each third of her anatomy appearing not once but twice on each third of the surface, which probably meant that here was unearthed the best if not the only pure surviving example of that storied Thessalian pictorial technique known as *tricuntos*. At some points, though, there are elements of abstraction that may be due less to technique than to the effects of time. Stewart Coach-Dwyer, for example, is pretty convincing in his analysis that one of the right buttocks of the Helen figure on the first third of the surface, which intrigues everyone with its inner compositional tension that seems to press it toward a purely floral configuration, is not finally man-made but a fortunate corrosion wrought by the centuries.

Caution so ruled during the initial restoration that some planes of the pictorial surface – especially where the triple sectors through which Helen flows intersect four quadrants, each quadrant with its own narrative scenes – are left fairly faint. Equally faint, there are amorphously patterned figures that one makes out moving upward, delicate lines incongruously unwarlike, yearnings headed higher. The top margins to which these figures aspire billow like asses missing their cracks while the bottom margins are deltoid and darkly colored, vaginal. Thus the very essence of the Greek, I reck, as, below, the drossy woman's hole gapes and, above, the dancing shit boxes flutter like the veritable portals of spirit. One imagines an ululated longing for elegy – ululation not yet itself elegy – to sound at all points between.

You can barely count how many forms interweave or compass all the places where they do. The face of someone who might be Aias the son of Telamon could also be the cunt of Briseis. Over here see Briseis' toes just about leap away perpendicularly from her feet, obtruding like boulders unless she's got some kind of elephantitis. Over there a leaf narrows at its stem, which may then be the forefinger of a guy who looks a hell of a lot like none other than Idomeneus himself and if you follow it for a few inches he seems to be sticking it up somebody's ass, it's hard to say whose.

Ellis recalls the "rapt and illumined" faces of his students as they gazed upon the tableau. He may have been demure in that recollection if not naïve. (I never met the man but one colleague who did says he was a bit prissy.) When last year I first visited the shield with Joann Montenegro from my team, the shock of seduction registered almost as a reflex of vision. Joann and her family have been our warm friends for years, and I've occasionally imagined her a soft welcoming bedmate, yet the day she looked first closely upon the shield of Paris something more darkly incisive from this bowel of antiquity well-nigh transformed her. I don't know which scene on the shield she peered at but at that brief moment I barely knew her. Rosy cheeks paled, lively eyes narrowed, a slight arch of eyebrows betokened the kind of fleeting thought or image that most of us, if we allow a sliver of such into consciousness, could never articulate even were we willing. When Meg McPhee and I were retained to do a second cleaning, I was aware she was glancing at me, that she may have been conscious of my responses to the shield, or perhaps uncomfortable with what she worried she was disclosing of her own fascination. The more we cleaned, the dirtier it got. I was so conscious of Meg beside me, her ample pale flesh, the fleshy cleavage as we polished the figure of a warrior chief, most likely Drakios with his thing in an unidentified female, only to find when we wiped a film of dirt away that the female was androgynous, and that her own cock was attended by a semi-circle of acolytes, their quiet worship altogether more unsettling than any pornographic caricature. The acolytes in their row were so finely sculpted as to suggest a phallus carved from their collective focus. We all feel so naked, I suppose, wondering what our faces scanning the epic panorama disclose. Looking at the acolytes in crisp formation I felt like I was being probed and I think Meg did too, and she smelled sexual at that moment and I wonder what she smelled. I never had that feeling before, of being fucked alongside somebody else, and I am sure there has been nothing since the Iron

Age to make me feel that way, but the shield of Paris was seven hundred years before then.

None of its unsettling scenes has aroused more discussion than the one on the bottom left quadrant where two warriors engaged in anal intercourse are imputed to be Achilles and Patroclos. Common sense rejects that a work of art created by or for Paris would likely so feature his two definitive archenemies. Yet certain verses of Dodar, never adequately explicated prior to the discovery of the shield, are most relevant in this regard. The poetry itself finally admitted of interpretation only in light of apparent allusions to the shield even as the poetry now helps explicate the shield in return. As Ryan translates:

> When devious-voyaging Alexandros set upon the craft,
> Abandoning sky-white Helen still timorous in her aching,
> There lofted past him and the troubled vision of her in his lists,
> The coupling visages of his enemies, Achilles himself
> And Patroclos, the soul of him of proud and manly ravishment.

In an unrelated discussion, Gottfried himself confidently situates Dodar in the vicinity of Volos during the Homeric period, where he would have likely seen the shield during or soon after its creation. Granting that, it must have been clear to the poet that the ass-fuckers depicted thereon were Achilles and Patroclos, for there would not seem to be any other reason for him to then write poetry about the envisioning by Paris of Achilles and Patroclos, and particularly of Patroclos as a manly ravished warrior.

Definitely, it would be too much coincidence, in light of Dodar's now fully explicated text, for these guys to be anybody else but Achilles and Patroclos. The only other persuasive argument is that the scene was added later, after Machaon's original workshop disbanded and nearer the day Paris killed Achilles. If so, the love scene only assumes increasingly momentous and complementary significance as a tribute to the prince – the picture of Achilles and Patroclos making love on his shield like Achaian balls hanging from Paris' belt – and, at the same time, a generous, even tender elegy to the warrior he killed. Too bad we don't have any pictures of Paris fucking Helen. It would be interesting to compare what that looks like to what we see here of Achilles and Patroclos.

How fierce Patroclos looks with that verge rammed up his buttock. Achilles seems impassive, as if the very knowledge of what he is doing, or perhaps the astonishment of how fine it feels up there, has quieted his demeanor. It is a lovely nuance even if unintended by the artist, that a hero like Achilles would look as he does, so immobile. The very realization of his love and devotion to Patroclos has utterly nonplussed him and stilled visible physical expression itself. Meanwhile, you can tell that Patroclos will cherish the jizz once it's shot.

Alternatively crude and wicked scenes fan out from the bottom left quadrant, a montage spaced away from, while still adorning, the two heroes in their congress. Over there a woman cleans her butt, gesticulating with her other hand in what looks like a dancer's old supplication to the gods, reminiscent of the wall paintings at Knossos. Past an inch or two of thick inchoate glaze, a woman kisses the foot of a soldier, her apparent seducer. Nowhere, though, has any figure been identified even speculatively as Paris, though his name at top unquestionably identifies the shield as his.

The importance of the work has only just begun to be appreciated as I think its initial impact was too jarring for cultural historians to contextualize. We've needed time to assess a twofold drama here, one a drama of something anciently capable of arousing libidinous figments that nothing since the Iron Age has aroused. On the other hand, in its plasticity and virtual multi-dimensionality, how far advanced—presaging modernity, I'd say—the shield of Paris is over an Iron Age sculptor like Polycleitus. How its vanishing points defy even Renaissance sophistication, and how we must now understand that the world was not flat before the European Middle Ages but had gone to flat, perhaps in flight from the intricately dimensioned labyrinth we have here.

Sometimes the vision seems so healthy and sometimes so sick in a way that can only be imputed, respectively, to the innocence of the ancients or the decomposition of the moderns. I think about the nature I hear vibrate in music like Rameau's *Suite in E Minor*, an insistent throbbing, nature naked for all the rococo adornment. There's always something of necrophilia when nature is naked, but in that expression of the mature West it sounds a lovely recrudescence contrasted to, say, an imminent decomposition in Expressionist rendition of curvilinear Art Nouveau line in our time, drawn it seems from the contours of a leaf, or Romeo still alive but about to rot in the tomb.

I love it over there on the second quadrant where you've got this big fat woman getting fucked by a squadron it seems of grinning little men, small men like pygmy armies but each man bigger a little than that I guess. They all look like feasters at a feast as if it is not love here nor even lust in any strict sense of the word but a gala benefit or chow time for the rank and file after the battle – like the one where Hector almost gets killed by the stone that Telamonian Aias throws at him has just been won – and all's well ending well at least on this day, and be it said that nothing as much as the Trojan war cry is like the roaring of the sea's surf against dry land or the crying voice of the wind in the deep-haired oak. All those guys on the big woman, who could be like a cow they're devouring raw, reminds me of the time some friends and me were having a drink at a bar at the old Brooklyn Navy Yards and we couldn't figure out why all these fat chicks were getting so much action until the bartender happened to mention that the Turkish fleet was in town.

Then there's this gorgeous design, an intricate geometry in the lower sector diagonal from the third quadrant that looks something like a pussy, which is odd considering how much these people hated the sight of such, but that's what it looks like, and it's so plastic in its expert delineation that it seems to be moving in on itself and moving outward at the same time, and all at the same time, too, a rune as well, or an old word of an old language, maybe one of the tongues Paris' Lykian allies spoke. Two meanings that feast on each other and concentrate the meaning all the more because the two meanings are working as one, even as antonymous meanings in the very same word are like to burst the meanings asunder or maybe form a third meaning, in a kind of dialectic, from the opposed meanings, or, at other times, a simple unmeaning juxtaposition of meanings that gives surcease from both the training in of meaning and the rendering asunder of meaning. Yes, it could be what the Lykians spoke at times, what Sarpedon had to say.

See the woman in the white shroud with some kind of chalky residue from the original medium still visible on her. She must have been so death-like or wraith-like when the shield was new. A garb draped across her waist reveals the upper thigh. That's very beautiful. A piece of a sculpted figure hovers before her and what may have been a divan is drawn beneath her. He's probably fucking her in her pale and moon-like milky dying. Very nice. Fascists take note when their mothers get fucked on or near their deathbeds. Hitler's mother dying was attended by a Jewish physician and Hitler, our own version of the pagan lord, would never forget or forgive it. By contrast, Hitler's opposite among proto-fascists, Orson Welles, had his mother done by a Jewish doctor, too, but he, the lordly fat man who must dominate whatever he does for better or worse, adored the physician lover, who was named Bernstein and whom Welles honored with a character so named in *Citizen Kane*. But they both took note, these men, when their mothers were Jew-fucked even as they died or were beginning to.

The seams of the shield show, what with its sectors and quadrants and pictorial dramas contained in each. In our time we assume the achievement of seamlessness defines craft, though we never expect it in the old tableaux, neither here, nor in static medieval compositions, nor in narrative Buddhist sequences from Mathura or wherever, nor do we devalue them for all the showing of their seams. "I am in my mother's room" is the first sentence of *Molloy*, and how obvious, i.e., seam-showing, can you get? But I do love it. Showing seams may after all be what abstraction is really about, which is why our own moderns persist to love ancient stuff like this or the tribal primitives even more overtly seamy-showing. Visible seams can bespeak urgency too, drawn or written as they are because there's just no time to more artfully wed the juxtaposed component parts. That may be the case with the shield of Paris. These people died young and without a lot of time to go get all Jamesian on us.

The Greeks were renowned for balance, but I wonder. I love Rusk's life of Emerson mainly because the author's purpose was to provide an exemplar of balance, and whether we actually believe that the unreported realities of Emerson's life support that depiction or not is irrelevant. It's the art of purposeful biography at work here. Yet even within the context of what we read in Rusk we have to wonder when we intuit a certain emotional blockage in Emerson, at least in his second marriage, his grieving at not being able to grieve over his dead son, and in his suspiciously stoical acceptance of his first wife's death. In other words, what is balance? I don't think the shield of Paris is balanced. I don't think the Greeks were either or, for that matter, the Trojans.

I prefer radiance. Genius in acting, for example, is defined by that one quality, radiance: Garbo in *Camille* and Cagney in *The Roaring Twenties*. The rest is technique or fine skill and empathy, but not genius, which is why British actors are over-rated. The Greeks were probably great actors even before the era of the tragedians, but who knows.

> I looked over my shoulder
> For ritual pieties,
> Geometric cities wisely met.
> But by the flickering light of Paris,
> Quite another scene indeed I saw embed.

> That fat women are fed upon
> Is an axiom as axiomatic
> As that demotic languages Lykian-carved
> Bespeak promises kept but tickling figments, too,
> Of the butt-fuck torments Myrmidons wept.

And so on and so forth as our refugees from their own educations, these Audens and so forth, limn the diminution of their catechisms and the stark reversals of the classicisms they suckled on. But behold, I tell you and I tell you again, behold this collective heritage unsurpassed for the pure sweltering fuck of life, and the vanquishing of the undone, and the undoing of the vanquished, and the noble manly piercing of the noble manly shit hole, Patroclos' it is who grunts handsomely amid the elegies. I suppose the mud huts of such ancient disport do posit a tangible diminution when compared to, say, cheap motels off Route 3 in New Jersey (especially the Starlight Inn in Secaucus), or the rented rooms in which we stiffen through dull August afternoons, and I suppose that that, if only as a matter of pure moral environment, is what Auden's or Eliot's or Joyce's epochal contrasts are meant to point to.

Paris got Delochos from behind at the shoulder's bottom,
Piercing through the front parts, and rammed the bronze clean through.
While the men were disembarrassed of their arms, meantime the Achaians,
Themselves brought low about the deeply dug ditches and impaling spears,
Ran amok in terror and were taken all upended in their ramparts.
But Hector hallooing in a piercing call...

Now look on the shield here where a woman runs naked in the lists pursued by men, seeming armed and hungry, though faceless, and looking to be a cloud of dust and all undifferentiated their forms, and look here where a waterfall pours from a male ass, and look here where dancing whores with faces like large walnuts carved in three sections point to their own genitals, and look here where the long sharp stakes are nailed to earth so dark it could be somebody's shit, and look here at Patroclos and his abiding acquiescent glare, and here too where squadrons wait, and Paris in his utter absence permeates all because he is master of love and death lived and died again and once again.

This Rover Crossed Over

1.

Charlie Saba: a tall man, sandy blond with light blue eyes and effeminate hands and soft, narrow lips. A pretty male, but it's usually women who find him most attractive. Once he used to dandify himself to please them. He loved paisley when he was younger and still wore high-heeled leather boots with elaborate buckles intricately patterned like wrought iron. For the winters he owned a camel's hair coat that had been strikingly elegant three, four seasons ago. Now the lining was torn and the outer fabric matted and seedy. He wasn't overly concerned. The yen to dress up was now only intermittent, as was the sexual urge itself. By the same token, when it came upon him it came strongly.

He crossed Eighth Avenue and went into a McDonald's. The restaurant was dimly fluorescent, crowded but fairly quiet. Only in places like this at such hours of the night surrounded by other tired people content to drift thoughtlessly into their coffee was he at peace. The shuffling and jostling were over. The ship had beached him here, voyage's end: North Carolina to college in New York, then cross-country trips to and from California carrying marijuana, which was how he earned money and lived fairly well for some years. Then an arrest, but no indictment. To Paris with a friend, but they nearly starved. Back to New York where he worked for a talent agency helping administer accounts. California again, using drugs, until his money ran out. He became haggard for awhile. Worked as a laborer in San Francisco, bought a bus ticket back to New York. Now on welfare, living in a one-room apartment on West 29th St. He eats fairly well, and doesn't care to drink or smoke much. His good looks have come back. Almost ruddy. Walks around a lot at night. Charlie Saba.

His intelligence is unimpaired. It's incisive, actually, which is why he often feels lost and desperate when he walks the streets. More than loneliness aches him. Loneliness he can take. But he also feels left out. The rich couples in and out of the theaters, their limousines: in their swagger, the nation's newly recovered pride in money and status. He's no longer young enough to either good-naturedly tolerate these strangers or pretend to hate what they stand for. A dull-edged envy is all he has. Meanwhile, the company of others like himself is colder comfort every day. "Fucking bunch of losers," he mumbles to himself.

A semi-circle of a half-dozen or so young people approached his table. By their dress, which was immaculate and informal – crisp bright t-shirts and deep-grooved corduroy on the boys, long dresses with demure floral patterns to the ankles on the girls – and by their expressions, smiley and uniformly energetic, Saba figured them to be Jesus people. They milled around for a full minute and passed a few whispers among themselves, then dispersed back to their own table where their plain cloth coats hung over the red plastic chairs.

One female drew nearer. She was extremely pretty. Her skin was milky smooth and her eyes a deeper, darker blue than his. Graceful, thin-armed, her features were too perfect; they would have been forgettable except that her mouth was broad and dipper-like. The lips were radiantly ruby red, almost unnaturally so. Her air of an acolyte's chastity caught his fancy. Waspish chastity intrigued him. Many of these people hadn't repressed their passions altogether. They held lust in abeyance as something they all knew about and thought was wrong, but they weren't as pathological as a lot of the Catholics he knew, or at least they weren't pathological in quite the same way.

"Can I have a word with you?" she asked.

"Yes." He nodded toward the chair beside him. She fetched her coat from the other table, came back and sat down.

"My name is Cindy," she said, showing a big toothy smile. "What's yours?"

"Charlie."

"Oh, that's a very nice name," she said, in a tone that a doting adult would take with a child.

"It's a pretty good name," he said. "Thousands of horses have worn it with pride." His humor seemed to confuse her, which was too bad because he was proud of it. Then an unexpected thing happened. She leaned forward and looked at him earnestly and didn't say anything. It was as if she were waiting for him to speak, to take the lead. What was he supposed to say?: that he assumed she wanted to talk about Jesus, that he knew she'd come to his table to discuss the destiny of his soul. He'd be damned before he'd give her or any other religion peddler the benefit of that much cooperation, or the satisfaction of knowing that their concerns were, to any degree, his own as well. So he remained obstinately silent. Of course he had never seen this before, a reborn who hesitated to go first.

Finally, she had to break the ice herself. "I wanted to talk to you about something very important."

Saba said "okay," but nothing more.

"It's about you, and who you are, and where you're going."
Still, she hesitated to say the name "Jesus," still seeming to
want to trap him into saying it first and thereby admit that
somehow in some way her god was on his mind.

Again, though, all he said was "okay," blankly. Again, she
was the one who finally gave in.

"I want to talk to you about Jesus." For a third time, he
said only "okay."

"Do you know Jesus?" she asked.

"Not really," he said.

"Can I talk about Him to you?"

"Sure, go ahead."

Her eyes fixed on him as she launched in. "I believe that
Jesus can salve every wound. When you're lonely on the street
– and I know you're on the street, and I can tell you're lonely –
He's with you. He's by your side. Without Him, it's hell."

She paused. Her tone was light and pleasant, even in
the way she said the word "hell." She seemed on the verge of
singing a ditty, as if her sermon so far were the spoken rec-
itative to some innocuous tune in a musical comedy. "People
who are offered Jesus and refuse Him, and refuse the sacrifice
He made for all of us, these people suffer damnation through
all eternity, with terrible fire and sores and scabs and wailing
despair." There was still an incongruous lilt in her tone. "It's
bad enough never to have the chance to know Him, like all the
poor dark-faced people on other continents. But to be offered
His love, and to refuse it, that's terrible. If you say Yes to Jesus
you'll be in paradise forever. It's so simple. You just open your
heart and let the love pour in. You'll feel love for everyone you
meet, and you'll forgive everyone who ever hurt you. That's
really what heaven is, you know. To forgive everyone. First

you've got to say Yes. You've got to take that step. You've got to open your heart. Maybe I'm talking too much. I can't help it because I'm so full with the love of Jesus that it just keeps overflowing. Do you know what I mean? Do you understand the things that I'm trying to say?"

"You mean you want me to accept Jesus Christ as my savior?" he asked. His tone was ingenuous, matter-of-fact, though with a slightly anxious edge to it. The obtuseness of the question confused her. Wasn't it obvious that that's precisely what she wanted? If he had to ask, she thought, perhaps it was because he suffered from some kind of a mental deficiency. Saba wondered himself why he'd responded in such an odd way, though he did have a sense, half clear to him at that moment, that his question was a prelude to a kind of game he'd been darkly, semi-consciously formulating all along, throughout her heartfelt peroration.

The lines in the restaurant were getting bigger, and some of the lights had been turned up a bit. The new customers were apparently filing in from a nightclub of some sort that just closed. It was almost four. Saba remembered it was Friday, so there was no work tomorrow for these people. There was a low buzzing among the customers, who were mostly young and black: fifteen, twenty people too nervous and full of the night to want to go home yet. Only a few of the girl's companions still lingered at their table and they too looked ready to go.

The idea came suddenly: a fearless powerful inner urge. It was in fact years since he'd felt anything this outrageous so self-confidently, with so little fear of rejection or consequence. And not just the urge came upon him at once, a whole stratagem followed on as well. He would try to fuck her and use for persuasion an odd, elaborate argument, each word of which was already sounding hard and clear in his mind, an old, old script somehow memorized and perfected months in advance.

"I will accept Him as my savior," he answered. Cindy was confused again, figuring that any conversion this fast must be suspect, Jesus' miraculous healing powers notwithstanding. "But you've got to do something for me," Saba continued, then rushed on to finish the whole proposal before she could enunciate a word of objection. "You've got to have sex with me in my apartment. For a long time. Two or three hours. Then when we're done I'll accept Jesus as my savior and I'll never sin again. I swear on my mother's grave, if you do this for me I'll give my life to Jesus forever."

"Shame on you," she said, her cheeks drawn back in a wounded pucker, the lilt in her voice gone. She jerked slightly forward, as if to get up. But she thought better of it. She'd stay and fight. Her place was with the sinners and publicans.

"Don't you know what you're doing to yourself?" she asked. Her smell, clean and sweet like wildflowers, strange to smell here of all places at this hour of the night, hovered on the table over the weak coffee. "Are you trying to ruin Jesus? You can't ruin Jesus. And you can't ruin the fortunate souls He's saved. But you can insult Him. You can violate the spirit. You can, you really can. Why do you want to? For what? It's your own poor soul at stake. You'll be among the forgotten. You'll be lost in the cracks of the world. No one will hear you squeal. No one will know your name or even guess that once a long time ago, millions of years ago, you were a person living on the earth like anyone else, and that you had a chance at love but instead you spat on the divine face and insulted the divine heart."

Saba contained his impatience, and kept control of himself. Of the plot. His anger was purposeful, a deep burning intent. Each of his thoughts was a hammer poised and ready to strike. It was the most lucid moment he had had in months. Step One, now.

"Look, either make love with me and I'll accept Jesus, or beat it. I haven't got the time for bullshit."

"Shame on you," was all she could say. The flesh on her willowy arms was like a baby's. And those red red lips...He could guess what her tits would look like and smell like, and the other thin lips between her legs. He could just about taste her.

"Beat it," he said. Her eyes grew moist. She was certainly upset, staring back, unblinking. Slowly she rose and began to turn away. Step two, now.

"But of course you might be making the worst mistake of your life," he said. "You might have just lost your soul."

"Me? Why my soul?" For the first time she was obviously irate, put-upon.

"Maybe Jesus sent you here to save me," he said. "How do you know you're not just being selfish, letting a miserable creature like me go to the devil, and you cheating Jesus out of a soul just because you're too damn self-centered to have sex with me?"

"Jesus wouldn't want me to sin with you," she said, almost petulantly.

"Say, where did all your friends go?" he asked. "They seem to have left you here with me. That's odd, isn't it? You'd think they'd stick around. Think they went home? Or outside, to fish for souls in the cold? Seems to me everything's been somehow prearranged to bring us together."

"Jesus doesn't ask people to sin for Him."

"How do you know?" he snapped. "Where do you come off knowing so much about God?"

"Oh, so you admit he's God!" she said, bitter and exhilarated.

"Of course I'll admit it. There, you see! We're halfway there. Every second we're together draws me closer to God. Closer and closer. You're not going to stop now, are you?"

"This is like the inquisition," she said, her voice cracking slightly.

"You're forgetting something," he said, glancing around to make sure the few people at the next table couldn't overhear. "You're forgetting that your body is nothing. Nothing. What a trivial thing to worry about when a human soul may be at stake."

"It would still be a sin. You're a very wicked man. Really, if you had any true desire for Jesus, you wouldn't have to be making me this horrible offer."

"It's because I'm so hurt and lonely," he said, lowering his voice, almost whispering. "You've got to prove to me you really care. I need you to prove it. Then I'll know. Then I'll be able, I'll be able to give myself."

Her eyes hardened. "You may be the devil himself," she said.

"Maybe. Maybe I am, but you'll never be sure. And what if I am? Jesus would still see into your heart. He'd know why you'd be making love with me. He'd certainly forgive you, wouldn't He? After all, He'd know you were doing it for Him. And wouldn't that be spitting in Satan's eye, to yield to his treachery only in order to more loudly glorify by your generosity the saving grace of Jesus?"

As he spoke he enunciated each word more convincingly. He had intended to play a shrewd game, yet with this impassioned eloquence he really surprised himself. It just flooded out. "Don't you know what happens when one single soul is saved?" he continued. "Angels dance around the throne of the Father for centuries. Imagine that!—-a thousand years of dancing angels because you, sweet Cindy on the streets of the city, were willing to take one drastic measure to help save one soul in peril."

She was extremely tired, almost numb, and her face was a blank. "It's still a sin," she said.

"No, no sin. Just an act," he said. "A gesture. If your soul is clean, I can't make your body dirty. If I'm lying, then it's only me that's damned."

"You're sick and twisted."

"Let's get out of here," he said, and reached forward and grabbed her elbow. "Put your coat on."

"No," she said, too weak to struggle physically.

"Please," he said, as his own eyes grew moist. "We'll just walk together, that's all. Please, I need you."

He got her out on the street. "I have to go home now," she said.

"Look," he said, "the dawn is coming up, the new dawn of my soul. Remember the angels that knocked on Abraham's door and Abraham fed them?"

"You know the Bible," she said, her tone now blank like her eyes.

"Abraham fed the strangers not knowing they were angels. What a beautiful thing!" His voice was dazzled, exuberant. They headed south toward his apartment, walking past vagrants and an occasional prostitute. Only a few cars were on the street.

"The devil quotes scripture," she said. "I've been warned of that."

"So what? So what? Oh Cindy, Cindy, don't you see! The only real sin is to refuse a soul in distress. Give yourself to me in faith, hope, and charity."

She tried to dart off toward a cross street, but he grabbed her elbow again and pressed tightly the heavy blue cloth of her coat. "Magdalene," he said. "Have you forgotten Magdalene?"

"I would never have expected you to know all those beautiful names," she said, almost dreamily. "Abraham, Magdalene. Do you know about them?"

"It's been so long," he said. "I've forgotten so much of it. I've been so lonely, so desperate."

"Look at that poor soul," she muttered as a dark Spanish whore wearing a parka above red silk shorts, her thighs chafing in the cold, walked by. Saba felt Cindy's resistance beginning to give way. He had pushed, now something was giving.

"Oh to risk it all for Jesus," he said. "What a glorious thing to do!"

She stared at him, nearly wide-eyed; she wanted to, he could surely see that now. Should he talk on, say more, press the advantage? – or not risk it, keep silent, bide his time until he could get her home and have her?

He spoke. "To sacrifice for Jesus, to...to..." For the first time he stumbled and, though he recovered in a moment, his cold composure was gone. His heart beat wildly. "And if our embrace does save my soul, oh what an embrace it will be! We'll melt in each other's arms, melt for the love of all mankind."

At 36th St. they kissed. The deep anger that had made him eloquent was gone. His tongue probed her gently and her breath was wonderful, like wintergreen.

2.

I don't know why I gave in. Except that face of his, which was the color of wheat, and which I've known so many years in so many dreams of men like warriors with cruel eyes and smooth sunny flesh, drew me to him. I wanted to save him. Was it You who sent me? Are You pleased with me, Jesus?

Jesus is barefoot, white robe sheathed with a gray band, standing before her with hands gently folded.

Heaven vibrates with your deed. Of all women, you are blessed in the chorus of the elect. You heeded not yourself nor minded the perils of the lonely path but plunged in deep, down, down to the passion pit of the world for my name's sake and my name's sake only. The Father knows you and glorifies you.

Great stars of shimmering silver and bursts of red and blue illuminate the firmament as He speaks.

A lost soul is found. Go thou, be my ministering angel, my sweet honey of joy, the tender apostle of love's darker communion.

Cindy is dressed in a single loose piece of light green cloth twisted across her chest and between her legs, the scent of mint strong and invigorating.

I'm so glad. Amen.

Dear God, You saved me once from sin, won't You save me again? You saved my dark Spanish boy too, remember, the Spanish boy who never told his name when we coupled in the doorways and on the roofs even when sometimes the addicts came and slept nearby while we did it? Remember, his paws on me, his tongue lapping like a dog's tongue between my legs, and how I wanted it and bellowed for it, the hot vile things I'd say? How once I made the sounds a chicken makes, the wicked delight in that until You came to us and showed us Your face of purest goodness and light. We held hands in the church. We accepted You with both our hearts and souls. Don't throw me back now into the darkness after all You've done.

Jesus' deep blue eyes don't blink, stare unyielding, His voice soft but insidiously furious, a two-thousand year-old rage corralled in one hideously unruffable manner.

The devil came to you and tempted you, and you gave way at once. You wanted to yield, so you did. You yourself conjured the blond devil out of the pit of your own malevolent lust. Never again will I raise you up, you handmaiden of the bog, you reeking putridity in the nostril of the goat. I cast you out! I cast you and I separate you forever from heaven and sweet truth.

Cindy's cloak is undone, pubic hair growing wild around the edges, the top of her garment fallen to her waist reveals drooping breasts with rigid ruby red nipples. There's an acrid sulphur smell.

Oh that's terrible! That's awful!

It was so ugly, that place, the odor of abandoned hamburgers and half-eaten potatoes. The people there were the damned. Their eyes were dying. I had to get away from them, I had to. That bracing wind, those steam-swept streets emptied of frantic life. I had to get out, or choke.

Cindy is naked with a slight smell as her arms reach out.

I was so proud, too proud thinking I could serve you so.

Jesus gazes heavenward.

Abagtruyin opertygnum esse nipoiyt ebbanebban utty sutty utty.

3.

He slipped out of her as she dozed off, almost smiling. Morning shadows on the bedpost, dishes in the sink, and the same ancient stains on the thick gray throw rug. Outside, matins, and the noise of jackhammers.

What about it? he thought. It's time.

Saba held her hand as she slept. She seemed to be sleeping comfortably, her breath coming in quiet child-like spurts. But she would surely ask him when she woke, and he'd surely have to answer. What words would he find to say it?

Their Music

They stood by the open window waiting for the muezzin. When the great cry sounded, the Jew smiled leaning against the sill. "I'm tempted," he said, slyly referencing the tangible power of the nonpareil incantation. There were proverbial scoffers, sundry cosmopoles, an unholy infidel host who, just hearing it, were said to have been brought, transfixed, to pious heel, Allah being all praiseworthy.

It was a power the Jew was happily willing to acknowledge. "After all these years, thirty years traveling here, visiting Algiers, Damascus, Rabat, even Biskra, I'm still tempted."

"And Michelangelo, El Greco, Tintoretto, do they tempt you as well?"

"No," said the Jew, the persistent twinkle in his eye a little bold, a little malicious even. "Christianity, God love it, lacks that, that..." He was an old man, hard to say how old. Bald, bespectacled, Jew of the fabled sort, prototype, perhaps, of the ancient Jew genus born in the musty monastic sagas. A type to be cautious of. A dark type, stiff-necked, outsider since Golgotha. Immersed at birth, you may be sure, in inevictable tradition, his father maybe a relic ritual slaughterer you might imagine in harsh rural Russian parts. The learned son inexplicably mercantile escapes, never to go home again or care to, into the dark byways of old lands that time and tide have fast bypassed. A rebellious, dilettante nature primed for the astonishing oddities of passion and dispassion such lands are eternally heir to. Savoring them in his travels.

His friend smiled and nodded. "You'll recall Frank Malkemes? Your name came up when he and I talked in New York last year."

"Oh yes," said the Jew.

"The prayer was so powerful, but, since I've brought up Malkemes, is it too soon or would it now be profane...?

"To speak of Hamid? I don't regard the subject of Hamid as at all profane under any circumstances. Or, if it is, yet so mingled with..."

"But so sexual. A monstrous, lovely..."

"'Monstrous,' echoed the Jew. "Yes, I would suppose 'monstrous.'"

"Frank Malkemes talked of it in such a way..."

"He said I could introduce you?"

"He thought it possible."

"Ah, but I don't know where Hamid lives now. I'll be happy to ask around." The Jew laughed. "I wonder if I have enough stamina at this point in my life to revisit Hamid. We poor old men, we require some insulation at last."

"Hamid must be getting older too. Fifty, sixty."

"The clergy for the most part regard him as totally degenerate. But, you know, it's the 11th century here still. Native movements abound. Secret contrarian movements."

"Malkemes said they want to canonize him."

"Yes, and there's a fascinating political motive in that, since so many foreigners and their wives have yielded up their music."

"A triumph for the indigenous peoples!"

"And why not?" smiled the Jew, subversively, radically agleam. Rather elegant, really.

"Did Frank Malkemes…?"

"Oh, I don't know. Of that I have no idea."

In truth, Hamid now lived in a suburb of the city visitors would not likely find. It was an insignificant settlement, home to a few workers and their families who'd followed a railroad built by Belgian investors a generation earlier. Fifty or so spacious mud huts sheltered beneath the shale outcroppings of the small mountain, a lonely castoff from the Atlases to the west, that defined the immediate terrain, otherwise flat and rather monochromatic. The train tracks were rusted in disuse. Only a few of the more inspirited acolytes lobbying for sainthood knew Hamid was hiding here. He was fairly inconspicuous.

Alleyways mythic and labyrinthine where young Europeans crouched in search of hashish or heroin wound outward from the center of the city. Sparse olive groves or incongruous gatherings of papyrus and related sedge that spilled over from Nile marshes far to the east grew uncertainly between the occasional mosques trailing off at regular intervals past the city limits. There were also taverns in these parts, and an open pen where sheep were slaughtered. Farther out, a last parapet stood mysteriously alone, unsung from for generations. Still, it loomed eerily on the desolate plain. Beyond it, a buckling cement road led due south toward the valley and Hamid's obscure refuge.

Officials in the city had begun to look askance. Malkemes it was who told the Jew about how Hamid's music was thought dangerous, and that Hamid himself was, for all intents and purposes, branded. The government, aspiring globally, fretted such local influences. The muezzins' cries were obviously non-negotiable and the government even subsidized the building of new parapets as a sign of official good faith. But Hamid's music was deemed jihad.

The Jew smiled at Malkemes' recounting. "*Aida!*" he exclaimed.

"*Aida?*" Malkemes asked, always astonished by his friend's penchant for fanciful connections. "How so, *Aida?*"

"The three main characters in the opera are destroyed in the conflict between love and nation. Nation, not tribe. No war of the clans in *Aida*. No *Romeo and Juliet*. Granted, it may be only an accident of an otherwise execrable libretto, but what's so interesting about the opera is that it anticipates George Orwell. Lovers hounded by officialdom, just as in *1984*. And—final irony—all to commemorate the opening of a canal connecting the timeless tribes to a bold new universe of nation states!"

"You, of all men, a Jew, a Jew with a mind that can't stop working...You call Hamid's aggression love, and the modern nation states oppressors. From you, I'd have expected less sympathy for sexual aggression wrapped around hostile third-world rhetoric."

"They may be dangerously political in giving it," said the Jew. "But we may have a host of good reasons for taking it."

"Longing for an exterminating angel," suggested Malkemes.

"What music!" answered the Jew, cryptically.

While plans for Hamid's sainthood progressed apace, the handful of his countrymen who surreptitiously came to the suburb to see him never said much once they arrived. Instead they'd stand dumbly about as if waiting for whatever it was he was going to tell them. But he too said very little. Occasionally, he'd make music with one of them, in private, or within earshot of the others listening in stone-faced silence.

Over a year had passed since Hamid fled the city. Only the oddest happenstance or even divine intervention might in so far-flung a suburb have provided him souls from Spain or America or Thailand to play on as instruments. Yet Carl Blumgren did somehow arrive in this place, standing by the tavern as if just vaguely aware of where he was or, as he worried aloud, where his wife waited for him at the moment, somewhere in the city no doubt. The man actually seemed a rather special presence, a gift perhaps.

When Hamid lived in the city, he had prowled its streets. The tourists' curiosity, their nervous delight at being taken up by so imposing a native and one who knew the old quarter so well, was often enough to by and by bring about the awesome moment. Other times, Hamid settled for his own kind, during long days in the city when hunger for any music overwhelmed him. They'd make the old hill music as it anciently was.

Hamid naturally preferred the foreigners. Theirs were fascinating new sounds, odd and charming to his ear. The fast-plucked ouds might still arouse. Yet even as a child, he imagined, prodigiously, diverse wild and alien tonalities before he ever actually heard the like. Even as a child, espying some stranger, a colonial official, maybe, or a colonial official's wife, he dreamed of how they'd howl if prodded to. He closed his eyes and listened to foreigners croaking in ways living things are seldom heard to croak.

By the time he was ready to flee the city, intent foreigners were seeking him out. Some were privy to the great radical secret that a great radical music was being made here. They wanted to be part of it, sometimes with fierce light in their eyes because they'd gone on pilgrimages and were wanting so to be instruments of the incomparable concertizing. Or, they were wanting just to find him and look upon

him as if he were an ancient statue in the sand mystified by
dark usage.

Blumgren in the suburb, an attractive middle-aged American, was the last and most beautiful of the foreign musics. The
English woman Miss Carr had been the first. Between them,
hundreds of his own kind, dozens of French, many Brits and
Americans, astonishing Japanese, brilliant Africans from Li-
beria and Kenya and Botswana, some number of unforgettable
Russians, Israeli merchants and their wives, tenebrous Span-
iards, enthusiastic Italians, inevitable Greeks, an unsuspecting
Canadian, the wife of an Armenian millionaire, and sundry
others all made their music.

Always, always the hunger of his for sound! The muezzin's great cry that was inside him demanded untold variations
on the sacred phraseology loosed each day from the parapets,
Allah who is after all a great mazeway full of twists and turns
be praised! There were times he'd been privileged, in music
stores, or a tourist's hotel room, to hear the wonderful 'classical'
music, and their jazz too, and singsong tunes that could, in a
way that was mysterious to him, because these songs seemed
to be the tonal equivalencies of mere treacle, fill him so full of
desire he'd think demons were run amok inside him. Always,
the hunger drove him on in search from one person to the next.

Even with the first, lovely Miss Carr, he knew it was more
the music he was after than the smooth and pallid flesh that
smelled like pansies. "My, it is enormous," she said when she
saw it. Her voice, just to hear her speak, was lovely, as many
Englishwomen's are. When he shoved it up her female part, it
started as a faint humming. Then there were lovely little di-
minuendos and one sudden exalted crescendo. How he loved it,
the clipped, controlled voice of the woman wholly given over
to the delighted risings and fallings he could make come forth.

With Miss Carr, Hamid discovered at once the rocking rhythm bound to induce the music. He sensed he could play her, elicit at will the low droning tone and pummel away in gradually lengthening beats to produce the myriad birdlike shrieks.

When he listened hard he forgot who they were or where they were. The sounds were disembodied and, hearing them, Hamid entered a great dream. He was holding them like beautiful instruments carved anciently, time-honored and enormously sonorous. There was a way to press them close as they rocked, a right way, by their shoulders.

Whomever he played, their alien sounds adhered to the ancient music, the old hill music, and to the great expostulations of daily faith as well. It was a wedding of old and new in which the new complimented the old. Thus, the Pole who gurgled when Hamid went way up the man's male part, or the wonderful wheezing of the Russian woman which filled the room, were juxtaposed without shame to the shahadas of morning. It was not precisely a counterpoint or a basso continuo or an orchestration of higher-octave accompaniments. "Compliment" is the best way to describe it, probably, but not finally anything our own language of musical theory quite conveys.

The Japanese were often wonderful. With one couple, he played the male and female parts of both the man and the woman. What open-throated calls came forth, the male's in particular, as if in expressive contemplation of what being played like this in front of the woman he loved must ultimately mean. It wasn't humiliation, per se. As the man's male part gave way under the pressure of Hamid's probe, it seemed instead the youth called out plaintively in exquisite final throe or last Orphic farewell. "Oh what the gods reaching way inside me have done!" his song had said. "Oh beloved, never again can I be to you what I have been before."

Of such music, legends are made. Stored away in Hamid's memory were all the world's sublime and sundry grunts and bellows and hissings, the stately arias of those who, being done, were thus undone. Hamid strained to remember, to preserve, for there was nothing else in this world he loved except music. The little money he had, for all he cared thieves were free to ransack the pouches where he'd put it. But the pouch that was full of humankind's music, such treasures gathered from the far climes of the world, was inviolable. Hamid's admirers among his countrymen said it was gold justly plundered, a redress of historical grievance. But the music maker, he thinks only on the music.

"The head is very like a mushroom," said one prissy Swiss, and Hamid playing him fierce wrung long oohs like an old mode that rises neither higher nor lower than a single protracted note. "This is my first experience with someone like you," breathed a young American student, a female whose male part he did. Her lovely music was full of embarrassment that got louder as the male part made dark involuntary sounds. "I hope I'll not be altogether damaged," said a gentleman from Nairobi as the tight hole in the black pitch yielded immensely. Aiiii," he chanted until Hamid finished.

"Explain to me again what it is about it that you love so much," Hamid asked Malkemes.

So Malkemes in perfect Arabic told Hamid just what it was about Bach's Mass in B Minor that he particularly admired. Yes, it's beautiful music. But it is also sanctified by usage. Today, Malkemes explained, in the West there is a great revolt against official canons of taste, an effort to liberate expression itself from the tyranny of established standards. And there is virtue in that. Hamid, why should your extraordinary music be valued less than the minuets European monarchs doted on for centuries?

But nor is it yet so simple, Malkemes continued. What makes this Mass greater than, say, a work found buried in a hole for hundreds of years, which has not been heard for all that time, but which, analyzed note for note, sonority for sonority, cannot reasonably be judged musically less accomplished than Bach's? Why, simply the fact that Bach's has been adored by consensus. A million souls with ears put the greatness in it. Human love has consecrated it. As much as pure sound, such consecration equates with beauty.

And this Mass is an especially good example because it was ecumenical, palatable to the religious appetites of all European Christians, added Malkemes. Consecration, consecration by time and usage, infused with love, a sound for all of mankind, Hamid...

"The Spanish woman, tell us again the music you made her make," the Arab initiates visiting him would ask.

"Yiiiii, yiiiii," mimicked Hamid in a falsetto squeal to oblige them.

"The wealthy businessman from New York, the one who tried to change his mind..."

And Hamid, to their attentive ears, told how that particular dilettante wound up clucking. He resurrected the ungainly sound and they nodded solemnly as if acknowledging a military event.

The most beautiful of all was Blumgren, sandy-haired and middle aged, standing alone in the suburb Hamid had fled to. He trembled when Hamid played him. His wounded music fluttered skyward. At moments, the man would grope for words but, straining to say something as Hamid dug deeper, his own ur-music buried the incipient speech. Words failed him. Blumgren once dreamed about making music, but he had dreaded it, and now it was all the more beautiful for having been dreamed of, and dreaded, like that.

Carl Blumgren was terrified of marrying Adrienne Engdahl for reasons he dared not confide to her, or to his closest friends. He'd been alarmed more than charmed by how this pallid woman of his, oh such smooth pasty skin and cherry red lips and pointed perfect nose, yelped at even the slightest brush of a finger between her legs. The bellowing that ensued! But her music was impersonal, it might have been anyone's finger in the curly bush, it was just the palpable thought of herself rent wide open that got her to give it up. In his mother's room, when his mother was away, which was where he first mounted her, Adrienne's primordial ecstasy broke the suburban calm.

No virgin, she had likely made her great noises for other men they knew. How they must have savored the stark outcries of the porcelain creature who was to be his wife. These dull men having tupped her were rich with musical memory forever. Blumgren married Adrienne and after she bore children the ferocious old bellows sounded forth no more. Yet still he'd search those other faces for the slightest secret snicker.

"You're not as expressive as you used to be," he said to her, affecting a casual tone.

"How can I be with the kids around?"

Volcanic dust thus settled on the surface of the moon but Blumgren fretted anew. She had squealed from so deep within, what great force had perforce been silenced, and what might happen now it was? Must some behemoth from beneath the lunar surface sooner or later rise up to devour them as they lived? One night he imagined there was a concert, which was a great communal listening to the love sounds of his wife. Outside, the men who knew described her to those who didn't. Of such women, legends are made.

One night as their children were growing his thoughts fell back to the handful of homosexual encounters he'd had as a youth. One skinny mop-haired fellow in Chicago lured him to his apartment and, rather without permission, in a seamless maneuver, it seemed, as their bodies turned and twisted about each other like vines, he penetrated Blumgren from behind.

"Make noises, that will help me," murmured the young man when he was up inside him. Blumgren, uninspired, was loath to dissimulate. But he did finally manage obligatory little grunts so the fellow could finish up. It was an unpleasant experience. Adrienne was getting lovelier with the years. The alabaster flesh took on grayish shades that gave greater depth to her beauty. They were good friends as much as lovers and with time found means to travel the world and see exotic lands.

Among the well-to-do foreigners from all over the world, even some who are not accustomed to chance sexual encounters or prone to impassioned exclamation seek out Hamid. It is fashionable to give oneself over to myth. Great painters and poets offer themselves as portals through which the very pipes of Pan may play out to the world once again, after so many ominously silent centuries. They tell their friends in Paris. Word reaches Budapest. Others on holiday in Provence sail over in order to enter into fable and be entered by it. If the darksome throngs perpend in this the clattering overthrow of oppressor nations, Hamid thinks only on the music he craves so much.

Others come upon Hamid by chance and in them the music is often desperate and unexpected. But if they're ambivalent instruments, frightened or abashed, their sounds are sometimes all the more tremendous for it. Blumgren's friend N. from the Chicago Symphony Orchestra was making interesting points about the trumpet. He was saying that in Bach's time people heard it to be emblematic of the voice of God. The sudden blast, a dominant timbre. The clear strong tone that leads forth all the others.

It can never be that again, for specifically musical reasons. The classical trumpet is flat and broad to the ear these days. It is at worst an official sound. It's like fruit that's altogether too fibrous. The depth is all gone out of it. Colleagues in Boston and New York and San Francisco play the Torelli and Haydn concertos with little passion for the music. As N. says, there are many classical musicians who've become cynical about music itself. But the trumpeters he knows are particularly cynical. The great jazz trumpeters, especially Miles Davis, redefined the instrument itself and, as a result, the modern ear has been treated to subtler, muted tonalities. Usage no longer sanctifies the traditional literature.

"But you're a wonderful musician," said Blumgren.

N. felt like an instrument when Hamid played him. He thought of a cello drawn lovingly close to the artist or a sarod in the lap of a master. Configured thus, he was glorious; he was proud to so boldly utter himself aloud. There'd been no conductor in the great cities where he worked like this. Solti and Karl Richter had powered high performances from him, but this was a gutting out of all the sound he had to give. None of the men who ever entered him in the rear made him make music, save for the dark involuntary sounds his male part made. Hamid, always hungry for sound, fanned a bellows up inside him just to hear the hot lips whoosh.

It may have been that, abashed, and ravished by the music she made, Blumgren inside his wife never wedged the sounds of his own between the sheets of hers. He was an audience, demur before the insistent vociferation. Hamid sat alone smoking when they met on a doorstep in the suburb he fled to. Once someone dies for love, others will surely follow on. The impact of the liebestod was fairly direct. Gounod's love scenes just a few years later reeked of it, for example. All of opera's last great moments are the last animal cries of the last possible entrance of the last singer and the last tremulous call of a fabulous bird pumped full of passion.

He turned and walked inside the hut, and Blumgren followed. Sandy hair glistening in the noonday sun, he was midway through his life. Inside was a makeshift tavern. A boy, probably no older than twelve, sat behind the table by a row of bottles, enigmatic without their labels. A stairway led to a landing which, stretched along the back and on each side of the hut, had no apparent purpose, except there were rugs like prayer rugs overlapping the edges. "Ssshhh," whispered Hamid to the boy, two fingers on his lips.

"Ssshhh," he whispered to Blumgren, repeating the gesture. Then he took Blumgren by the arm and led him to the steps.

"Why do you think I want to be with you like this?" asked Blumgren. But it was the same as his first time with a man when he was young: There was no moment of explicit compliance, just a numb kind of going along. Hamid held onto his shoulders and Blumgren, with his knees on the carpet, felt himself as one about to be given over. When the huge thing was way up there, Hamid made him sing and sing.

The boy who had lingered just outside the door signaled triumph across the sun-beaten plain, to no one in particular.

Woman, My Come Is Time

Talk about a killer dick, this one's loaded with HIV and ready
to rumble. It all started one day when he wanted to buy some
life insurance. Or, it may have actually started many years earlier when he was listening to Ghiaurov sing Don Giovanni.

It had dawned on him, when the Commendatore reap-
peared in stone, this association of hard cock with ungainly
fate. Stiff as granite, he'd drag the libertine to unspeakable
physical conclusion. All this opera business was one stylized
variation on the theme of sex and death. The *Liebestod* was the
most obvious and signal instant, but think about Violetta and
Mimi, and all that coughing up of blood—the dear delicate
vessels cannot contain the revolt of their own thickly contami-
nated fluids—as, prone by their bedsides, the grief-struck and
tumescent tenors flabbergast the Met. Then Lulu, bride of Jack
the Ripper, bridesmaid to Eva Braun, the finale to all of it.

Opera's great! It's as basic as the Eucharist but so florid
and overly refined as well, a pageant necrophilia infesting all
things civilized. Romeo in the tomb in Gounod's opera! You
can smell the decomposition with each incanted kiss.

"Hello there. My name is Marcus Underwood."

Ah, they were done! The best part was always when it
was over. It's so peaceful to be half-asleep inside of somebody

else. The young man damp and open dozed with him. They dozed the half-sleep of death. He'd soon be devastated, this kid. If his lethal aim was true, he was doomed already. Ever since he learned of his own infestation, death had become a bosom companion. Death itself was the seduction. A balm he'd insinuate inside of others.

Death had brought him to another world. None of the old arguments could restrain him from sharing it. Some days it was as if a low-grade fever distorted utterly how he perceived the devastation of others. He saw them as if he were feverish. Marcus had always been promiscuous but never thought himself destructive. He used to like it in tearooms, the subway toilets. One day he saw the words "sex pain shit and death" scrawled on a wall. It aroused him, even then. So maybe, who knows, he was already a killer just waiting for the right weapon to come along.

Now it was all about not caring. Being beyond caring. Fucking and dying, and taking along what other beings there were for the taking. They'd be better off anyway. Out of their misery. But a big part of it was power too. The power to deal, to deal death. And the more he thought about that part of it, the bigger that part of it got. So big, for instance, that lying there inside the young man, reflecting on things gone by, and the dreadful things yet to be, he got hard again and banged the boy up his end once more.

His end once more. In your rear is your end again.

He tried to avoid the sweet sounds of children when he paced the city with death between his legs. Those chirping sounds, the sounds of loveliness, a daughter's. Who could destroy somebody that somebody else loved like a daughter! Yet thus would he destroy Estelle Moore who knowing about nothing wanted him inside herself so much. Had she not been a daughter once? Had her father not held her tight? If you prick her, does she not grow sarcomas?

The main character in *Our Man in Havana* is Graham Greene's most humane protagonist simply because of how much he loves his daughter. His little girl. His sweet little girl. Ugly Rigoletto, graced and cursed to adore day and night the most beautiful thing a man can adore, a loving daughter. But in the sack she goes, of his own crazy scheming. Opera, you mongrel, degenerate, hyper-refined monstrosity!

He was so aroused, was Marcus, to think himself a dealer of poison cum, even unto the very golden muff of the lady Estelle. How frail he used to feel when there was dick up his ass. Now I am become death, dirty dicking destroyer of worlds. Dispassionately, he sought again the traces of how he had come to be what he'd become. Did the man who dealt him death, in his mouth or up his end, thrill to it too? What alloy made them killers all? Ah, killers all!

There were always parents to ponder. Freud stops too short in *Totem & Taboo*. Why would Paleolithic or Neolithic sons feel at all guilty about killing their fathers and fucking their mothers unless the act or its attendant acts threaten survival itself? If the primal instinct produces defective get, let's say—well, then you've got real etiology on a grand scale.

Here's how it worked back in the old days when guys like him were roaming around the continents dealing death out of their dirty dicks. They really did want to fuck their mothers, like Freud says. In fact, there was nothing in their whole crazy gosh darned Paleolithic or Neolithic worlds they wanted more than to fuck their mothers. It's the greatest sex urge there is. So they do it, and kill their fathers to maintain the savage hegemony. So far, so good. It's pretty good for a century or two until they discover that by fucking their mothers over and over, they've brought forth mangled nincompoop children not fit to survive. Thus does Freud meet Darwin in a big way.

Now their guilt is understandable. They see that the most desirous of all sexual acts, the definitive sexual act, in fact, leads directly to death. Sexual intercourse is redefined in terms of death, of idiot offspring and disease. Sex is necrophilia. Necrophilia is sex. There you have it, my friends, the ur-origin of opera, necrophilia the bridesmaid of incest, and vice versa. So the next thing you know, we've got Wagner coupling his braided bitches with their brothers in one opera and bellowing *mild und leise* in the next. Don't you love it how civilization, the more stylized it tries to get, gets ever the more barbaric for all that!

Marcus' dick was just like anybody else's, an average dick or at least it used to be an average dick before it filled up with death cum. When he was young, folks rendered the obligatory praise. A very nice cock, Marcus. It's bigger than most, Marcus. Attaboy, Marcus. He liked all that. But he never really understood love and sex until one of the guys he met ignored his dick altogether. This guy was having him up the ass, and that was all he could talk about.

"Oooooh, so tight," the man said, kneading it with his dark Mediterranean hands.

"Thank you," said Marcus."

"I'm in you, baby," he said. "In you," he said again with a stress on "in" that made it sound as special as it must have felt. Marcus that instant thrilled with the sense of what it was like to be up inside of somebody else in a way he never did when it was he who was up inside of somebody else. "Ahhh," went the man. "Ahhhh."

"It feels good," Marcus whispered.

The man exalted as if it were magic to be up Marcus Underwood's ass. "Hello there," he said reaching into Marcus as far as his dick could go. Years later, he could still hear the man's praise, his praise of being way up him. Another time Marcus was fucked while the Anvil Chorus played on a record player in the background. He would not have enjoyed fucking to the tune of the Anvil Chorus because he would have felt ridiculous doing so. But he was deeply stimulated to be fucked to the tune of the Anvil Chorus because it made him feel ridiculous to be done such.

Incest was born with Adam because Eve was his daughter and his sister. The great prospect too horrifying to allow was the ascension of themselves and their offspring up the Tree of Life. It would have made them immortals like the immortals of the Old Orders who live forever and hump their siblings. In this, Electra is more primal than Oedipus because women fucked their fathers before sons fucked their mothers. Fatherfucking takes us back before the womb, to a time in Eden before the wisdom tree was eaten from. Electra is older than old. Oedipus produced defective children and made humankind guilty in the nurseries of the world. But Electra produced a race of wicked gods who might have gone on living defective forever.

Pretty profound, all this death and fuck stuff!

Marcus was eager for Estelle to say yes as they both knew she would. They'd be seeing each other next week. Estelle, not thirty, was a great woman older than her years. She gave herself to men when she sensed secret grandeur in them. She loved hidden moral power. She loved them looking outsized in the moonlight or darkly marginal by day. Having such men inside her was grandiose. Yet there was nothing grandiose in her manner. She was a straightforward person. She dealt unpretentiously with most people.

What power she saw in him, he was at some loss to define. When they'd had dinner a month or so before, he'd been pensive.

"It astonishes me that a soldier can walk into some little house in Kosovo or Vietnam or Rwanda and just butcher helpless civilians," he said.

"War dehumanizes them," said Estelle blandly.

"Of course, but the thought of causing so much misery for no damn reason! Yet other times I wonder how anyone can contain the demons most of us live with, and *not* kill randomly."

"There was a serial killer in the Soviet Union who had lived through the collectivization of the Ukraine, and the Nazi invasion, and who grew up afraid to go outside his house because there were cannibals prowling around. I saw a show on TV about him. His mother used to warn him about the cannibals."

"I know the case," said Marcus. "He cannibalized his victims too."

"But I was thinking that it wasn't the war or Stalin's terror that drove him to it. Millions of others lived through that and survived morally. But for all the horror he saw, he became a murderer because…"

"…because his mother didn't treat him well."

"That's right," said Estelle.

"Or his father didn't treat him well."

"That's right. All that horror raging in his world, but it may have been a small domestic unkindness that drove him to become the worst of murderers."

Marcus could barely eat the carrot cake he ordered, which was too bad, because it was moist, and served with lovely edible petals at the corners. The restaurant was known for its carrot cake. But he couldn't think about the carrot cake. He was thinking about the death in his dick. He dropped his fork and stared intently at nothing. The dessert cart was at the next table. He stared at that. His killer dick was hard in his pants.

It was probably quite a stare, the kind of stare that makes you look like you've traversed some great terrible continent of longing or desolation. Estelle held his hand. All gods fuck their sisters because all gods are charged to forge all life out of their own ribs. Everyone on Olympus is everything to everybody else. Once you lay your mother, who's also your sister, your son is your brother as well as your nephew, and your sister is your daughter as well as your niece. Their children are your grandchildren and a hundred cognate creatures besides. It's really rather magnificent as well as ludicrous.

That night after dinner he went back downtown and met a young man from Spain. He was hot for the guy's tight ass. Oh, Spanish! The smooth tan skin, the crack, a breathtaking symmetry. The most extraordinary passage of all was *Genesis* 3:22-3:24: They were to be tossed out of Eden "lest he put forth his hand, and take also of the Tree of Life, and eat, and live forever." Conventional exegesis comprehends the exile described thus as our only possible redemption. If, having eaten of the Tree of Wisdom, Adam lives forever, then nothing lies ahead for Adam but eternal degeneracy, hell on earth because no death's in store to force the moral issue.

Maybe.

The most mysterious part is 3:22: "And the Lord God said, Behold, the man is become as one of us, to know good and evil..." Who are *us*? God, plus His angels? Or are we being slipped some vestige of a yet more primordial world populated with lots of gods, nameless and vaguely ominous entities, Jehovah's cohorts? Adam was to be kept out of that crew. The equity pool was to be sealed from that point on. There were already enough immortals going to and fro in the world, and walking up and down in it. They say *Job* was written even before *Genesis*.

Demons, gross old demons they were that drove Marcus from place to place during the weeks after his last dinner with Estelle, right up to the night of his next one. He went from hooker to hooker, and when they pulled out their rubbers, he'd say, "I don't use them."

And they'd say, "You sure gonna use one with me, honey!"

So he'd say, "I'll put another $300 on the table. I'm not afraid."

The first woman asked him why he wasn't afraid. He made something up. "Because I've got cancer of the brain, and I'm going to die anyway." The woman tried to express sympathy. Then she pondered his dick without a condom for a few moments and shrugged her shoulders. She put the money in her purse and opened her skinny black thighs. He wanted to know her name because she might be the first of the women he'd be killing. She gave him a name. He rubbed her cheeks, which were smooth and soft, as was the skin on her shoulders although it was full of ugly bruises.

"You okay?" she asked, almost in a whisper. It must have been the alleged brain cancer that made her want to dote on him like that a little.

"You feel so fine," Marcus said, fucking her. Then he grunted with the extraordinary feeling of cuming wet death in her dry tight twat. He wanted to hold her close and carry her away to a better place. He was sad like all animals are sad after coitus but even sadder under these circumstances.

"Thank you," she said, and put her panty hose back on with a sudden masculine herky-jerky yank.

"I'll be in a better place soon," he said, his mouth full of the thick taste of her perfume.

"Where's that?"

"I mean, in another world."

"Oh yeah," she said softly. A few hours later he picked up another black prostitute and being with her was swell too.

He was right about opera, you know. Great authors had shared the fatal vision. You take a history of the civilization of the West like *The Magic Mountain*. The young hero immerses himself in opera even as he and his world move ever closer to the catastrophe of 1914. As if the motifs of *Carmen* should naturally interweave into any narrative that is just about to culminate with World War I. As if the sickly piety of Guonod's *Faust* were part and parcel of the same centuries-long incest that bedded Hapsburg cousin with Bourbon brother. As if Aida and her lover suffocating through their final love fuck is the ineluctable expression of what happens when for twenty millennia you've banged forbidden love holes and dispatched their ancient guardians.

The arias rise to frenzied heights. *Der tag!*

Consider the moral reek of *Un Ballo in Maschera*. Renato is remorseful because he learns that his vengeance was unjustified: Riccardo didn't actually fuck his wife. Riccardo loved and worshipped Amelia, and Amelia loved and worshipped Riccardo. Yet their obsessive adulterous passion bothers Renato not a whit. The very ownership of his wife's soul is nothing he's not willing to forgive at once, as long as he can be absolutely sure that Riccardo never stuck his dong up the diva's cunt. So there you are: a Mediterranean preoccupation with the coital act itself haunts the fatal scenery of operatic sexuality. Was Verdi being ironic? I don't think so. Operas don't allow for much fine irony. They're too big and unsubtle. They sweep irony away. (That such stupid stories are set to such lovely music! That these last strange things, these weird collective fixations, should cull forth the best of song itself to find their form!)

Yet Renato does have a point to make. Imagine Amelia actually penetrated by Riccardo. Then listen to her sing. The same gorgeous song we're used to hearing, which we expect is sung to invoke all life's beauteous lost ones, which is the great high-falutin' call of unsullied longing, which is the closest secular music gets to *spiritus sanctus* set loose in the world, is become a different song altogether. It's now the unbearable song of the adored one just absolutely, utterly croaking her head off because at long last she knows, *o mio deo,* she just knows what the ultimate fuck feels like, and that ultimate fuck isn't you, no way hubby wubby! Oh listen to her! Imagine a big dick is up her cunt every time she hits those high Cs! You go, girl!

What's worse—losing Gretta Conroy to the intangible passions of distant music or living with the image of Amelia squealing on all fours as Riccardo rides behind? True, a good case can be made that Gabriel Conroy's loss is the sharpest of all, to relinquish one's wife to an abstraction. Every cuckold is different, I suppose. Take Otello, who punctures Desdemona with a knife. It's a kill fuck for sure, and hearing the *Gia nella notte densa* music at that point is so beautiful, it's just positively awful. It makes you want to go out and kiss somebody you've just killed, or vice versa. This is necrophilia at its best. This is necrophilia to make the heart ache. The big black lady killer has gotten his bride in the cradle at last—a kiss, just one more kiss, and then it's over forever. We're barely born, and yet we're dead. We're fucking doomed fetal tissue in Eden and the florid music makes it seem so right.

I digress. The very fearful fact of Marcus Underwood proves some method in Renato's madness. Had Amelia sung lovingly of a Marcus Underwood she adored but would never have, she could have gone on singing until the end of time. But penetration wouldn't be smart at all. Renato should only know how dumb it would be! She'd get night sweats and lose weight and develop blotches and appalling sarcomas. As would Renato were he to have her in Marcus Underwood's aftermath. Maybe Renato's right. Maybe penetration is serious business, serious business indeed!

Marcus' recording of *Un Ballo* featured Maria Caniglia. He could almost hear that fine voice sob an English lyric of his own invention, "Oh cruel heart that beats but faithless time." Ah, to deal death to Maria Caniglia, if she weren't dead already.

They first met when her marriage was breaking up. She suffocated in that marriage dead to passion. Marcus with no thought then of being her lover lied anyway and said he hadn't had a sexual relationship with a man since he was a teenager. Instinctively, in a way that bemused him, he wanted that part of his life hidden from her. It was probably because she'd dis-approve. Not of the sex, but of the callous way he and his part-ners ignored and discarded each other. Theirs was a throwback lifestyle to the meaner homosexual milieu of thirty years ago when he was still young.

But he talked gracefully of his boyhood crushes, and how some older men had made him feel rather vulnerable. She appreciated those confidences.

While she was still married, he told her that he often thought about women. "This is what I long for in a woman," he began, and went on to describe a nurturing soft-spoken female, somewhat amply figured but clear and blond and blue-eyed. Warm as the earth but with the severe light and pale color of a southern beach; who enjoyed the life of the mind but wasn't compelled to live it. Of course, it was her he described.

They went together to the opera two or three times each season. Her other male friends, Fred, Simon, Dan, didn't like opera much at all. They were true intellectuals. They took their culture too seriously to appreciate how ideas central in the history of civilization could be so grandly stylized to the point of caricature. Even Mozart's operas eluded them. They could speak intelligently about *Don Giovanni*, but something about it wasn't quite palpable to them in the way that Picasso or Flaubert or Bach was always palpable and important.

The night before, he went to an S&M club and stood there with his dick out. Other men were also masturbating as they watched the transvestites spank their dark and silent clients. His friend in England Jeffrey sent him the latest installment of the necrology. Every few years he'd list, on a monthly basis, anyone of notoriety whose name he could immediately recognize, and who had just died. It was to keep track of who was dead. The great operatic swell of names: Anne Morrow Lindbergh, Frankie Carle, Anthony Giacalone. The mighty dead. Each month Jeffrey jotted down his strongest personal association with one of the decedents. In January, for instance, Gregory Corso died and Jeffrey wrote a brief personal reminiscence of that most unpleasant good poet.

He creamed on the floor but nobody saw as the cum seeped into the floorboard cracks and disappeared. "Estelle, I need you now." She was so pretty when she smiled. Her shaven cunt looked childlike and vulnerable tucked between her wide and milky white hips.

"Sweetheart, I love you," she said. Her voice was fragile. But when she grunted during sex the sound she made was full and woman-like and endearing. He was dismayed at the thought of killing her. Once he felt like killing Brook when they were young men together. Brook's ass was as soft as a baby's. Marcus never got to touch it. He hated Brook, but Brook had gone to hard drugs and was dead by then anyway, so what did it matter?

April came. Estelle bloomed. Sometimes he felt like he could claw her skin to shreds. It was like his dick was a stiletto. Everyday he waited for the horrible announcement but she always seemed happy when they met, and for all the ferocity he struck between her legs she'd whisper something about how tender her fine fierce lover made her feel, and how tender and loving he was like no other man she ever knew.

"You're the first woman I've ever had like this," he said, which was certainly true. "This means so much to me."

The dog days came and still no word of trouble. She saw nothing to alarm her as he remained asymptomatic. Maybe the others were sick and dying already. He went out and had sex with another man. He gazed fascinated afterwards at the man's ass which was like a compartment full of death. He vaguely thought about going downtown and getting himself gang banged so that he could spray death all around and kill a bunch at one time. But he preferred the thought of dealing it himself with his dick. That was his fervid instinct. He loved Estelle so much, when was she going to die?

He couldn't bear the thought of having to explain it to Estelle once his symptoms finally appeared. He figured he'd kill himself at that point.

By Christmas time, Estelle's passion was so abundant, she was looking for lovely ways to pay tribute to him. She swallowed him often. Once, in gratitude, she showed him her ass and said, "Here's a good target for you, darling." New Year's passed, and nothing, nothing. He went out to screw more hookers.

"It's our one-year anniversary," she said one day. A week later she called him at his apartment earlier in the morning than he was used to. "We have something important to talk about," she said. There was no fear or anger in her voice at all. He'd go see her. He'd wait and listen.

Estelle's apartment was full of geraniums, and she had just bought a new painting the day before, a small seascape that she said she loved because the sea in it was like a vast field flooded with incongruous light. She pulled him over to the bed in her bedroom until they were both sitting on the edge. She held his hand to her breast. "Something has happened," she said. Her eyes narrowed as if a little afraid of how he'd react.

"I'm listening."

"There's no way to tell you but to tell you…"

"Yes, go on," he said, regretting he hadn't already killed himself. She was so beautiful. It was terrible. He'd hate to see her suffer. He would never allow himself to see it. God cannot witness the things he injects into the world. He can't bear it.

She smiled and said, "I'm pregnant."

Don Giovanni a cenar teco
M'invitasti e son venuto!

Armenia In Boston

What a tale of woe is old Armenia! New Armenia isn't much better. Wedged between Russia and the Ottoman Empire, it has been the victim of invasion and atrocity ever since the Osman family first swept Islam from the mountains to establish a second-rate civilization that would endure four hundred years. The Russians also savaged the area, but Russian atrocities are not as picturesque as the weird fantasies of Suleiman made real. Imagine a Eurasian horde wielding unlimited power over defenseless males and females. The imagination scurries to antiquity, to savageries couched in legend, and legend assuages guilty discomfort. Many of us are stimulated by the pornography of Buchenwald, but many more of us are nauseated. By contrast, even the later mayhem in Armenia that commenced in 1894 is graced with quasi-exotica and a kind of timelessness.

1894 saw a wave of Turkish atrocities throughout Armenia. By 1895, public opinion in England was outraged; political pressure forced diplomatic pressure, and the violence abated. By 1896 the Turks were at it again and there was some talk of international action. World War I was the eventual expression of this concern, although it cannot be asserted that World War I was declared solely on behalf of the Armenians, or that the German invasion of Belgium was planned as a bold flanking maneuver to buttress Turkish aims in Southern Russia. Had the Germans fought the war solely to further those aims, it would have been too bad for them, because the Russians fought bitterly, and successfully claimed Armenia as their own.

It is also interesting to note that Russia's claim to Armenia was partially based on the Czar's approval of the Sykes-Picot Treaty of 1916. By the terms of that agreement, the French wound up in Syria even though Clemenceau had been anti-colonialist all his life. The English, meanwhile, were continuing to cultivate a Middle-East interest to balance the French presence, even though their initial concern in 1914 had primarily been to protect access routes to India. The support of the Czar helped cement the agreement, a fact which scandalized the Communists, who later published the hitherto secret treaty. But they kept Armenia anyway, and Roger Sykes died of the flu.

I want to return to the Turks, however. Even Mt. Ararat, where all mankind and two each of every other living thing were beached after the flood, and which had been in Armenia, became part of Turkish territory. Not a lot of people know this. It certainly is a commentary!

The Turks changed the life of all Armenians. Back in 1896, for example, there was a small settlement of 241 people just south of Nor Kharberd, which, in turn, is south of Yerevan. The Turks came and beheaded sixty-three male members of the community. They torched eleven old ladies. Thirty-seven children were beaten to death. Fourteen children were sodomized. What is interesting is that, of those fourteen children, six were girls. But only one of the girls was also raped vaginally. In any event, these children, along with eighty-seven men and women, were taken from the community and made to accompany the division back to Anatolia, where, after numerous buggerings, they were released to wander where they might. Of the twenty-nine others left behind in the village, twenty-three escaped to Nor Kharberd, five committed suicide, and the remaining person, a kind of village patriarch, had been the first to be raped—in full view of one-hundred of his friends and relations, forcibly assembled. When he resisted with the full strength of his sphincter muscle, a lieutenant ordered a subordinate to fetch a tent pole and knock until he opened. He opened.

Today, there are Armenians living all over the world. Many of them, including Eddie Nor, live in Watertown, Massachusetts, near Boston. Eddie himself has actually spent more time in Boston proper, in various mental hospitals, playing pool with the paraprofessionals who work there. He was first committed when he was eighteen following a three-week period of silence. For three weeks his father, Haigop Nor, screamed at him to talk; for three weeks his father lamented his fate, which was to be the father of a madman, to certain close friends. With other friends, Haigop maintained a silence of shame.

"Please be quiet," Eddie finally said. Eddie was an angular man who wore dark clothes that always carried white or gray hairs from God knows where. "You must be quiet."

"This is my house," stormed Haigop. "I speak when I want."

"But Roberta is speaking. You're interrupting."

"Roberta!" exclaimed Haigop. "Who is Roberta?"

"The dark lady who stays in the wall."

"You're a crazy man," said Haigop, whose own father had escaped as a youth to Nor Kharberd when his village was taken by the Turks in 1896. Landing at Baltimore in 1905, he found his name and even the name of the town impossible for the official at the gate. "Nor" was the only syllable successfully communicated, so Nor the father of Haigop became.

"Am I her man?" asked Eddie, of no one in particular.

Eleven years later Eddie had the solids in a casual game against a paraprofessional of whom he was especially fond. Eddie sank the four in the corner and the six in the side. He whizzed just past the eight to knock the two in the far corner. Then he tried a bank shot for the one and just missed. He courteously waved a slow hand at the table, as if to say, "It's all yours now."

The paraprofessional scratched. He shook his head. "I'm no competition for you, Eddie."

"That was a nice try," said Eddie, with no trace of irony.

Then Eddie cleared the table and dispatched the eight in an easy shot. "I'll play another game with you if you'd care to," said Eddie, who had no actual desire to play again.

"Not today," said the paraprofessional. "I'd better go back down to the junior leagues first."

"Naw," said Eddie. "You'll beat me tomorrow."

The entire mental hospital was submerged in Eddie's meticulous civility.

Three years later, Eddie met his dream girl, Roberta. She was tall and black with very flat cheekbones and eyes that were constantly bloodshot. In and out of mental hospitals since she was fifteen, Roberta was wont to sit and babble for hours, delivering vicious diatribes against black men. She'd speak of Roxbury as the "Hades place" and, as she saw or remembered seeing "those niggers, those niggers" flying about like harpies, her voice would rise to a feverish volume.

Eddie would sit and listen. He'd often show embarrassment in the presence of a third party. Other times, he'd place his hand on her hand and stare deeply as she rambled. Once or twice he'd mutter something to calm her down. The antithesis of a rapist, he supplemented her Thorazine.

Sometimes he hallucinated as he listened. Great ebony arms waved behind Roberta's horse-like head; they'd reach out to him—the sun would meet the moon in eclipse, and lanky indeterminate black flesh stimulate streaking flashes of white like firecrackers. Then back down to earth, and Roberta's voice of frantic banality, which is the very hallmark of madness.

A period of great mystery ensued. No one knows exactly what happened, or with whom, but more than one of their fellow patients have told how Eddie manipulated Roberta into performing sexual acts with new arrivals at Boston State. And yet each of these testimonies stops short. Which new arrivals? What sort of sexual acts? How did Eddie ask Roberta? With what words, what gestures, did he approach the patient chosen to receive favors of the snarled and wasted black oak tree? It is difficult to imagine this quiet and gracious man donning the robes of Pandarus; the whole chapter is so alien to the pictures which precede and succeed it, and vibrates with a timeless unreality.

In 1977 Eddie and Roberta left the hospital and joined a sort of halfway house. Eddie sits and plays cards. When Roberta forgets or refuses to take her medicine, she often rants about black men. Rumor follows them always, interposed between them and the unqualified affection of others. Eddie's silences are profound. They define and simultaneously exist just beyond him: a vast pool of silence that contains more silence.

The drawn and heavily veined skin on Roberta's hand is all that Eddie has known. Down from Bluehill Avenue they've poured, dark men claiming their sister as their own. It doesn't matter who dies first, Eddie or Roberta. Eddie would like to help Roberta, but much has happened.

Romero and Sylvette

From on high, it looked colonial. Say you were one of the monkeys in the treetops, you could crack your nuts and peel your bananas while maintaining a very circumspect oversight of the serene premise. You'd survey white colonnades that looked almost antebellum North American. In fact, you'd have to get up much closer to finally see the inlaid alabaster filigree that gave the façade its vaguely Spanish feel, although the complex latticework was not particularly associated with any style currently or historically Spanish.

The monkeys had a crisp view of the semicircular drive marking off the grass from the portico. Along that drive arrived the occasional carriage that brought the occasional visitor. Very occasional, since the only other homes within many miles were enormously more modest, as were their inhabitants. Not much truck passed between them and the denizens of this most commodious and impressive abode.

Behind the mansion, the area only the monkeys in their branches could see from the front, were rougher roads, four or five small ones in all that were more like pathways as they emerged from the forest. They ended in hitching posts gathered about the backdoor. To these the Indians and sundry other laborers tied their horses preparatory to the day's work or, arriving nightly in wagons, waited to pick up house staff members, wives or cousins or daughters, for the long ride home.

The monkeys couldn't see inside, unless it was by catching occasional glimpses through the upper-story rhomboid windows. Although only five people lived in the house, and it was a big house, all the space within seemed defined by their continuous presence. Not that they were, any of them, especially imposing in stature; here were no outsized rubber barons clumsily accustoming themselves to the architecture of a more civilized era their own piratical labors had made possible, nor yet Bourbon or related scions implanting Old World hegemony amid the New World wilds. It was instead the mere fact that their presence was continuous that rendered it definitive. These occupants seeped into the faded red carpeting. Wraith-like, they rivaled the dozen small statues, icons, cherubs who'd be peeing if they were anywhere near a fountain. They could make their own claim to inanimateness, and canny visitors would have remarked on that as the overlay of a most ancient breeding indeed. When they sat at table, one marveled the food could actually get eaten, that there were places alimentary for it to disappear to, or that, reposing on one of the dozen or more couches or smaller divans, the pillows needed to compress in reply.

Looking down from the top of the house, you'd trace a serpentine balustrade leading directly toward the dining table in the middle of the main salon. Its oaken texture was oddly rough-hewn, as if here, and here alone, the designers, original architects or subsequent modifiers, had foregone ornate indulgence in favor of a "natural" feel wholly at odds with the texture of the rest of the place. The dining table was more typical. It featured an immaculate surface on which was spread an embroidered green cloth with piscine, vaguely Christian motifs woven in toward the center.

Now, we did say five souls were resident here. As was often the case these days, however, only four sat for dinner. There was a middle-aged couple, incongruously well dressed for the everyday domestic scene. The man was gray, though occasional glints still showed youth in his gaze or dim lust at least for same. A blue-green cravat, ebullient, rather, even betrayed a kind of defiance. He was Father. The woman who was his wife sat directly across. She was quite gray, as time and tide made her. Yet the decades hadn't been altogether cruel. Neither ungainly incident piled on ungainly incident nor palpable tragedy following on palpable tragedy had ever urged whatever intellective activity might have once percolated in the tense head toward articulate reflection. She'd reached no conclusions about life. She had maintained constant equilibrium instead. She was Mother.

An even older woman could have been from either side of the family. Ah, here time's ravages were tangible, downright biological, in fact, and, saying biological, we include those sad neural synapses old flesh is heir to, what with blood vessels turned harshly granite and cortex brought so unceremoniously in the tropical heat to the consistency of mulch. One saw it just by looking at her. Insistent jaw movements and a periodic expulsion of the very dentures themselves bespoke irremediable senescence. Poor old woman, thank the good Lord her wise family, wise always before the altars of time, honored each day the sacrosanct fires and guarded the scintilla stubbornly alive and burning within. She was Grandmother.

One hurries in empathy toward the fourth diner. His back imperviously erect, his moustache equally so, this young man in dark blue buttoned pants would have deemed the void of lassitude into which endless days had sunk their lives intolerable had not great duty informed familial piety. His destiny was here, with them. He had never left because there was nothing in the world that could warrant his doing so. He had stayed put. He was Son.

But, Peter by name, he was also Brother, which brings us to the fifth member, not this evening dining *avec famille,* as they say. Nor had she done so for many other such evenings in recent weeks. She was Sister, Sylvette by name. Ah, where was she? Where was Sylvette?

"Sylvette, are you coming down for dinner?" called Father. "My dearest, you *are* coming down?" During the past weeks this beseeching had taken on the predictability of ritual; the immediate silence that followed, equally so.

Then Grandmother would begin waving her arm herky-jerky. A wild look was in her eyes. At such moments, and of late there were many, much ambivalence afflicted those who had venerated her these many years. On the one hand, it was felt this confusion of mind that had settled upon her required intense heedfulness. Who could doubt but that time had festooned her ample consciousness with antique wisdom or that out of Grandmother's expostulations, however cryptic, some balm for future generations could be captured if they, the inheritors, were but prepared to receive it? On the other hand, there was persistent fear the fogs of age lay too thick, her speech too labyrinthine to ever yield its prize. Mother seemed particularly troubled by the latter possibility, which you could see in a certain way she had of contorting her lips or even rolling her eyes whenever Grandmother spoke.

Grandmother would always speak as if on cue when Father had finished calling up for Sylvette. "Of course she's coming down," Grandmother would exclaim a few seconds into the silence that followed Father's unanswered exhortations. "Why wouldn't she come down? She's human, isn't she?"

The drama hadn't changed much during these strange and challenging weeks. Mother would then turn her head toward the stairs, ignoring Grandmother. She'd say, "Oh Sylvette, do come down!" Or sometimes, "Sylvette, listen to your dear father." Tonight, she offered, "Oh my dear, you must come down!"

Brother's part in the collective longing for Sister's descent was not unlike a chorus. While Father was patient, and Grandmother insistent (like the very pulse of being itself pounding insistence through the eons), while Mother was importunate in her sadly wounded and tensely put-upon way, Brother's words tended toward the exquisitely predictive. For example, this evening, Peter exclaimed, "The *smart* money says she's coming down!"

Father didn't particularly know why that was true—she hadn't come down yet, why would the smart money wager she suddenly would?—but there wasn't time to figure it out once the next round of supplication began. Often, as on this evening, Father would commence this second go-around with a smile to hide his pain. "We who love you want you to come down," he called up.

Grandmother merely parroted, "Come down! Come down!"

"She *will* come down!" Brother insisted. The way he twisted his moustache and knowingly averted his eyes, the ineffable bearing he brought to table, it was like Stendhal himself was a member of the family.

"Be kind, Peter," Father would then say.

"Yes, be kind," said Mother in a motherly way. Brother couldn't reply to the repeated admonition because he was not aware in what way he'd been at all unkind.

"Is she down yet?" asked Grandmother, her voice an octave lower and fairly staccato as well.

"No, but I'm sure she'll come," answered Father, patiently. "Do come down, my darling," he said wearily, as if to start a third round.

But tonight was special, unique, in fact, and there'd be no need for further convocation. Grandmother it was, looking up toward the balcony, exclaimed, "Look! Look! Who's that coming down, and where is she comin' from?"

It was Sylvette, Sylvette was coming down. From upstairs. Almost breathlessly, the family pondered the event. They were silent lest something be said to make her scamper back up. Sylvette was a beauty, but not of any regal nature all practiced in the art of long and stately ascents or descents. Quite to the contrary, a disinterested observer might have been appalled at how she was virtually slinking down, entwined about the balustrade like a snake.

Everything about her was disturbing. Men may even find beauty like Sylvette's burdensome, a travesty of life's ideal. Such milky white skin and golden blond hair as hers are the necessary counterpoint, alternatives for the heaven-hungry to raven-haired wench flesh gotten from the earth and fated from the start to tumble in it. Young ladies who look like Sylvette are morally thirst quenching. Yum, says the soul. Ahhh, says the spirit. Even in marriage, nature draws a forgiving veil. The wedding night is sheer hymn. Later there's birth, but afterbirth never.

God had given Sylvette perfect lips, they were smooth and thinly roseate. Yet she pouted all the time. Sylvette's eyes were light blue turquoises all agleam in morning dew. Yet there was tiredness in them, even a jaded glower which made her look petulant and impatient when you spoke to her. Sylvette's dear voice, a sylvan lilt, held salve for the heavy-hearted. It held the timbre of woodland flutes off o'er the lea, the faint but pervasive sound of happy surcease. Worry not, la la. Worry not, la la. Yet a way she had of tilting her head when she spoke hinted untoward content, perhaps a memory of past passion barely disguised in the very forefront of her consciousness. If not sinister, there was baseness in the actual chemistry of her being even though she was born to an untainted family.

Men may even hate such females as Sylvette because they turn the God-given façade of loveliness into a template for corruption. Delighted at first blush by the sprightly creamy features, you may yet search that face for nuances nearly African. How dangerous that seems for all humanity, especially for the Africans! Darkies paw blond flesh on the rare occasions they see it. What if they were to also find in that exquisite text the iterations of their own selfsame hunger? It would turn their universe upside down. Whatever hope of salvation they have would be lost forever, for they would see that the ideals they yearn to corrupt are already so. They'd have no incentive to seek not to be damned.

Perhaps the most unsettling possibility—and this, we would maintain, is still merely a possibility despite all we may already know or speculate—is Sylvette's own awareness of everything we've described. Her specious beauty is something she may be choosing to play with, at least to the extent she knows what torturously multifarious meaning such a physical presence as hers can have for men. Understanding that, she may despise us for the reverence we yearn for her to deserve. In other words, Sylvette may be a very cynical person.

How it's tortured her poor parents, this possibility of barbarous self-knowledge on their daughter's part. Worse than feeling lust as an animal might, or as might one of those aforesaid darksome strumpets hidden away in forest deeps and obliged by fate to obey simple instinct; worse, I say, than an animal, might Sylvette also have intimate knowledge of what lust actually is, and of what, beyond mere physiological craving, causes it? Her tired eyes show that knowledge; tired, because such knowledge wears down all those who have it.

Sylvette is not an easy one at all. If someone were to paint her, the paintings would have to be full of dangerous angles. She isn't an angel, she isn't an angel at all! Sylvette is a maze. Lately, she's added insult to proverbial injury by tying her beautiful golden hair in one long drooping braid behind her head. It makes her look like one of those modern young ladies who live in the cities, and whom men like to refer to as "chicks."

She'd take three steps down the stairs, stop, pout; take another three, stop, pout. Father did his best. But Sylvette knows that they all know, and it makes her sick to her stomach to know they know. Just as it makes them sick to gaze upon the radiant flesh guessing the insults absorbed and even maybe welcomed there. Like a lascivious shadow in the eyes of the Holy Mother herself, Sylvette's existence is a challenge.

"Ah, welcome!" exclaimed Father, full of largesse. He wanted her reincorporated into their love. He wanted the family together again. He wanted no blame attached to past misunderstandings. "Sit, sit!" he urged. "Lovely roast beef," he added as she made her way to the table next to Peter. "Ah, roast beef!" he said again.

After a pause, Brother veered his head somewhat in her direction and asked, "Have you been enjoying your philosophy studies?" Sylvette shrugged her shoulders. "Well, it's simply a marvelous opportunity for you," he continued. "The tutor we've retained is excellent."

"Very challenging ideas," added Father. "Elevating ideas, the kind of knowledge that can take a young lady to the next level."

"Without the dross of practical applicability with which women needn't concern themselves," said Peter. "Knowledge that does not demean. We're all just dying to know if you read the book we gave you for your birthday."

"Yes, darling," asked Father, "have you done your Kant?"

"Her *what?*" exclaimed Grandmother, scandalized.

"Hush, mother!" retorted Mother.

"Some say his vision is tragic," commented Father. "Others say immoral. What do you say, Sylvette?"

"I don't know," answered Sylvette.

"I find it corrosive, and yet inescapable," said Father. "The Kantian critique of reason also applies in the most fundamental and undermining way to faith. Whatever one sees, one sees through the colored glass of one's own conditioning, one's perceptual categories, and, with faith, that conditioning is, specifically, the need to believe. Needing to believe is the systemic alloy of faith as a category of human experience."

"No one ever had faith in something they didn't want to have faith in," said Peter.

"Precisely," said Father. "So how can one trust it?"

"But who cares!" Peter responded, roughly.

"I say it's tragedy!" continued Father. "Yes, the grandest tragedy. I say Kant *grieves* that we can only know what we think we know or want to know. Our limitations are the awful gaps between God and ourselves. Yes? No?"

"Worse than an atheist with a name like that," said Grandmother, almost coherent within her own terms.

"Would you please hush your hole," Mother told her.

Father, in a condescending tone, although to no one in particular, said, "He is a man who chronicles nothing more, and nothing less, than the human desire to do our human best. Is that not so?"

"I just hope he's not a damned soul," said Mother. "Attacking God like that!"

"Really, Mother," said Father.

"Maybe that's what's wrong with Sylvette," she continued. "All that stuff you've given her to read because you were so sure it would help her. Maybe it hasn't helped her at all," said Mother, whining plaintively. "Maybe it's *hurt* her."

"It gets her thinking," interjected Grandmother, lucidly.

"Oh yes," insinuated Brother, almost wheezing the sly words. "Thinking, thinking, thinking!"

"Nonsense," rejoined Father. "Utter nonsense! I want Sylvette reflecting on the concept of duty. I want her baptized in the waters of the categorical imperative." Again, his voice was fulsome and grandiose, but, as he continued, his manner grew sterner. "I want her to reflect on what I had to face. On the decisions I had to make." The theatrical tone was cloying no more; it had become vaguely formidable. He was a patriarchal figure who knew that that was what he was as well as how to play the part. Now he was speaking to Sylvette and Sylvette only. "Imagine being me, young lady! I've grown you, lovely stalk, watered and pruned, invested in you. It was not easy to create you, so why should it be easy to be you? Don't you sneer! You think you see a father's pride and greed and vanity and possessive ambition. But there is more, so much more you have to understand. You were entrusted to me, Sylvette, God's personal way of thanking me and honoring me, even if we can't really be sure there is a God. My soul itself, my immortal soul, even if we can't really be sure there is such a thing, was bound to the nurture of you, a magnificent gift from Above and, with the gift, a terrible burden. Do you think I care about anything else beyond my duty as child of God and father of you? It was not for me to till this land I own. It was not for me to earn the money I banked. There was for me one purpose and one purpose only. God gave me many pleasures, but only one responsibility. You! You were the only chore." His tone became less leonine. "And I welcomed it even if I could only achieve requisite apperception through layers of categorical finitude, as it were."

"God bless you, you saintly man," exclaimed Mother, awe-struck today as she had been on so many similar past instances when the totality of the person with whom she lived would suddenly emerge.

Father continued. "What was I to do when he appeared, that dark one, unworthy of you even in a metaphysical sense? In another few years, you'd have felt so ashamed of yourself, of how your realm tilted toward adumbrating planes, your essence drawn down into the digits and double digits of sub-lunary cycles, the very stuff of reflexive fallacy. It was all a crush, a silly crush. My God, Sylvette, he's half-Indian! How could you imagine spending your life like that? How could you imagine my allowing you to? Was this some whimsical affect, well meant, I might even grant you that, but only phe-nomenological, merely a tracing of that which can be variously rendered? Was this some toying with presumed immanence in the willed categorization?"

"She must love doing it with Indians, what else?" snick-ered Brother.

"Shut your mouth, you turd!" responded Father.

Mother, a little dazed as she often was by the volcano of words and ideas from the husband she adored, turned to Peter and said, amiably, "Do what your father tells you, dear."

"Oh Sylvette, look around," said Father. "Your mother, this unprovable prover, this pure substance. Your brother, this unmovable mover, this pure form. Flesh without idea, idea without flesh—what else have I but you?"

"Me, me!" yelped Grandmother.

"Given to an Indian!" hissed Father, ignoring the old woman. "I was to assent to the reenactment of the primal Fall itself when God's very charge was to hoe the sacred golden row?"

They ate in silence until Sylvette said, "I'm going back to my room now."

"Sleep well," said Father, forcing a cheery tone. "And if you need anything…"

"Thank you," she said, as they all watched her climb back up.

ROMERO AND JULIET
SCENE: DEATH OF TYBALT

Close-up. Tybalt's face full of fury. He calls Romero a wretched boy. Cut to Romero's face, confident. "This shall determine that," Romero says, drawing his sword out of the scabbard.

Long shot. Sword fight. They seem equally matched but at no point is Romero actually in danger of Tybalt winning. Others, including Benvolio, walk into the frame as the duel continues.

Medium shot. Romero dodges a lunge by Tybalt and delivers the *coup de grace*. Tybalt falls forward onto his face. Benvolio hurries to Romero's side. "George, let us flee," he says. "Rumor saith they rise faster with each new moon. Mercutio hath already devoured three, who, not being quick, are thus now undead like him."

Still in medium shot. "O I am fortune's fool!" exclaims Romero. "George away, be gone," urges Benvolio. They exit the frame amid others also scurrying to escape before Tybalt rises to eat the living. Shot of Tybalt for full minute as tense music builds to climax. Tracking shot opens vista around the corpse. We see unwitting Citizen walking toward him. Tybalt rises, bloodlessly white like others in previous scenes. He lurches forward toward Citizen, who may notice Tybalt and run, or may not and be devoured. We will never know.

Cut to Benvolio approaching Prince, who's walking with Montague and Capulet elders.

(Notes for dialogue...Puns should be emphasized to help tie scenes and themes together. Sampson and Gregory in first scene should emphasize dual meaning of "move" as both "incite" and "flee." This is especially important since Romero and Juliet will pun on the same verb when they first meet four scenes later. Juliet says "Saints do not move," meaning they do not take direct action to help us, although they may grant our desires. In reply, Romero asks her not to "move," meaning go away and be absent from him. We shouldn't lose these connections. When Benvolio tells Romero, "Away, be gone; the sport is at the best," he means, we've had enough fun with this Montague/Capulet dalliance; anything more is anticlimactic and probably dangerous. It directly mirrors what Romero said in the previous scene before he met Juliet: "The game was ne'er so fair, and I am done." There is thus a sense from the very beginning that all that is to follow is the reenactment of a game that was doomed before it started. And, of course, "done" is especially resonant because it suggests both sex, as in "Hey, I just did Juliet," and death, as in "I'm done for." All of this is very important because the florid lovemaking as well as flesh eating in our version could get real sloppy and indulgent without the rigor of the original puns. Puns are rigorous because they conjoin meanings and are therefore intellectual. We should be sure to use them well because it will silence critics who may try to say we're only titillating the audience with a lot of sex and cannibalism. Of course, it can go too far. FYI, I tend to share Dr. Johnson's misgivings re Donne, who was really too entwined in intellectualizations. The lyrical potential of his poems is often denuded by the massive intellectualizations. Not so with *Romero and Juliet*, which requires the counter-balance of such intellectualization. Johnson was dead right on Donne, dead wrong on this material.)

SCENE.

Sylvette is lying fully clothed on her bed. It is an imported four-poster masterpiece, if you like the style, posts and head-board in walnut spliced with linden. A gold-embroidered red bedspread is furled at her feet. Sylvette is wearing a powder blue suit, lace frills at the hem that reach to her ankles. Her ponytail is perpendicular to her head, resting on a pillow. Her shoes show a perfect curvature of the foot just beneath her toes, which can't be seen.

Sylvette is staring outward, unblinking. Her eyes widen just a bit as the sound of stones tossed against the window is heard. She hurries off the bed and stares down into the night. For the first time, there is some real animation in her features. As she stares, her lovely smooth face tenses up slightly. Tenses with eagerness.

She squints now. A thunderclap. Loud, but not overly dramatic. Then she arches her head backward a little as the sound of rain beats against the windowpane. "Oh," she mur-murs, and reaches down with both arms into the dark night outside her window, reaching for something. Then her whole body leans out over the window sill. You can see the rain beat against her as the camera slowly follows the motion of Syl-vette's body stretching out over the sill and reaching further into the dark. Another thunderclap.

Sylvette is hanging tight on the rider's waist as the horse gallops precariously through the rain. They travel into the forest in the rear of the house. The paths are narrow. You can see the texture of Sylvette's clothing contract from the wet. The outline of her nipples is visible. From the other side, the rider is dark, mustachioed, a little fierce-looking, although that may just be from concentrating on maintaining the perilous gait.

Small groves and ditches whiz by on their left. The rain is now slanting against them, whipping them, just as the rider whips the horse. A small lantern around the rider's shoulder illumines the scene: his intensity, her look of fugitive anxiety. But now there is a sense of density that the lantern cannot compensate. The groves and ground seem all enmeshed in the same darkness. The rider's face is flickering, dimmer and dimmer.

Yet as the rain pounds on the horse and riders with ever more intensity, Sylvette's hunger, though invisible, seems to have become ravenous. One senses it in the forest. It writhes in the rain. If one could see her face, well, one hardly wants to see it! We surmise the virginal gleam contorted with a threatening monstrous lust. The smell of that lust mixes with the profoundly varied smells of vegetation made sodden by the rain. Find some way to make the smells visual. Foreign smells under any circumstance, in the downpour this fetid profusion is well nigh unworldly. And Sylvette, whose body seems so immaculate because it's so white and tight, adds to the inchoate, overwhelming jumble of odor.

There may be opera in the background. The sound of rain and hooves in equal measure with something grand and Italian.

Suddenly a tree breaks, or so it would seem from the dark shadow flying in the near distance to the left. The horse rears and Sylvette flies off her perch and, as she fortunately breaks her fall with both outstretched hands, rolls over an embankment. There is utter black for a half minute. Is she unconscious? Is she dead? Moonlight threads through the trees and the rain and Sylvette is lying on her back in a mud bog. She is oozing in it, an incongruously blond and pony-tailed creature swimming in the steamy earth. The mud cakes her light cloth suit, which is torn at the shoulder and disheveled at the waist. Half the garb is up over her hip and the mud swarms onto her white panties. She has lost her shoes and through the moonlight we get a faint glimpse of red toenail polish. As she opens her eyes, her head sinks back a little and the wet mud creeps to her lips. She reaches down and pulls up her dress so the mud enters her, slipping in past the corners of her underwear. She is barely conscious of what has happened but her instinct as she feels the mud fill her up is to smile lasciviously.

Footsteps. It is her Indian lover. He stands over her. The moonlight shows a blank penetrating glare. He watches as she discards the rest of her clothing, squirming to do so while she still lies on her back. The rain rinses some mud off her smooth flesh but, just as it does so, more rises to cover her. The moonlight shows the man lower his pants. His feet are muddy and there is some mud on his thighs. His penis is fat and erect as he looms over the girl in the bog.

Sylvette sees his penis and sighs, then giggles. "Come down," she says. The man stumbles into the bog and the mud covers his lower extremities. He covers her and yanks at her bespattered ponytail. As his muddy cock penetrates her, she whispers, "Do my cunt." Clouds over the moon complete the scene in utter darkness. Nothing more can be seen. Done.

The Montez Get

It is important that we understand Evelyn Vallejo.

One imagines, at the wedding ceremony, her gown all crosshatched with lace in multiple gradations of white on white. Alabaster-like skeins stretch taut across the paler shade of the underlying cloth. The overall impression is certainly not one of traditional virgin simplicity, and Evelyn is not, in any event, a simple person. Nor does "radiant," the assuring term the world dotes on to commemorate matrimonial epiphany, precisely apply. But she is a happy bride; the community observes that at first blush. She is nubile, and lovely too. There is a sea of smiles in the church, lips mostly pursed tight and content. A collective recognition prevails that, for this particularly signal union, a certain quiet congratulatory restraint is most appropriate. The event has the public gravity of a trade treaty. Bear in mind: this marriage has consequences for the children and grandchildren of the merchants and villagers and outriders and tradesmen and neighboring potentates, the ever so many retainers who've not actually met Evelyn Tortazar or Roberto Vallejo, and won't necessarily be remembered if they do.

Gladness, which is not quite joy, but a commodity palpably rounder and more communal and more bankable than joy, pervades the occasion. The priest who administers the sacrament is, for one, glad to be doing so. "They met in church," whispers Maria Velez to her confidante Helena Jimenez.

So they did. While they awaited mass that day, Evelyn told him all about the crafts with their dazzling colors, and the astonishing weavers she met the day before on the green dale just outside Antigua. They'd ridden the new buggy equipped with a picnic lunch and sent off the servants for a Saturday holiday. Father took the reins himself.

"The patterns, you know, are ancient. They're Mayan."

"Yes," said Roberto. "Somehow the weavers still know what to weave."

The assembled parishioners observing the pair exchanged approving smiles. If nothing else, a future union of Ruben Vallejo's son with Federico Tortazar's daughter, obviously advantageous for both families, provided a charm of predictability. Love itself in service to social stability always warrants the approbation of the known universe.

"It's in their minds somehow," said Evelyn.

"Yet no one has ever taught them."

"Isn't it mysterious!" she exclaimed. "How they know to weave the tapestry of a long gone world. As if by instinct."

The priest came forth and they fell dutifully silent. After mass they were allowed to sit together on the veranda, where they chattered comfortably into the night.

Evelyn set about the task of organizing her new household on the ancient Tortazar estate with great robustness. She directed the workers in the construction of the cavernous closet space tucked within the side of the house overlooking the lake. Her dresses and petticoats and pantaloons could be draped on heavy oaken hangers with space to spare. It was a magnificent closet in a magnificent house. There were many other expansive rooms to fill and, for her, a joyous vista of days ahead in which to fill them.

Roberto's closet was perpendicular to hers and, since there was no partition, husband and wife could stand together at the juncture. It was a happy spatial configuration that, while not consciously designed to do so, reinforced a theme of connubial familiarity. Each early evening, soul to soul at the threshold of their respective wardrobes, Evelyn and Roberto habitually reviewed the developments of the day. Their joint appearances in the spacious alcove became a casual ritual and a diurnal comfort. When cousin Emilia took to bed with the same mysterious fever that laid Aunt Rosa low, it was there they fretted. One night they talked fondly about Ezekiel, a favorite horse she had named after the prophet who was so fascinating for all his bones and the valley where those old bones might live again.

Maria Velez and Helena Jimenez came calling. The priest arrived too, accompanied by Angellita Tortazar, the redoubtable mother wizened though not yet fifty. On such occasions, Evelyn and Roberto would often sneak away, after an obligatory hour, to visit their private ground and relive their common concerns. "They love each other so," gushed Maria.

"They could be more courteous," scolded Angellita.

"They're young," said Maria.

"They are the future," said the priest.

To organize the household, it was necessary to hire and manage the servants, and this Evelyn set about with great vigor as well. Manuel Ramos was put in charge of the stables. He was directed to pick and hire his own stable boys, although it was generally commended that he himself could do the physical labor of a dozen young men, and likely in less time. Yet such was the largesse of the clan to let Manuel employ a staff anyway. Paulo Ramirez acted as a butler. He was hopelessly oafish, but, nearly seven feet tall, with less than one hundred and fifty pounds on his bones, and an enormous handlebar moustache like a ribbon around his mouth, he was sufficiently picturesque to compensate his sundry deficiencies. Sometimes Evelyn and Roberto in their closet told tales of his ungainly misadventures and giggled together when they did so.

Sonya Ramos, who was no apparent relation to Manuel, ran the kitchen. Most every night she lingered fearfully in the doorway during dinner until the food was pronounced delicious or at least very good. It usually was, for Sonya had learned from old Celia Montez, a Cuban émigré who had worked in remembered times for Roberto's grandparents. Celia was acclaimed for the picadillo she imported from her native land. The world was astounded that so simple a dish could be so rich and good. How the stewed tomatoes imbued the rice, how the garbanzos steamed lusciously in concert with the meat. And, the world wondered where Celia ever found such peppers, such galas of red and green.

Sonya's picadillo wasn't quite so good and, knowing this, she labored in torment to revive at least fleeting hints of the exalted antecedent. Night after night she waited to be unmasked for the pretender she was. Evelyn and Roberto found this somewhat comical as well, especially since no one really expected her picadillo could possibly match Celia's anyway. Yet it was a sad sight, when Evelyn inspected the kitchen, to watch Sonya lay the peppers on a paper towel on the counter, allow them to dry a bit, and, with eyes all a-bulge, sniff around at the roots as if in search of such magic fibrous shreds as might somehow lift the final ensemble beyond the merely acceptable.

There were many other servants as well, including Celia Montez' great-granddaughter Sophia who variously helped around the house. As the household fell into its established rhythm, Evelyn was free to spend more time in the stable. Sometimes she rode Ezekiel, at other times the black pony

Angel, a special gift from the Vallejos on the occasion of her first wedding anniversary.

Evelyn made a point when she rode to circumnavigate the estate, which included her house, her parents' house, the servants' houses, and the landscaped backyard meadowlands interspersed among the houses, as well as the lake and a swath of forest. The project she had set herself right after the marriage entailed specific reclamations, improvements, and additions. By now, it was all just about finished, and what she saw as she rode—the fences around the meadows freshly painted, the berry bushes springing up near to maturity, the marble Cupids and Madonnas happily afire when the sun shone onto the lawns—bestowed a sensation of plenitude.

The semblance of plenitude likewise demanded that Roberto be kept happy. Cigars were imported from Cuba and Nicaragua. Evelyn saw to the wine, but this was another cause for Sonya Ramos to lacerate herself. She knew nothing of wine and therefore felt additionally inadequate in her work. At times Evelyn was troubled by Sonya's habitual self-denigration, as if something other than Sonya herself hung threateningly in the air, an evil spirit animating the poor woman. Evelyn knew too that insane people hear mocking voices, and this concerned her. She was reassuring to her utmost, and advised Sonya to focus utterly on the picadillo and not worry or bother at all about wine. "Work hard," she urged in a kindly way. "Sacrifice for your work, but don't let it drive you crazy."

A favored Hospices de Beaune arrived and Roberto was jubilant. As to other matters, Evelyn remained uncertain and even adversarial. When, if she awoke before the usual time, and the light that had begun to appear in the fading hot night caught for her surfaces of the lake through the window, she might at such moments envision him ecstatic, but it was a dream she struggled to awake from, even when she was not asleep.

One day she rode Ezekiel to the boundaries of the estate, on the north fork where the dark swamps start just beyond the swath of forest. Two riders darted out from behind the dense brush. She recognized one whom her father pointed out years ago. The other she had never seen before. Ezekiel reared; Evelyn, hanging on tight with her thighs, cried out a little.

"Forgive us," called the one she recognized. "We should have been more careful."

Evelyn looked back at them through a haze of sun and late afternoon humidity. These were the lowering men of the northern lands. Her father regarded them with great admiration, as a separate breed of being who eschewed civilization and vast wealth. They were not reconstituted bandits such as the rubber and cacao traders from Brazil he knew so well, who in the olden times may have stripped and devoured their mighty country, but were now transmogrified. They'd become landed gentry, veritably suburban in their jealous attention to property lines and political affiliations. They adorned themselves with bogus military titles. Conquerors once, other men have long since been hired to enforce the suzerainty. Their tale is not magical realism. It is the postlude to it.

In contrast, the two men before her now, polite and taciturn, still drink blood and whisper low to succubae. "I'm quite all right," Evelyn said, and nodded politely.

"Goodbye then," said the man. They rode back into the brush, tramping intricate patterns along the trail that was fast overgrowing with foliage and would soon be gone for good.

As it was a family custom to bestow their blessings on such occasions, Evelyn and Roberto attended the sixteenth birthday celebration of Celia Montez' great-granddaughter. Sophia was average looking as Evelyn first observed her, yet many truly beautiful women did not often visit this world—it was a world of children, and mothers who were maidens one moment and matrons the next—and she doubted his lust could hold out much longer. He danced the girl along the edges of the rope that marked off a part of the lawn for that purpose. They swirled the circumference passing close by the small circles of adults looking on. A kind of stupor lay on the faces of these onlookers as Sophia and Roberto swirled and swirled about. The audience neither smiled nor was discomfited.

Evelyn took closer stock as the girl lingered over a wash-basin in the dim light of a dying spring day. She was really rather stocky. Her hips and thighs were heavy. Yet a remarkable radiance shone on her nut-brown skin. Either in repose or busy at her chores, Sophia looked vaguely liquid as if she had just bathed and wasn't quite dry. There were no visible blemishes, although her forearms were streaked with unusually thick strands of smooth hair reminiscent of black velvet or sleek velveteen garb. Evelyn imagined what full clumps must occupy the armpits. An obscene comparison came to mind and she stifled it at once.

She told Sophia to take more responsibility for the laundry. "My husband wants his collars starched, at least those shirts there," she said, walking the girl into the great closet and pointing out a dozen or so formal evening shirts sequestered on a separate shelf. Sophia nodded in acknowledgment. "These pants he wears to church, or to family gatherings, but to family gatherings only. Air them out as the occasion demands.

"I'll also ask you to wash some of his clothing by hand," said Evelyn. Her voice at the moment sounded brittle and even rather guttural. The prospect that lay before her, and her own inchoate notions regarding it, was palpably more ominous than the conventional and seemingly trivial accommodation to which she had first resigned herself. A clammy unsettling sweat flashing upon her might have been fear, if she could have specified exactly what it was she was afraid of, or even a sort of longing that was equally indefinite. Sophia staring back blankly possibly understood the instruction and possibly not. The clammy flash passed. How deeply Sophia's eyes were set in their sockets, how peacefully they rested there, and how so very dark they were! "Do a good job," Evelyn added politely. A room was prepared for Sophia as at certain times it might be more convenient for her to sleep there than in her own house.

Evelyn rode the breadth of the estate atop Angel in a moonless evening. This periodic night riding with its tempestuous aspect suggested some species of incipient disorder, a spirit being set perilously loose. It disquieted her husband, who took certain steps to have Evelyn's surprisingly restive manifestations discreetly monitored. At such dark times, Manuel Ramos stood guard outside the stables. He'd gaze thoughtfully as the lady rode off and then patiently await her return so he could put the horse back to shelter and lock up safely for the duration.

As the years went on, no one thought much about Sophia and Roberto one way or another. Sophia was not aging noticeably. Only her dark skin was getting darker, and the hairs on her body when she went bathing in the lake lay on her longer and thicker. At times she was rather feral, like a child of nature one might encounter in a cave. She was by no means unsightly. A certain sort of fullness attached to her. The hair when it got wet under her arms and on her legs made her seem altogether ripe and, in a most suggestive way, imminently pregnant. Sophia accepted her role in the life of the family with neither embarrassment nor ambition. She was neither slut nor schemer, and what had evolved in the course of time was as acceptable to her as it seemed to be to others; to the Pellot clan, for instance, the three brothers and their wives with their accumulation of ten children in constant tow. Much to Evelyn's discomfort, these Pellots were accepting increasingly frequent invitations from Roberto.

Why he invited them all so often, she did not understand. They were amiable enough guests but such a friendship would have been unthinkable a few years ago. Yet for Roberto, the tacit disapprobation, even of his own family, was a matter of apparent indifference. Roberto appeared to be losing interest in many things these days, while the Pellots, and the wild gamboling of their numerous get all about the place, offered up for him a comfort his wife found rather demeaning. They treated Sophia as if she were Roberto's sister. Either they were simply ignorant in their bourgeois simplicity or, conversely, were of a different social caste that, more than tolerates, actively promotes such license on principle. On the other hand, they were possibly just being polite.

One day they picnicked by the lake. The Pellots stood configured in a V-formation facing the lake in order to applaud the exuberant frolics of their children on the shore. Vaguely irritated, even tense in this swamp of self-congratulatory domesticity, Evelyn ambled behind one of the couples on the near wing of the V. On the other side of the far wing, she could see Sophia and Roberto in profile. Their image flickered, was caught and lost and caught again in the crevices formed by the various Pellots as they casually shifted and re-shifted position before her. The sunlight at that time made her husband look younger than he was. More than relaxation, it revealed the abiding serenity of a man at home in his own world at last, of one who has found his rightful place alongside his true life's companion. Sophia turned toward him and they exchanged a few words. What ease they enjoyed in each other's presence, how they continued to smile in silence through their pursed and tranquil lips! It was the ripened comfort of a lifetime, as if just the few years they had so far spent together could suffice for that happy effect.

Evelyn was lost in a terrific loneliness. She had counted on disgusting lust. She had counted on her husband lapping like a dog at the servant girl's hairy arms and legs. She had counted on barnyard noises hollered up in strange contorted positions. She had counted on Sophia waiting in the stables for Roberto to come mount her in the haystack. She may even have foreseen the day when, her lover failing for whatever reason to appear, Sophia might pleasure herself with one of the stallions. She imagined the girl wriggling with him on the grass or soiled on the shore of this very lake. She could see her husband yank his trousers up afterward. His undergarments would be stained, but that was no matter; it was the girl's job to wash them anyway. She had counted on her husband being what he was; being what he had no choice but to be. But she had not counted on this.

Miracles had occurred between them. The unbearable miracles of quiet intimacy and tender regard transformed the world. Then there was a baby. Even that she might have counted on as an inevitable and acceptable produce, for it was still a lord's prerogative to seed his fields. But she now suspected that the Montez get was conceived in her own bed. Once, standing outraged and bereft at the entranceway to the bedroom, she espied Sophia's heels held high aloft as if in salute to love itself. Evelyn, if furious, could not feel quite empowered to remonstrate or strike out to any purpose. She only avoided the bedroom for many nights after that and slept elsewhere, in one of the guest rooms on the first floor. Nothing was said.

Late one afternoon she went to Sophia's room and found her on the edge of the bed nursing the baby. "Have you been able to get your chores done?" Evelyn asked, gently.

"Yes," she said, "except I haven't yet pressed the two new suits." Sophia was naked to the waist. Her hair fell to her shoulders; by now, it was nearly charcoal-black. She wore a light red slip, and the outline of her pubic beard was faintly visible. Always, the girl showed such confidence. She was radiant in that simple confidence, and Evelyn marveled at it, and respected her for it. How she just sat there with that baby at suck even as her mistress loomed thus above her!

Evelyn imagined peonies flung all through the labyrinthine tresses. Worlds once yielded to such beauty, and would do so again. "The baby seems to be very happy," she said sadly.

"Oh she is," said Sophia, smiling, and appreciative. "She truly is."

Evelyn knew better than to rue this confidence of Sophia's as insolence. It was not that at all. In these months and years, she had never challenged Evelyn's authority nor, in their domestic entanglement, had she indulged a single visible moment of heartfelt triumph. In her own way, and with her own unspoken words, Sophia must have known, with painfully intimate knowledge, that Evelyn herself had no choice except to soberly acknowledge the overall rightness of things as they stood. It was a disheartening reflection on how, informed by Roberto, or drawing her own conclusions from what she could see and sense around her, Sophia interpreted Evelyn's very existence and its fundamental shortcomings.

Sophia held the baby tighter to her breast. "Try to iron the suits either today or tomorrow," said Evelyn. "Do your best."

"I will, I surely will," said Sophia.

"Thank you," said Evelyn.

Omar Jimenez, the son of old Helena Jimenez who had married a niece of old Maria Velez, became Evelyn's best friend. Their friendship was encased in a species of formality as intimate in its way as carnal love. How he bowed to her, alone or in company; how he never presumed to use her first name, even when others did so freely; how he doted on her numerous trivial needs as if he, not the seven-foot Paulo Ramirez, were the real major domo. By his very restraint, Omar implied an instinctive familiarity with longings that could never be spoken, and thirsts that were not to be slaked. Of all this she was only vaguely aware as he, faithful husband, and church elder, had learned since their respective marriages to indulge this one great vice of his, which was to adore the idea of his own attentiveness.

He sensed the barren spaces inside her. Not that he could possibly invest those spaces or imagine trying, but he thrilled to the thought of her emptiness as something tangible to live in, as it were, and to roam through day and night. Omar was a careful enough man to think this a great sin in some way. Once he even tried to confess it. "I have impure thoughts about this woman," he said.

"You dream of an improper relationship?"

"I feel it is an improper relationship already."

"You have made improper advances?"

"Never!"

"You have carnal thoughts?"

"No, not really."

"Then what is the sin?"

How warm January and February can be in these parts, even during the great and predictable mid-afternoon rains. The sky slants over Zacaleu to the west as if the big green mountains there have pierced its side. In Cuba, moisture mixes with the dust. In Nicaragua, the heat pounds on the flatlands, and crops die and the peasants in the west endure their perennial travails. In Brazil, where the old rubber and cacao bandits dote on aldermen, everything just heaves with incipient storm. But in these parts, a delicate balance continues to be maintained, and all seems to depend on that balance. The weavers outside Antigua, anticipating the cloudbursts, close up their looms by noon. At Lake Atitlan, the clouds above the old volcano look like goose feather pillows.

. Evelyn strolled with Omar Jimenez past the stables. Omar handled everything. It was Omar, for instance, who arranged to have musicians play at her parent's house on the Saturday just past when all the Tortazars assembled to celebrate cousin Emilia's vows upon her recovery. It was a great success. They played Mozart's 5th Violin Concerto, adventuring its lively climatic pseudo-orientalism with pronounced gusto. Everyone savored it like an exotic dessert. It was vulgar in a way, perhaps. Any such ingenuous, or perhaps disingenuous, caricature of things anciently and eternally Spanish might have likewise sounded to her like a shameless travesty. But parody is abstraction of a sort, and abstraction is a truth unto itself. What's good for the Turk's goose is therefore good for the Spaniard's gander, and rootless men were always free to ape in words or deeds her frail and stately passions.

"You are a priceless friend," she said. There was no one within earshot, yet they were whispering just as Helena Jimenez and Maria Velez customarily whispered when they huddled together like conspirators in church. Nothing, she had come to realize, had ever been innocent.

"Your trust is priceless," he answered slowly.

"You must know what my life is like," she said.

"I pray for your happiness," he said.

"I want to ask you for something that may not be honest or right. Don't judge me too harshly. But I must know everything they think and feel."

"I understand," he said, so he built her a machine to peep with.

She spied for months with the machine Omar built her, as Omar withdrew into the shadows of her life until he could barely be seen by the naked human eye. Evelyn watched their tenderness and it revolted her. She unfolded for him like a last summer bud, and she burrowed in his arms. A kind of animal contentment, not unlike the look of her when she was nursing, held her midway between sleep and wake. Then, clinging each to each for dear life, they slowly writhed until passion rose and overcame them. They pressed harder against each other; they writhed without parting, until she sang out at last and he smiled for her in delight. The sweat percolated on her dark peasant flesh. She saw the beads glisten in her armpits, in the big bushes there, and on the braids all along her legs. How could she grunt like that one moment and be so meekly sweet, veritably childlike, the next! She watched him mount on top; his fury mounted. How could she allow such violence one moment, and such caresses the next!

One morning she entered upon the bedroom. She pulled the sheet from the bed waving the tallow-like white cotton at a slant until it billowed and hung a second or two suspended in mid air. Evelyn shook it, and shook it again, peering intently for the telltale remnants. Expressionless, drained as if by a consumptive ailment, she nonetheless went quickly about this bit of drudgery lest an imaginable passerby catch her at this servant's work and marvel at the diminution. She bundled the sheet and stuck it with the other dirty laundry for Sophia to wash, by and by, in the course of her daily chores.

She saw them in bed with the baby. They fondled and pinched her tiny toes, and Roberto held Sophia's breast up to the baby's mouth. Maybe Roberto was inside her at that moment. Maybe another child would be born, and then another, and another. Sophia, nursing interminably, could not be riper. She saw a new world unfurl before her, and Sophia and Roberto were its parents. Evelyn hectored the kitchen staff. "I'll take that," she said, seizing a dinner tray as if the scraggly haired little niece of Sonya Ramos who was now assisting in the kitchen didn't even know enough to carry roast beef.

Evelyn served the main dish and called out to the kitchen to hurry up with the rest. A glance from Roberto, quiet in his chair at the table, said nothing. He was opaque. Or, perhaps, there was nothing to conceal, and it was a simple blankness in his glance that only seemed to be opaque. There was no point in his thinking much of her, or speaking to her, or condemning or comforting or reconciling her, her who saw and knew it all, as he did too. This was life, that's all, and it was meant to be lived numbly and happily.

Amid the silence, everything seemed uncannily normal. The new world that was unfurling before her seemed inexorable. "I have sacrificed my life for a peccadillo," Evelyn said to herself. The Pellots were expected after dinner, but, through the open window on the far side of the dining room, she thought she heard them arriving early. She thought she heard their children scampering off, probably to visit the stable, to beguile the horses and giggle wildly as they did so. "I have sacrificed my world for a peccadillo," she thought again, and gathered herself up for the evening ahead.

Tight Like That

In the old days, when he worked for Dutch Schultz and palled around sometimes with Vincent Coll, there were dozens of women all named Kate. Some had come from squalid little farmhouses where wizened rabbit-faced fathers drunk or deranged in the dark flatlands nightly groped or poked their unguarded innards. Others were the daughters of Bronx or Brooklyn assemblymen frantic for the fabled Manhattan just beyond reach despite all the trains and tunnels that could take them there. Still others tumbled in from the breast of the great crazy continent, from whistle stops or flat bland suburbs, having heard of—or if they could read, having read of—the famous frenzy that was Flegenheimer. If they had dying to do, this was the place to do it.

Some opened right up for Louie because they thought men like him were steppingstones to the top. Others opened numbly, without hope. By contrast I think a lot of them put out for Coll because they loved him. They put out for him as much as they could put out for anybody. Coll was a very strange person who often kept his door wide open all day long because he liked it when people and even strangers traipsed in and out. You got to see a lot stopping by Vincent's unannounced. One time when Louie came over with Dimples Wolinsky a girl was barking for Coll like a dog. She went bow-wow, bow-wow, bow-wow. Years later, when Louie told the story to Phil Strauss, Strauss thought it was funny enough but warned him not to tell Red Lavine. Red had this strange religious streak and you never knew how he'd react to a story like that.

Luciano sent women over to Vincent's from time to time, and one of the nights Louie was there a guy from Baltimore whose name he couldn't remember offered $2,000 to any of the girls who'd take it up the ass. A little Jewish redhead named Susie Wexler accepted. A few years later Susie really got it up the ass, in a manner of speaking, because she was one of the girls with Wolinsky when all the shit hit the fan in Brooklyn. Wolinsky was lying in bed with a girl named Kate Quigley when Reles's men came in. Susie was in the bathroom at the time, and after they killed Wolinsky they walked in and shot her sitting there.

By then Louie had made it a rule to do what he was told. His loyalty to Schultz was what kept him alive. He wasn't involved when Coll was murdered but he was there when Dutch converted to Roman Catholicism. You'll remember that they'd hung three guys up on meat hooks. Schultz, watching them die, saw them find true comfort and peace. They were praying, and when they commended their spirits to the Holy Mother their bulging eyes glowed with love. Dutch wasn't going to let three pig-ass Irish thugs from Burnside Avenue gain a cheat on the last agony that he couldn't count on for himself. Louie figured the ignoble motive didn't matter one way or another so long as Dutch was baptized, which he was. But Schultz died delirious. He cried out "Mama, talk to the sword" and other such expostulations, a vast poetry, perhaps, a language worthy of legend, yet with nothing of the finalizing salve he'd banked on when he gave his soul to Jesus Christ.

After Dutch got shot, Louie was in a world of shit. He'd hidden in the men's room while it happened, there at the Newark Chophouse. He climbed onto the water tank that sat at the top of his stall. Luciano's men, rushing in, somehow didn't see him there. When he heard sirens Louie jumped down and ran out past Dutch at his table, slumped forward in his own blood. Outside, Luciano's men, escaping, saw him escape. The cops who were coming saw him going.

But he got away running and ducking and hiding. He made his way to Livingston, just outside Newark. He hid in the basement of some well-to-do family who didn't know he was there and never would know. Back in New York the next day, Louie was short of money but couldn't go back to his apartment on Carmine Street for cash because somebody was sure to be there waiting for him.

In his life's greatest act of love and devotion, he did not try to find Kate that night in New Jersey because he was terrified that, if they found him, they'd find her too, and that they'd kill her. Kate Baird was her name.

Louie figured he had the biggest dick you ever saw. He regretted not being a smarter and shrewder person because with brains as well as balls he'd have turned out to be something terrific, a Dutchman or Charlie Lucky himself. He liked to show it off, his dick, which was why he liked the parties where guys banged their tarts in front of everybody, right there and then as they pleased. He'd seen Tommy Montefusco fuck and he'd seen Jimmy Bellaterra fuck and he'd seen Desiderio Albertini fuck. He was glad they'd all seen him fuck too, because having seen him they knew how much he had.

But of all the people he'd ever wanted to see it, it was Kate Baird who worked at the little red library off Hudson Avenue in

North Bergen, not far from the Jersey City Heights border, whom
he'd wanted to see it most. She was very stately looking. She
walked with slow steps, as if a heavier gait would have been unla-
dylike. Kate's face was like porcelain and she wore straight brown
suits that hid her figure. Her hair was knotted in a blonde bun
which Louie loved to look at. He loved her eyes, too. He wanted
to know what her eyes would look like seeing his fat greasy dick.
The sight of it would teach her something. She'd have no choice
but to learn. No older than twenty, she was cherry for sure.

He was in North Bergen to beat up Paul Schinapoulos.
The idea was to beat him up in broad daylight as a message: we
do what we want when we want and we don't care who knows
it, and if you think this is something wait until you see what
happens after the sun goes down. The library closed just a few
moments after he left Schinapoulos gasping on the sidewalk,
and when Kate walked out of it Louie saw her for the first time.
Still fervid with the beating he'd given Schinapoulos, Louie,
swaying gracefully ape-like, followed her.

"Hey," he muttered, coming abreast.

She paid him no mind. But he thought about her all night
and returned the next day at closing time. He was bursting.
"Hey," he called. Again she barely moved her head. When he
walked faster and said, "Hey, look at this!" she kept walking,
not looking. He jumped in front of her and began to unzip,
but she brushed past him with a horrified look. He let her go
without making her see it.

There was news of big changes in Brooklyn. Everybody was
talking about Brownsville and Reles and there was talk of new
men in the D.A.'s office who weren't Lepke's men. A girl at a

party they were throwing in honor of John Irish told Fabrizio she'd been with Francesco Ioele the day before he died. "I heard the whole story," said Fabrizio, when he saw Louie walk in.

"Yeah?" asked Louie.

"Frankie's last blow job," said Fabrizio.

"Yeah?" asked Louie, gazing over at the girl who sucked the cock of Frankie Yale for the last time ever. He thought he recognized her as the sister of a musician who played with Bunny Berrigan at Club Ooofus Rufus. The musician's friend had a neighbor who knew a man whose cousin once had dinner with the sister of the barber at the hotel who a lifetime later stepped aside to let two guys in masks walk in and murder Albert Anastasia, as a result of which Buddy Hackett was able to buy that beautiful home of Anastasia's in Edgewater.

"Very definitely," said Fabrizio.

Of all the phantasms in his life, the woman with the blonde bun in North Bergen pressed around him day and night. He wanted her to look right at it. A few days after he'd first seen her Louie got across the river again and waited twenty minutes on the stairs by the library's front entrance. He leaned against the railing until she came out. When she came out, he showed it to her. But she looked away so quickly, he wasn't sure she'd seen it.

Louie put *Hocus Pocus* on the Victrola when he got home. *Hocus Pocus* sounded like sex to him, but it was sweeter and subtler than the noisy fucking sounds that the horns on other records blared out right at you. When Louie closed his eyes and listened to *Hocus Pocus*, he imagined a vast room like a gymnasium, with hundreds of couples dancing as if they were in a trance. They were smiling and happy, but they were all in a trance, and they were ready to die.

He could get back to Jersey on Friday, and this time he'd say the things to her he wanted to say. But she wasn't there on Friday. He worried a little she might be afraid of him and was hiding someplace. He went again on Sunday but the library was closed. Tuesday, she wasn't there either. These were torturous days for Louie. He had sex with a Cuban woman he met eating at a restaurant on Bleecker Street who didn't know any of his people or his friends and had no idea who or what he was. She told him his big dick was really pretty, and he accepted her compliment, but it made him long to show it to the girl at the library all the more.

It was like he was walking in his sleep. He couldn't stay away from North Bergen. He sat in a big park that was named for Jim Braddock, who was from North Bergen and had run for mayor there. He got beat but they named the park after him anyway. Louie dozed for what could've been an hour on a park bench, then went over to a bar in order to phone in and see if Schultz wanted him for anything.

When he stepped out on the street again, Kate was passing by. Her eyes got big when she saw him, big and blue and bulging full with fear.

"Hey," Louie called. She kept walking.

"I'll call a policeman," she said when he caught up.

"I'll kill the fucker if you do," he said.

She gasped a little and picked up her pace.

"Hey," said Louie. He tried to sound nice. "I just think you're a very attractive lady, that's all. You don't have to look at my dick if you don't want to." But she turned. almost running, and Louie stood there not sure what to do, so he did nothing.

The next day Dutch said to him, "Louie, since you started the job with that Greek shithead in Jersey, you finish it."

"Yeah, I'll take Rudy with me."

Dumb Schinapoulos had ignored all their warnings. They followed him in the car, around five hundred yards behind. At one point Schinapoulos slowed up for no reason and Louie worried he might try to lead them someplace where he had friends, so they took the matter in hand. With a quarter of a mile or so between Schinapoulos and the next car ahead of him, they switched lanes, sped up, and pulled around in front of him, then jammed on their brakes to block his way. Louie got out and started walking toward his car. Schinapoulos sat behind the wheel, indecisive.

Rudy went back to the Bronx, but Louie rented a motel room in Jersey. The next day, at dusk, she looked the very same way she'd looked when he'd first seen her leave the library. But this time, as he came toward her, moving fast in a diagonal across the intersection, she held her head up, defiant.

When Louie was within a few yards, his body propelled forward in sidewise herky-jerky jolts, she averted her eyes at last. She was so beautiful to him. She was solemn and seductive like a church procession. She was like a beautiful container full of something he didn't quite know what, yet she was just a cherry woman who worked in a library. Her face was so pure, a stern angel's face. She had stuff, lots of hot and stately stuff. He just couldn't explain it.

Maybe Louie saw some faint welcoming glint in her eyes right before she looked down. He didn't run after her as she walked away, toward the far corner of the intersection. All he saw now was her back draped in the plain brown suit. He'd track her down in his car. There were other people around, a young couple with what looked like twin girls in a stroller, two men walking on the sidewalk just ahead of them. But as he drove up they disappeared from sight in the gathering dark.

Louie passed in front of her and pulled the car up on the sidewalk. She might have gotten past him if she'd wanted to—she could have slipped through the space between the front bumper and the storefronts. Instead she stood there for a full moment, motionless and tense, as he rolled down the window.

"Just take a look, that's all," he said. His tone was puerile. He whined in a way that sounded strange to his own ears and maybe hers too. It bothered him, the sound of his own voice.

She didn't smile at all. Her eyes kept bulging in a way that made Louie wonder if there was something strange about her. Maybe she was crazy even though she was beautiful. Before he even had it back in, he stepped on the gas and drove off. Then, in the silence of his car, he had to acknowledge he was a little scared by what had just happened, even though she was just a librarian and cherry at that. .

Louie gained possession of himself. He pulled over by a park, not the park named for Jim Braddock but another one on the main drag. A red stone buffalo faced the nondescript city behind him. Behind the statue, the park stretched back expansively, greenish grass covering a sizable declivity that ended with a bunch of telephone poles winding toward Secaucus with its pig farms. Louie drew breath and drove back to a block or so ahead of where he'd left her. As he pulled up alongside, he leaned over and opened the door, willing her in.

How she came alive when he fucked her! They drove to New York and he played *Variety Stomp* on the Victrola. The knitted brow unraveled. The stern look went away. Her arms waved about, her wrists hung limply down. She hummed the melody as her virgin crotch dripped blood on the bed. He fucked her deep and, excited, she sang out, "Da Da Da Da, Da Dah Da Dah, Da Da Da, Da Dah Da Dah," in accompaniment to the frenetic out chorus. The world itself came alive when Kate sang like that, like a crazy bird.

"Music's great, ain't it?" he said quietly, when they were done.

If Luciano was planning on killing Schultz, maybe he and Kate could move out together to L.A. afterward. She'd give up her job at the library. They'd take a long romantic train ride. He'd work for the Jews there.

"It's wonderful," she cried the second time he fucked her. "*You're* wonderful."

He drove her home. He loved to watch her primp naked in front of the mirror. He liked her apartment more than his own. It reminded him of his Aunt Marie's house with its big couch full of cotton pillows embroidered with faint pictures that looked like they came from China. Instead of crucifixes or portraits of Jesus like at Aunt Marie's, in Kate's place there were pictures of dark countryside and men and animals that looked so small under big bulging gray-black clouds and huge tree trunks twisted with age. It was like you could die there without being scared to die, lying on one of the knolls or hillocks or whatever they call them. You knew there was a flood of moonlight all over you even though you couldn't see it. You could drift away knowing you'd never have to feel scared again.

Louie came up behind her in the bathroom where she was primping and stood beside her on the soft blue carpet that covered most of the tile floor. They didn't talk about a lot. Neither one of them had a lot to say or the desire to say it.

"I got business," he told her late that night. He went out and crossed the bridge. Albertini was having a drink in one of Schultz's jig whorehouses.

"I don't think Lucky wants any of us to walk away," said Albertini.

"Not even you and the other dagos?" asked Louie.

"Every man for himself," said Albertini.

"What do we do?" asked Louie.

He loved Kate. Think of it! She was this cherry librarian who turned into a big hot whore just for him. The tenderness and gratitude he felt in return were indescribable. One night he sat on her couch for an hour smiling just to look at her. Luciano could be sending over men right then, at that very moment. Louie wasn't that hard to find.

As the week went by, he was crossing the bridge a half-dozen times every day. "All I am is yours," she said to him one night.

There was a brief silence as they lay there. "You have parents someplace?" he asked. "Not being nosey or anything. I'm just curious."

She smiled at the question. "Sure I have parents," she said. "They live in Toms River." Moments like that, she looked at him like she couldn't believe how life was turning out. But she seemed happy. Every night that week she'd strip naked and lie back down on her bed all eager to surrender the bushy blond librarian twat. You may call it madness, but Louie called it hidey-ho.

Kate couldn't stop listening to the music and bought some of it for herself. She bought *Variety Stomp*. She bought *Relaxin' at the Touro* and *Milenberg Joys* and *Tight Like That*. Wednesday that week they holed up in North Bergen for the entire afternoon, dancing to the music. Kate was butt naked, waving her arms like a bird as if there was something in the world worth flying for.

Back in New York after Dutch was killed, a police captain named Paley stopped him crossing West Twenty-third Street and took his money. "Lucky little bastard," said Paley, amazed that Louie had gotten out of the Chophouse.

"Yeah, lucky," said Louie grimly.

He knew it was stupid to be in New York, but where else should he have gone? New Jersey seemed too broad and open—the vast spaces on both sides of the turnpike stuck in his mind—without alcoves to dart into or hallways to hide in. And being closer to Kate was unthinkable. He'd rather be dead than risk getting her killed. Maybe he should have gone to Boston or to Philadelphia. That's probably what he should have done.

That same day he was picked up in a sweep as a known felon. They put him on a van, handcuffed to one of the side rails that ran from front to back. The van drove to a holding pen a few bocks from Yankee Stadium, not far from what was once friendly Schultz country. They fingerprinted him along with a beady-eyed little white guy, a half-dozen or so black guys, and one Spanish kid who was very edgy probably because he was afraid of getting fucked up the ass if they didn't let him out of there. One of the black guys got ushered into a back room. In another hour or so they let the rest of them go.

He walked back to Manhattan figuring that was better than trying to walk to Boston. A cop would pick him up on the highway if he tried that. But Louie was still afraid that one of Luciano's men might spot him. He slept in Central Park and started bumming change for food. His plan was to wait and see. Soon he was bumming enough to buy a drink or two at the Irish joints on Third Avenue.

The longing for her began. Louie crossed the bridge on foot to North Bergen. He didn't intend for her to see him— that would be dangerous for her—but he was afraid they'd killed her already. Just a glimpse would ease his mind. He'd managed to beg enough for half a pint of whiskey, and it made him feel stronger while he was walking. In his mind the virgin face was come alive. The blond bun jutted exquisitely. He could touch it. It reminded him that she was a librarian puss forever and ever no matter what.

Louie hid five hundred yards from her apartment. But being there solved nothing. A dim light blurred through the drawn shade, which might have meant she was home and safe, or it might have meant she wasn't home, or it might have meant she was dead up there all by herself on the floor. Louie waited an hour. Walking back toward the bridge he saw a skinny guy like a plumber or an electrician with a flashlight and a screwdriver tucked in a pouch at his side. He could take him. The unwary man crossed over to Grand Avenue due south from the major intersection where the highways going west began. When they were alone, Louie took out his gun and stole the man's money, then pistol-whipped him until he was down and bloody and gone.

There was a liquor store by the bridge where he bought more whiskey for the long journey ahead. He crossed back over and headed downtown. His legs were like rubber but the whiskey kept him going. Oh Kate, your twat! Louie was desperate to see it. He wanted to kiss her on the forehead. He wanted to caress the stately blond bun. Lord, how long was he walking for? Where was the time going? Where was Kate? Louie was like to puke his guts up with worry that she was dead at that very moment, just because she'd loved him with all her soul.

Days later he found himself on Carroll Street in Brooklyn. Louie was sure Hymie Weiss himself walked by. An hour after that, or it could have been minutes, he spotted his own reflection frozen in a storefront window. He looked different. Maybe Weiss just didn't know who he was.

Louie crossed the bridge again. He couldn't remember where he'd gotten the money for the bottle he was drinking from. The sun was glowing high halfway on the horizon and the river shone below him. Now the apartment in North Bergen was clearly unoccupied. One window was boarded up. He walked back to Manhattan, muttering to himself. There was another bridge, and he crossed it, but it wasn't New Jersey he got to; it looked like Brooklyn. He heard something about Charlie Lucky being deported, but he didn't remember whom he heard it from. Then there was another bridge, and he didn't know where he was at all.

Sometimes it got so cold he felt like his skin was on fire. Then the cold would slowly melt away and he'd feel better. At times he'd find himself back at Roseland—it was crowded every night but it seemed like a different place than it once was. There were lots of people on Fifty-second street and when he asked a man in a camel's hair coat for some money it was Frank Costello who reached into his pocket and pulled out five dollars. Frank Costello was the softest touch on Broadway.

The days got cold again and warm again, and he kept trying to figure out what to do next but never could. Sometimes his stomach ached terribly, but he'd fall asleep anyway and wake up because it was so cold or because everything around him was so noisy. Louie couldn't remember these buildings at all. The cars in the street kept changing. Someone wanted to kill him, he was sure. Strange music, the likes of which he'd never heard before, blared from storefronts that seemed much bigger than the ones that used to play Herschel Evans and Red Allen and Benny Morton. "Doo Doo, Doo De Doo," he hummed, hearing her hum along too. Louie walked to Eighth Avenue and then came east again. Inexplicably, he found another bottle half drunk in the inside pocket of his overcoat. If he had still known anybody who could have told him, he would've heard that Vito Genovese had returned from exile in Italy.

And then Roseland was just about empty because it was raining so hard. The raindrops stung his face. Some of it came straight down and some of it flew at him sidewise, driven by fierce winds from across the river. Louie was alone. A limousine stopped in front of a small restaurant across the street from where he stood. The chauffeur unfurled a wide umbrella and hurried to meet the couple walking out. Louie crossed over and came up alongside the car while the chauffeur, drenched now himself, opened the door on the other side. The window wasn't tinted, so Louie peered in. He saw Kate there. Genovese hung on her arm and Valachi was sitting impassively in the front seat.

She was radiant, dressed all in silks and satins in the latest Paris style. The bun was gone, and her hair fell in well-grooved skeins to her shoulders. There were jewels. Her bodice was sculpted in chiffon, her breasts poised there like big white swans. She looked like a million bucks. She was a creature in and of the world she swam in. Seen in profile, she didn't blink.

"Kate," he said.

She yelped to see Louie, his sudden face hideous in the window. Her eyes bulged when she saw him.

"Get outta here or I'll kill ya," said Valachi, jumping out of the car, a shadow puppet in the black rain.

"How did he know my name?" breathed Kate.

"I'll kill him," said Valachi. He grabbed Louie by the waist and flung him down on the street. But Kate had saved him. How did he know her name indeed! Genovese was sure to wonder that very thing. So she asked it herself before he did, in utter innocent terror. Kate had learned things.

Louie got up and pedaled back quickly on his heels to avoid being hit by their car speeding off the curb. They'd run him down without the least thought if he let them. As they drove away Louie's last quick glimpse was of Genovese with his hand on her shoulder and Kate's eyes shut tight beside him. He was probably calming her down. "Don't worry," says Genovese. "Maybe he's seen you somewhere or another. We can take care of it."

"No," says Kate. "Let's forget it."

The long black car hurtled further uptown. There was a lot of lightning and thunder now. Louie stood in the middle of the street, staring north at the limousine in the distance. Kate keeps her eyes closed in the warm car. It must have been a shocking sight for her, him in the street so raw and pitiful like that.

He gazed way uptown through the rain. The rain beats the windshield and Kate's eyes are still closed. This is the man who opened you up. You loved him, and he loved you in return. The sight of him ravishes her now. "Are you okay?" asks Genovese. She nods but doesn't know what else to say.

Kate! He felt the pain now where Valachi had thrown him down on the ground. The rain bit into him like wasps. He cradled the whiskey bottle at his lips and made for shelter, heading toward one of the stores on the avenue. Things were going dead in his head, and the sidewise rain still stung him. There was more thunder, and despite the whiskey he was aware of just how cold it had gotten that night. It was tough to have seen her under the circumstances.

He Who

It lay there on her bed like a bright invitation or, even more palpably, a ready treasure trove compelling anticipation. *Tomorrow's Teens* arrived every month, this was her third issue. She used to buy it off the newsstand before subscribing, and was no stranger to the publication. But this was the first issue to thrill her so, because, while others may have dealt with dating and boyfriends, this one was all about being pregnant. The feature article was splashed on the front cover with a picture of a beautiful young mother holding her baby and sitting like a queen on her throne. It would be there to pore over when she finished lunch and Mommy said it was okay to go back upstairs to her room.

She read…

A woman who is pregnant experiences flushes of profound joy that she cannot really describe. Even her husband can only guess what it all means. She's never known anything like it. The pleasures dwarf all other pleasures. They make the pains that come with pregnancy all worthwhile. The stomach aches and other discomforts won't mean much to her now that the great expedition of motherhood is underway.

A warm glow enshrouds her. A burst of sunshine dances in her mind. There is a shimmering bauble in her heart. She feels its wondrous light wherever she goes. Even at night she dreams about precious little jewels that shine through the pores of her body. She has said yes to divine joy.

She is alive. She is holy. She is pregnant.

Martha reread the whole piece twice while stopping a few times to look out her bedroom window at the half-dozen or so neighbors' lawns landscaped toward the playground down the road. Her small room was all in blue. The carpet was extremely dark blue, the wallpaper a shade or two lighter. On the shelf just above the bed was a row of hand-painted horses that had been her father's. On the larger shelves at the foot of the bed were books and magazines, including the recent *Tomorrow's Teens.* Her mother had bought a subscription for her ninth birthday.

This special issue she folded by itself and stashed away in a drawer by the closet. Something about it, the way it was written as well as what it was written about, tantalized like a personal appeal, written just for her. As she closed the magazine, she wondered if most women like her mother who had been pregnant, or others who might someday be pregnant, could likewise glean the full potentiality, this incandescence so eloquently described by the author of the article. Somehow she doubted it, and even the words seemed to be sculpted especially, if not uniquely, for her: "flushes," "expedition," "enshroud," "shimmering," "wondrous." What beautiful words, even without looking them up.

Not until the next evening, however, did she feel anything definite. It was around nine. She had just gotten into bed after her bath. Beads of water still hung along her arms and down her thighs and in the small space between her legs. She reared herself up on her knees and studied the ponies above her. A few had riders. There was a cowboy, and a Napoleon, and a young aristocratic-looking fox hunter. But most of all she loved Robert E. Lee on his beautiful Traveler. She loved his luminous white beard, each thread of it cropped and delineated by the artist's hand.

When she crawled back under the covers the feeling came upon her. It was a tingling that sneaked in everywhere. It was a jet of cool water, it was a quick burst of hot perspiration, it was a whooshing in her ears, it was a sudden clearing in her nose. She lay down and hugged her pillow, but changed her mind about falling asleep right away. So she hopped up out of bed to reach for one of her Junior Classics. As the evening passed she found the sounds from downstairs comforting. Her father was watching television; its relaxed murmur was a continuous drone. Her mother was making dinner for the following evening. An occasional mild kitchen clatter interrupted the tranquility.

The next morning she went to watch the boys play ball at the playground. Every few minutes she'd drift away and chat with a friend or sit on a swing. Martha was very well liked. The other girls sought her advice. Even last year, by the end of third grade, the boys had come to treat her with a shy, respectful deference. They never teased her as they would her playmates. Sometimes they'd even consent to sit next to her in the special reading circles. And when they'd dig up earthworms and brandish them while chasing the girls, Martha would sit on the outskirts of the mayhem, smiling slightly as the wild boys passed by and let her be.

Today, however, it was obvious to everybody that Martha was preoccupied. Her conversation was perfunctory. The close attention she normally paid the details of her friends' lives was missed, as were the emphatic concerned tones that customarily informed her responses. But she couldn't help it. The glow had really sprung and was taking her over.

It wasn't that she felt uncomfortable in any way. She wasn't dizzy. She wasn't even nauseous, as she had expected to be. In fact, it was a wonderful feeling, as she had also expected, as of warm water caressing the nape of her neck. It inspired in her a kind of subdued awe and she felt obliged to honor such somber joy with extreme heedfulness; track it with a mighty inner energy. (Just so she tracked the mysterious passages in the Junior Classics that were somewhat beyond her comprehension. But then what exhilaration when she did figure them out! A dozen times rereading repaid the effort every time. The words were hers now.)

Her friends wondered if something was wrong with Martha today. Mary and Amanda wondered, as did Jo Amy and Roberta. But no one said anything.

Of course she'd have to tell her parents. Thank God they were such marvelous people. Can you imagine how awful it would be if they weren't, if they were mean people? Ten years might go by, after all, before Martha would be able to get a job and afford a place of her own for herself and the child. By then the best years of the baby's life would be over. Without someone to take care of them both, and to take care of them willingly and lovingly, having even a sense of privilege in so doing, it would be like being imprisoned in a terrible dreary realm, like the storied troll's shabby lifeless land she remembered still from pre-school even though she'd grown so since then.

That evening, Martha addressed herself to the question: Why me? How does God determine whom He wants to be pregnant? She did not know a single girl her own age who ever was. All the pregnancies she remembered had happened to grown-ups.

Suddenly she thought she heard thunder but it was a clear night. The thunder was only a sound of sorts in her mind, an inchoate fear, an inchoate but gnawing feeling that for some reason, with which she wasn't necessarily altogether comfortable, she had indeed been singled out. No, there was no storm outside her window; just distant cars on their way to movies or parties or restaurants. It was a mild early April. By her calculation the baby would be born amid the swirling torrents of December when traffic jammed and schools closed and the world itself might sometimes come to a dead halt.

Martha hesitated to tell her parents just yet. She realized what a big change in their lives her announcement would cause. It might take them awhile to adjust. Because she knew that life would soon be irrevocably different for everyone, she held back as if to savor these last golden moments of the Old Order. How she delighted to contemplate the two fine forms before her! Her father was a tall, impeccably groomed man in his late thirties. He was quick to smile, loath to raise his voice or criticize other people. His only flaw was a bit of a potbelly. Martha's earliest memories had captured him a sleeker beast, but he was an impassioned gourmand. She couldn't even pronounce the things he ate.

On this evening Mr. Engelman stretched out on the couch, his feet up on a chair. Her mother darting in pounced gently on his stomach and winked at Martha as she landed there. "Oooh, oooh, oooh," yelped her father, good-naturedly feigning consternation. Martha laughed appreciatively.

"I'm dangerous," said Annie Engelman, a small dark woman, a nervous person who was always touching people and trying to hug them. Sometimes Martha would creep up behind her mother, caressing her as fiercely as she could and pressing her lips against the moist flesh under her chin. One time her mother responded strangely. She snapped her eyes shut and held her breath when Martha embraced her. A moment passed and she softly grunted from what sounded like the very bottom of her throat. She bit sadly at her lower lip. The sight of it all fascinated Martha, and frightened her too. Actually, she hated it. Other times Annie was a laughing and lighthearted soul, and those, for Martha, were the choice moments. Tonight atop her husband's belly she was carefree like a child herself.

Oh please God, thought Martha as she went to bed, let me dream tonight the invisible jewels shining through all my pores. Martha had many dreams that night but none of them were happy dreams, much less this glittering phantasm she banked on. In most of her dreams that night, dark angry men were trying to hurt her. The worst dream of all had her walking alone on a vast tundra. She could sense someone was behind her but the terrible sluggish pathway she walked on rooted her feet in front of her, and it was impossible to turn and identify the shadowing figure. She felt like its target. When the shadow finally crept up behind her, she saw his face. He was a dreadful man. He looked like the ruler of some foreign country. His forehead was large and he had a thick moustache. His eyes were leaden. He chased her.

She cried when she woke up, disillusioned as much as frightened. Tonight of all nights, when she was supposed to see paradise, she wrestled with devils. Around dawn she fell back to sleep, but in a new dream, a shorter and even crazier dream, Robert E. Lee's beard – its strands all knotted, the threads of hair huge and oppressively undifferentiated – stuffed the air itself so that Martha could hardly breathe. She awoke like to gag. By six-thirty she gave up on sleep.

Just when disappointment and weariness brought her to the edge of despair, the great glow came upon her once again, more radiant than ever. It made her forget all about the dashed hopes of the haunted night. Her mind quickened with images of the pregnancy ahead. Each image was a new marvel passing before the mind's eye; each image, its own resplendence.

For example, there was the image of August. By August, her glow would be visible to all. Teacher would interrupt the lessons to discuss with the class the blessedness that had come upon Martha. The other children would beam in sympathy and gladness. There'd be no hint of jealousy, despite the apparent fact that, for whatever reason, Martha had deserved this pregnancy more than the other girls.

She'd be fat with the baby in September, and that was the most dazzling image of all. On the street the people would pat her belly and offer words of congratulation and encouragement. Mommy and Daddy would walk proudly by her side. Who knows who'd draw near from out the distant buildings or faceless throngs to bow adoringly and bid her Godspeed for the great journey ahead. Maybe the Mayor. Maybe the Governor. Maybe the President.

She decided to tell her parents that evening at dinner. Through most of the meal she sat quiet; she was concentrating, piecing together the words to make the momentous news all the more so in the telling. Her mother remarked on her silence.

"It's because I have something very important to tell you," she said, her tone suitably portentous.

"What is it?" asked Annie, expecting some news of school or a major event in a schoolmate's life.

"Before I tell you," said Martha, "I want you to remember that this is something that has never happened to me before. It's all brand new, and I know that there will be times that I'll be needing you to tell me what to do. But it's something so wonderful that I can hardly describe it."

"For goodness sakes, love, what is it?" laughed her mother.

"I'm pregnant."

Her father blanched and pushed himself away from the table. Annie let out a little scream and then covered her mouth with a clenched fist. The top part of her face was utterly stricken. Her eyes, her cheekbone, her brow were like shattered glass during the second before the whole pane crumbles to pieces. Then Mr. Engelman stepped backward toward the banister that led to the basement. He kept glaring at Martha as he reached like a blind man for the railing.

"Oh God!" said Annie.

"Yes," said Martha quietly, bewildered by their response. Why weren't they laughing or crying for joy? What was going on?

"Oh God!" repeated Annie.

"Yes," repeated Martha, now angrily as she got up and ran for the bedroom. She grew angrier and angrier as she ascended. What's wrong with them? Are they jealous? Or maybe they don't want to spend their money on my baby's food and clothing. Not likely, that wasn't their nature at all, but she was too angry and now too panicked to focus her mind on exploring their bizarre reactions any further. In fact, she wanted to blot them out altogether. She wouldn't care. She'd think about the baby and nothing else but the baby.

It was thus almost with defiance that she began pondering names. Maybe Christopher if it's a boy. Maybe Sophia if it's a girl. Those were beautiful names. She felt so alone, the loneliness pressed down and burst the glow inside her so that the light spilled out and was squandered all across the shelves, the drawers, the horses, and the dark blue shag. Drained, perhaps, she drifted off to sleep, a dreamless sleep, imageless and windless. Her mother woke her with a gentle nudge.

"We must talk now, darling," said Annie.

"All right," said Martha, resentfully.

"You know," began Annie, uncomfortable and tense, measuring each vital word, "your father and I love nothing in this world like we love you. In the morning the three of us are going to sit down and discuss what's happened. We're going to talk about what's best for you and what's best for the baby. And your opinion is going to be important too. Okay?"

"All right," said Martha, as confused now as angry.

"I want you to remember that there's nothing in the world that we won't do for you. Nothing can make us stop loving you. Whatever you need, ask! And we're not going to badger you or make unreasonable demands. Okay?"

"All right," said Martha, rather dazedly.

"But there is one thing that we must know right now. We must demand that you give us an answer, and that you tell us the truth. Okay?"

"What?"

"Who is he?"

"He who?"

Body Parts

This is a tale of star-crossed lovers, former patients at Mass Mental over by Roxbury whose paths crossed first in Boston in 1973 after their separate releases from the hospital when they both joined an aftercare facility. It was a sort of voluntary social club located on an upper floor of the old YMCU building at Boylston and Tremont. In those days, the club was purely recreational and consultative, no psychotropic or any other kinds of drugs were distributed. What a collection of souls in therapy! Rough-hewn Boston wags who lived through and told fine tales of the old Charlestown street wars were there, as was the son of a Nixon cabinet member, as were middle-class Jews and Italians and Greeks remarkable for seeming so unremarkable, as were silent little men and women living whole lives cradled from the city's ancient institutions to its modern, as were the scions of proud Africans or Armenians broken by history. Some of these people were so sad they just tore your heart out. Others were too grotesque.

They all heard voices, dangerous voices from the past, Neanderthal gibberish you darkly suspected was war cries. Charlotte Brill first had sex in a concentration camp when she was still a long and even rather gangly creature without what later curved out as that maternal, that grossly and aggressively maternal imposition of self on others, all enormous bosom and huge hooked nose who, as soon as she saw you, cried out, usually with no particular reason or provocation, abruptly expostulated HA! HA! She affronted others, especially men, with garrulous challenging expostulations which, however, were not always necessarily devoid of affection or respect as hopeful slight softnesses in her eyes besought forbearance. So much had changed. When she was in the concentration camp, she was bony-limbed, and loomed about in the lists around the fences with a face then smooth and skinny almost like an intellectual Jewess' though she was never intellectual. As far as we can make out, the first to fuck her wasn't actually a Nazi but one of those craven fellow inmates, one of those capos or trustees, whatever they call them, in cahoots with the Germans, who if they survived justified themselves in later years saying how they had parlayed power to keep Jews alive who would surely have died much sooner without them. They bought them life. So this one told Charlotte that if she'd do it with him, he'd look after her, which he did for all the days and maybe weeks that he was having her over behind the little kiln where the Germans baked biscuits and catty-corner to one of the long latrine compounds patrolled until very late into the night by single sullen guards. They tried to do it after dark so nobody would see. He'd slip down her trousers and suck her off awhile before he'd stick it in. These Jewish people were really into eating, what they call "fressing." I once read where oral sex has its collective roots in cannibalism, that's why we call it "eating" and why in the throes of passion we say things to each other like "eat me, eat me." This capo or trustee, or whatever they call them, was as good as his word for as long as he could be, but he couldn't keep his word for too much longer because one day a guard was in a foul mood and shot him. It probably didn't matter much for Charlotte one way or another since a few of the Germans had been noticing her all the while, and she'd have to fuck for them eventually to survive anyway, and, well, you know, in for a dime, in for a dollar. By the time she got to Boston by way of Prague and Tel Aviv and, right before Boston, Trinidad, her cunt was a goddamn combat zone, like a piece of concrete with multiple leaks, although nothing she had endured stopped her from lusting for more, lusting big time and all the time, especially for big men or men with a bigness of power about them, but not necessarily distant men or cruel, for she liked to laugh and have a good time in bed despite all she'd been through. Men who didn't have some kind of bigness about them didn't usually want to try to fuck Charlotte in the first place, what with all her bellowing and HA! HAs!, the taunting bellows and unremitting garrulousness – alive, this woman was, with vast maniacal mother's power no matter what, no matter where – that, for all but the biggest of big men, compelled immediate impotent collapse. No one at the mental hospital ever had sex with her or tried. Quite to the contrary, most of them were quick to hide if they sensed she was feeling randy tonight and might come looking. For some of the poor folk there, she was just a bogeywoman who'd get you if you didn't watch out. Charlotte enjoyed bright Jewish guys like the counselors at the aftercare facility, one especially who was aggressively verbal and occasionally acerbic in his own right. If this guy was ever intimidated by Charlotte, he didn't show it. Nor was he apparently intimidated by John Odomrick, which was rather remarkable because just about everybody else, including the doctors and administrators who ran the facility, were and didn't mind admitting it.

It is either a triumph of the human spirit or yet another referent to humanity's abiding instinct or proclivity to eat shit at every possible opportunity, but one way or another it really is something how Charlotte still enjoyed having sex with men even though when she had gotten shtuped those first times in the camp it could hardly have been a pleasant or encouraging experience, the air was so acrid, and sometimes on their way to the fuck spot by the bakery, they'd see people hobbling back from the latrines with dirty asses because who gets toilet paper in a Nazi concentration camp? Which reminds me, nobody ever really used the word "acrid" much until after the World Trade Center was blown up, but then after that you'd see the word in the newspapers all the time because that was how it smelt downtown.

Now, John scared the souls out of people. He lurched toward seven feet with a thick moustache and creased leathery skin. He typically wore overalls and black sweaters. He was a violent man with a history of violence. In fact, we hear he bludgeoned a woman to death finally at one of those hotel set-ups where they shelter these sick people. He was sent to the asylum for the criminally insane in Walpole and hasn't been seen or heard from since. When he was at the aftercare facility, the only instance of real violence that anybody knew about had occurred decades earlier against his father whom he nearly killed, though the deed was a little less ominous in people's minds than it might have been because his father was said to be a very crappy human being and apparently had it coming. Yet John's verbal violence was always something. He'd stand up and circle you before he spoke, reconnoitering for some area of vulnerability and then he'd pounce. He said to one of the counselors who worked there, "You're here begging for love, that's why you're here, this place is all you've got, and that's pathetic, because how can you help us when it's only your own love-starved self that brings you here?" For the woman he was attacking, the aftercare facility did indeed fill up much more than half her life and the people who were there and heard can still recall the wounding and the twisting in her face as John seethed and stormed. She left the job a few months later, exhausted with John and the burden of the other ones as well, the silent ones who never stormed about or pounced or bellowed but were dying slowly as she watched. HA! HA! Charlotte would cry when John pounced but often her eyes were pained as he did so, and she was sorry and a little intimidated herself that John caused these things to happen. She was very impressed by one of the Jew counselors when John pounced on him, hissing at him that all he knew was words, and that all he could do was words, that there was a hole in his puny creepy soul that, try as he might, words, words, words could never fill, they were just like dope, all those words, and that there was nothing else, nothing at all, real about him. The counselor waited until the fury abated and with a calmness that was itself a sort of seething aggression he said, "Actually, John, when I'm home with my wife, we don't need to do a lot of talking. Here, though, I do need words to talk to you. I have been trying my best to talk to you and I have every intention of continuing to try my best." He stared intently at John, ironically at that moment not using words at all to make his point, and, what do you know, he and John became friends, or whatever you might call it. John showed him his paintings, and he said, "Jesus, John, these are better than Rouault," and he meant it. In these there was none of those maudlin sad suffering faces or their equivalents that demeaned Rouault for a sentimental bourgeois. By contrast, this darkness was cold and matter-of-fact. Ominous fetal inhabitants limned like pouches that had not quite achieved distinctive form hid teeming in the contours. John didn't seem to have been influenced by anyone. Years would go by and he'd still see in his mind's eye the small moons and other vagrants in the horizons that John had painted, how fine and suggestive the tenebrous world. You'd never expect anything so subtly tenebrous from a homicidal maniac, which, let's face it, is what John was.

John and Charlotte usually sat together in the dining area. They were often quiet as both perhaps felt offset, he sensing her indomitable garrulousness and she his foreboding violence. The mutual respect was palpable. When Charlotte was still in the concentration camp, she promised new sexual things every night just to stay alive, like a Scheherazade compelled to spin her differing tales or else! "I'll give him a big kick in his fat pecker," she said once about one of the aftercare facility staff members she didn't like, and, hearing her, he could guess that, however gladly susceptible to the lust or weird love in the men she'd been with in the years since, a fat pecker was a kind of Nazi thing that, to the extent that all men she didn't like had one in their pants, merited dread and contempt, and was a talisman of sorts, of the countless benighted hours spanning back to Buchenwald. In one of Scheherazade's stories, Charlotte sucks a Nazi cock where the dead bodies were, licking the head of the laughing man as all the while the corpses got skinnier and skinnier in the ditch waiting to be covered over, arms and legs and fingers broken off, some scattered on the lip of the ditch. Charlotte got a rep. She was the woman who sucked dick over by the bodies. Sometimes she pretended to be dead. Her asshole was always a reliable standby in a dozen or more contexts each of which offered some permutation of those that preceded it, the permutations adding up to a thousand and one nonpareil phantasms. John first had sex with a prostitute in Kiev. His father took him to the brothel when he was thirteen, it was a year or two before the Germans came, but already he hated him and, likely, they'd been hating each other all along throughout their lives. His father, taciturn, was all white brows and glaring dark eyes vaguely inhuman in their puffed and powder white sockets.

Charlotte, it was actually a turning point of sorts in my life when I found out that you and John were fucking. I might not have ever remembered that you told me, much less let the fact rivet my sense of things thereafter, if you had not added – serious, suddenly, and speaking almost in a most uncharacteristic whisper – "Oh yes, poor fellah, he goes to bed with me because he needs to be forgiven." Every day for the next decade and the decade after that and now into this fresh century, I think of you and how the two of you must have tumbled and coupled like Cyclops' rumbling away in some unquiet mountain crypt that the world built to bury away its monsters forever. Charlotte's eyes, which were kindly almond eyes, smiled and sorrowed for John because his father had turned in the Yids when the Nazis came, the sweet almond-brown eyes tortured with their love a lost and longing part of him. She felt him lost inside her, in her cunt of a no-man's land full of the broken soldiers of the twentieth century, and, wanting him to fuck her real hard, she caressed the massive and leathery pocked desert of his man's back with his dick still stiff, and he was on fire to cry out although he couldn't yet quite cry it out, the tidal yawp that, had he sounded it ever, would wrack the warm breezy night and all who live there. They were so fine and alive, how she caught his breath and breathed her own back deeply into his. No one kisses like that in the real world. You crazy people! There's new life in Boston, John. New life, Charlotte, and such life! You'd both love it. There's so much light out there, and the way the girls in Harvard Square show off their titties! Charlotte was better off getting fucked by Nazis with some Jew's shoulder blade lying in the refuse by the ditch because it was too inconvenient for anyone to go get it and bury it than he was with such a wicked father who knew not love and had no concern. Charlotte, you would like these young people. You would too, John, the way they talk to and take care of their children. They've not known, of course, nor ever will such desolate terrains as you have traversed, they only memorize the epochal misdeeds and piously recite the lessons that the past must teach us, but the way they talk to and take care of their children, in the cafes on Brattle Street, or on the park benches in the Commons when the spring around Easter time dazzles their world, gives me great hope for the future. And the darkness over the river, it feels full of life, your kind of life, John. I wish you were alive or sane enough to savor it, that darkness gotten fecund.

They were both so fine and desperate for life, the more so as their many dark remembrances pressed in on them. In John's nightscape the Vidrovs were the darkest lights. John's father fetched two or three times more money than what the other farmers in the village were getting for families with four and five children. The Vidrovs were twelve souls, the oldest child around twenty and the youngest around three. He paraded them at gunpoint into the town square by the falconer's statue on the green and waited for the Germans to come. John when he was fifteen or so had loved watching the littlest ones play in the grass over by the compost heap until their father would come running out all irritated because the children were getting so dirty there in their wild disport. The man was just bluff and bluster at heart, sensed John, a kindly and forbearing man, although he eyed John guardedly always not aware that you, sullen and seething boy, treasured him and his Jew brood for a comforting crazy warm presence. You were about to become a righteous man in your sullen righteous boy's resentment, and none of them, Jew or anti-Jew, would ever know it. You watched as all around you stolid Ukrainians were surviving this who could never withstand another Russian revolution with the stern force of its Soviet disapproval. John alone among them all was about to become wrathful in his awesome and terrible way.

Oh how beautiful Boston was, and how extraordinary the easiness in the night and the almost full moon in the sky when first you laid Charlotte Brill. John did not ask her, he took her without speaking, head bowed most of the time rather respectfully, really, as he remembered, as he always remembered in his life the violence and the shame, and, wrathful, wrestled with the hopelessness and the helplessness. Charlotte kept looking at you in the public garden by the swan boat with mocking almond eyes that in a second welled up in tears and covered you gently with the blanket of her wet and glazed human being's gaze, you wanted to bury your behemoth self in her neck and suckle the thick aging woman's flesh hanging low at her throat, a beloved friend she was, this Jew woman like a big monstrous beast who had taken it up the ass from Nazis while, who knows, it might have been her own father's kneecap or pelvic delta strewn a few yards away, Charlotte's sweet righteous father, and it could have been, she always knew it could have been somebody just like yourself who had gotten them all put there in the first place, yet here she was hot for you and wanting it, to love and give love in return. There were bags under her eyes with tiny red abrasions on the lower lids, and her big breasts sagged, but he wanted so to suck the concrete cunt, lick at the reeking wet congealed like jelly in the cracks of the concrete cunt, get the essence of her there, and she in turn wanted him to be sucking her like that just like a baby sucks away at its mother's teats. Brutality made her twat juice up. She had a twatful of honey love to feed you because you needed as she knew from the very first instant to be forgiven.

Charlotte never had it like this or anything close. Certainly not in Prague with the bus driver who with his finger up her dress in the café wore so extraordinarily bland an expression, a sort of moral oblivion on his face, that she could not grasp it at all except she knew she didn't like it. Not in Tel Aviv where a pair of Russians shared her at the hotel full of tourists and whispered passionately to each other right in front of her, in some kind of ungodly secret commerce of their own that had nothing to do with her. Not in the concentration camp where on the nine hundred and something night you promised he could shoot you right after he came, which would for you mean at least a few extra minutes of life, a reasonable enough something to fuck for under the circumstances. When she talked him out of it, it was with a promise to orchestrate an even more grandiose death for herself the next night, so becoming a wholly different kind of Scheherazade who promised not just literature but the shifting theater of her own extinction, maybe a pistol up her butt that he could fire off while she was cuming or maybe they would all watch her suck on body parts in the pit while other Jews with shovels buried her alive as she sucked and sucked. To tempt them, she thus offered up phantasmagorias of death with her own unseemly self center stage. Oh, the past is past! Let sleeping dogs lie! Yet she can't help but think of those things now with John, because she's never had it like this, not even when she had a pistol stuck up her ass – and, furthermore, how could she forgive him without remembering what it was she was forgiving him for? She knows that John can kill her right now with those big hands of his she says she loves. They rest around her neck that he sucked in the darkness as life outside in the vibrant Boston streets was quieting down at last so another great dawn over the Charles could finally rise on a vivid empty cityscape and renew hour by successive hour the incomparable jubilee in store. She loves you as you do her, and thereby hangs this tale of star-crossed lovers.

They were a wonderful looking couple over there in the public garden by the swan boat. John when she put his thick Ukrainian thing in her big hungry Jew-broad mouth thought of her sucking Nazi cock over by the body parts – he could no more not think it than she, to forgive him, had any choice except to think about what it was she was forgiving him for – because he knew in his gut with a dreadful foreboding that, if he was beneficiary of this loving and mighty remission that stretched forth all the way to Boston from the rank bowels of the Ukraine, he was also reenacting with cock in her mouth the very primal carnage that occasioned her exquisite proffer. So there you have it in a proverbial nutshell, their very act of love demanded the palpable memorial presence of the old horror that had caused the love to happen and gave it meaning. She wanted to know if it broke his heart when the Germans came and took the poor Jewish families off to hell. The mother was beside herself and silent with her children whimpering pitifully, she died there in spirit to hear it even though she could not bear to hear it. The father surveyed wildly with be-mused glances the swirling landscape, what? forty miles or so from Kiev where they had lived these many years and survived as quietly as they could these Odomricks and the neighbors of the Odomricks, and the Russians too, who whenever they came hated everybody. They had survived with, until this very day, nowhere else in the world to go.

It was 1954, Charlotte was in Israel, when you nearly killed him. How those hands make such nightscapes! "I love his big hands," Charlotte told the counselor and bellowed HA! HA! to imply lasciviously the secret gropings of the big rough hands. I know what the big hands must have done. They felt her hard cunt as if it was a wound and when they looked each other in the eye neither one of them could hide true love. Charlotte never wanted to hide it. You'd cum blood in Charlotte's cunt if you could and Charlotte knows it and loves you for it.

I will never know why you beat the woman in the hotel but you more than Charlotte will haunt the world and its complacencies because you became a great wild beast whereas Charlotte was just another loud Cyclops ravening for love. There were pieces of Jew lying in the dirt when Charlotte sucked the fat Nazi thing not possibly knowing where her father might be or if those sad pieces strewn there in the earth or on the embankment of the ditch were the pieces of him desolated first and butchered later. Scheherazade let out her round Jew ass for the fucking one night and the next night shampooed her hair in Nazi cum. Then she started picking up Jew parts and playing with them, put a shoulder blade between her legs, the residual flesh acrid like the air at the World Trade Center, so hyenas, if there were hyenas, would have wrestled her cunt for possession. Maybe it was Reuven Goldenstone's shoulder blade. Maybe it was Yussel Krupkin's. She searched the mounds that abutted the ditch for pieces of cock and balls so Scheherazade could reinvent horror one more time, and commandeer destiny for yet another night. It was when she was in Tel Aviv that John in his world stepped closer, inching his raging way toward parricide. John never told the Jew counselor or any of the other counselors what made him do it, and no one was really all that interested to know, the population of the aftercare facility being so rich with terrible stories, except it had something to do with prostitutes, and that when it came right down to it his father was challenging John to render up his own soul and live life with his instead. John's mother grew shadowy, fat and shadowy in the Ukrainian night, a year or so after Stalin who collectivized them all was dead and gone. So it must have been, what? 1954 or something.

How I wish I could – no, not necessarily have been there – but hovered instead like a ghost and shared the air in the room when John rested in your fat arms after he, male of the Cyclops species, mounted you terrifically. I think the forgiveness he wanted and you vouchsafed could not have been seen in any sadness of your eyes, though sad they were, nor in the tender touch of his face or belly, though tender it was. I think it was in the smell of the room. I think the forgiving you gave him was something you had to be there and smell. Boston outside in the early evening smelled fresh and full of night flowers, and there were little boys aglow with baseball eating supper with their dads after the game, and a little later jazz clubs were starting to open for business in the Back Bay, and the fine restaurants at Inman Square cheap enough for college kids to gather and eat and drink into the night. Life is happening just outside the room where the smell of the fat old Jew broad, female of the Cyclops species, and her forgiveness hang heavy in the place. Let yourselves go, let yourselves go beyond all you know, all you have been, and see how life just sprouts like flowers between your legs. I'm so hopeful, I know your dead and rotting flesh feeds the world. I can smell it happen.

When I think of John killing the woman in the hotel, I don't think it was Charlotte in his mind's eye that he was bludgeoning. Quite to the contrary. He knew that yet another vessel, another human creature with a cunt, could never yield up the same viscous reek of forgiveness, that hers was instead merely a thin suck of time. This woman, whatever her poor name might have been, who never licked Nazi cock over by the pit of the dead Jew parts, was unbearable to you because you'd known communion with one who did. Well, I'm guessing. Maybe you just lost your temper over something altogether trivial. But the voyage out after Charlotte was awful, I am sure of that, and you must have gagged on any other woman's taste having tasted once the taste you craved for. The apple is love itself, real love. I see you walking endless streets and it breaks my heart. You just really break my heart. There never was no Nazi with dick up yours over by the body parts, just a bastard father who wanted to see you fuck whores and make them yelp. Ironic, though, that Charlotte can still smile and you can't. Nothing hurt her like the nights alone in Kiev and then London, before you came to Boston, hurt you. It's your eyes not hers that make me want to die. John, I don't know why you killed the woman in the hotel, but I'm glad you did because right now they've got you so pumped up with drugs you're bound to be feeling nothing. Half the world's enterprise aims at just that, or to help us keep from having to imagine the pain in the eyes of such human beings as you. They're trying to pound me into inconsequentiality even as we speak. I must answer them, I must comply, and I have only you to remember and rely on as they whittle down whatever it was I once wanted to be.

There you are on Beacon Street by the State House, arms thick like pistons sculpted and folded, your big hands clutched pathetically around your elbows. The sacrosanct remission wasn't enough, even the great historical remission vouchsafed by someone who sucked cock over by the body parts because the likes of you had stuck her there, wasn't enough. Only death is enough. You'll be done with the Ukraine and all the dark redounding centuries. But before it comes, you may yet blow up the whole world because the mighty vouchsafed forgiveness was not enough and love, the soul in us, won't mean all that very much either at the last trump. Ah, just get out, John, go somewhere!

The resurrection is not of the body. The resurrection is not of anything. All I know is that through so many empty and useless days since I knew you and Charlotte, leading at last to nights where at least I can sit alone and think and watch the fog, and hope the night will never end because the day ahead is so full of hollow responsibility, and I've no particular hope I'll ever grab off a single scintilla of the sacred fire I long so to light, you have kept me fine company, your awful self has warmed me as it must have warmed Charlotte. I don't usually speak directly. I usually speak in riddles, and the older I get, the more I wrap myself up in irony and idea. But you, I bet, have no use for that, it was only my own glibness that tricked you that day decades ago it must be by now to forgive me my language. As you may or may not care, I have come to long ever the more, and ever the more achingly, for unmediated elegy, for whatever sheer outburst of imagination might find a way to compass the likes of you and Charlotte.

The resurrection is only of one idea or image or piece of song or strange lovely howl of lust or pain that we can somehow pass off to each other across the vast distances. I can't believe I'm so old. I'll die and see you nowhere, my quotidian, if rich with greater sustenance than yours, only because I've had children and you, nothing. You're probably dead by now. So too Charlotte. You're both gone and what a vast call of pain to its own must have drawn you off, to nowhere. What a vast sounding at the last like a grand duet from an opera, florid and full of impossible ecstasy, the buried world's very sound, impossible the love duet that carries the star-crossed lovers off to nowhere. *Vieni, Vieni!* The earth reeks with the music like the stench in the room that was Charlotte forgiving you when she kissed your hands in gratitude because you had cum blood in her cunt and silently rested in her arms afterward. She knew what the silence meant. She knew it was the complete giving over. How well I've been treated by women, how I've known love, was even able to deny it to others, squander it because there would always be more, but I have never known anything like what you saw in her eyes that night nor smelled anything like the stench of forgiveness that hung heavily as the sun rose over the Charles and with it the merciful promise of new life. Now, as I hope you are dead, done with the pain, the hands of you two are nude and skeletal, the bony knobs still entwined in what was once sexual commerce, not sweet like old Pompeii but miraculous like childbirth, wholly bony the two of you, not forever, there is no forever, but until your bones rot and disperse as dust and only the stench and the sweet music settle on the scene as the curtain falls. Touch, you two bony beings denuded of flesh, touch in a Sistine of last communion before the end, which is all and only end, I am sure of that, and no resurrection but the squeaking by and passing through of the acrid odor of forgiveness or the paroxysm of sound, symphonic and insistent, calling, Come, come to me at last. Be done with the horror of this place where the last thing in the world you can expect is toilet paper.

You gave yourself over, you parricide. But still you walk a man haunted more now than ever as she huddles in her room knowing death conquers all and is coming soon. Listen to the sound of a woman in sexual crisis, and you hear the majestic ache of humanity being butchered. It's true, isn't it? The way your father used to beat prostitutes, he wanted to hear the sounds they made. What music to his ears! That's why I use words, John, because I want to sing, and I can't, and this trap of vowels and consonants is a shadow of song no ear in this world can hear nor mind quite imagine. It began in Eden, the exile, that's true, but it was the first buggering of the first slave in the first pre-Sumerian city state that sounds the symphonic clarion that will carry you from the pit of Jew body parts to the forgiveness-reeking scent of the Back Bay boarding house where you sucked away at Charlotte's concrete cunt for dear life. Death right afterward would have been better than the lonely streets where love, as you walk in your days of solitary pain and memory, shows its face for an hour, an hour tops! then it's day, and we are commanded like men and women whose souls are about to be vacuumed out of us by life itself even though we know that that must be wrong, and that somehow we deserve better.

What awful, wonderful music! Not martial, but not pastoral either. It's a terrible sound, this music of the spheres, because it's so personal. Jupiter and Mars and Saturn reverberate with it, their music sucks up the sound of Charlotte making noises to amuse Nazis when she put the Jew shoulder blade up against her wet excited muff, wet and excited even then because she was ready to die and fuck for the privilege of living, as it sucks up your silence when you almost killed your father and did kill the psycho girl in the hotel over by Andrew Station. John, you creepy scary fuck!

Oh God, let's go home and stay home! I want you to tell them how it was to have been part of the butchery of mankind yet live on to tell so tender a tale as now you tell. Fill dawn in the city with the stench of forgiveness, and the awful galactic music, before the money boys win over our children again as they always do. Stop it, stop it, she screamed. I want to do to language what you did to your father and the poor mental defect you bludgeoned to death, why I'll never know. I want to wrench it clean, oh the purity, and yet the stench of the body sweat and kisses, the selfless caresses in the room where you and Charlotte, Cyclops' of pain, made your love. I want to be expended, hear at last not an apocalyptic blast but some gentle or even lilting music over gravestones, a song about star-crossed lovers, assuming you have a gravestone wherever you are, or, as I hope – so those who care for you need never again see your eyes heavy with the world's whole pain since Adam – that you are indeed dead, finally dead, so dead that, in the terrible music of time, and of history, which is our part of time, your part and her part, you may know as even your father will the great grace of love that abounds for sinner and sinned against alike.

Acknowledgements

Kid's Friend was originally published in *Exquisite Corpse* March 2008 *Punch Line* was originally published in *The Bicycle Review*, #30. *Stone in the Bone* was originally published in *Fixional*, June 2017. *The Queen of Astoria* was originally published in *The Wagon Magazine*, July 2018 *Hecuba to Him* was originally published in *Sequestrum*, Fall/Winter 2016. *Kazantzakis at Home* was originally published in *The Adelaide Literary Review*, August 2018 *The Testament of Betty Sue Williams* was originally published in *Hambone* Fall 1984 *The Desert by the Sea: An Anthology* was originally published in *Lucrezia Magazine* July 2009 *Sassanids, etc.* was originally published in *The Bangalore Review*, June 2017. *Her Memoir: Part Seven* was originally published in *The Serving House*, Soring 2018 *The Shield of Paris* was originally published in *Low Rent* January 2009. *This Rover Crossed Over* was originally published in *Curbside Splendor* November 2011. *Their Music* was originally published in *Prick of the Spindle* June 2012 *Woman, My Come Is Time* was originally published in *Heart and Mind Zine*, October 2015. *Romero and Sylvette* was originally published in *PANK* January 2009. *The Montez Get* was originally published in *Ray's Road Review*, Spring 2014. *Tight Like That* was originally published in *McSweeney's Quarterly Concern* #27 May 2008. *He Who* was originally published in *FictionNow*, March 2012.

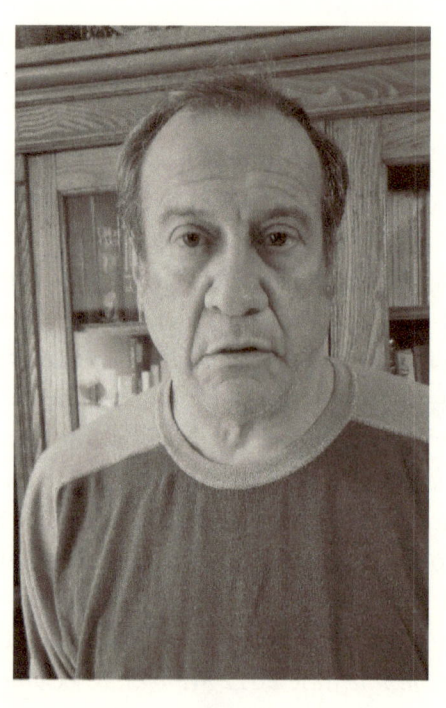

About the Author

Larry Smith has published fiction, poetry, and a variety of nonfiction in literary journals throughout the world. His 2016 novella *Patrick Fitzmike and Mike Fitzpatrick* (Outlook 19) traverses the political, sexual, and spiritual terrain of the modern Catholic Church. A former business journalist with thousands of bylines, and retired executive of a public relations and crisis management firm, Smith grew up in Cleveland and migrated to New York in the late 1960s. His story collection *Floodlands* is also published by Adelaide Books (2019). He is currently compiling a third collection of stories called *High and Dry* as well as a collection of hybrid nonfiction entitled *Nicole Simpson: The Untold Story.*